Praise for Margaret Miles's

TOO SOON FOR FLOWERS

"Miles weaves a wonderful spell . . . the glowing
descriptions of colonial life and the mystery itself
are bound to dazzle readers."
—*Romantic Times*

"Miles's clever dialogue satisfyingly contrasts
superstition and religious fanaticism with a steadfast
enlightenment belief in reason and science."
—*Publishers Weekly*

"A superb colonial who-done-it. The wealth of detail
that makes the decade before the revolution seem so
vivid to the reader . . . makes the novel shine."
—*Amazon.com*

Praise for Margaret Miles's brilliant debut

A WICKED WAY TO BURN

"An entertaining read."
—*Tales from a Red Herring*

"A bewitching adventure . . . this New England mystery
of 1763 should certainly round out the historical
mystery scene nicely."
—*Mystery Lovers Bookshop News*

Bantam Books
by Margaret Miles

NO REST FOR THE DOVE

TOO SOON FOR FLOWERS

A WICKED WAY TO BURN

No Rest
for the Dove

MARGARET
MILES

BANTAM BOOKS
New York   Toronto   London
Sydney   Auckland

For Rocket,
who, like Jeoffry, is
"a mixture of gravity and waggery."

He that hath found some fledg'd bird's nest may know
At first sight, if the bird be flown;
But what fair well or grove he sings in now,
That is to him unknown.

— HENRY VAUGHAN
(1622 – 1695)

Chapter 1

⟶ Milan, Italy
Late spring

ONCE AGAIN, A glowing sun gave new life to the fertile Lombard plain, while the streets that ran like veins through Milan's medieval heart darkened with rustling shadows.

Still, the surrounded city maintained a musty aroma born of its thick stone walls. More noxious odors permeated its narrowest passages, but lessened as these merged with broader avenues . . . avenues that led, ultimately, to the pleasant relief of open squares.

In such spaces lined with plane trees, the city's residents strolled to exhibit trappings of a more prosperous age. On their fingers gleamed gold, as well as old gems proclaiming wealth—though rarely the love of current fashion. Clad largely in black, with linens the color of antique ivory, they went proudly about their business or pleasure, watched by statues with smooth, protruding eyes.

In an avenue adjoining one particular square stood a house just taller than the rest, whose upper windows reflected the spires of the city's vast cathedral. Suddenly, the walls and roof tiles of this dwelling and those around it began to throb with a clamor of bells—a reminder to both the religious and the worldly. However, this was ignored by a collection of urchins who ran through the square below, laughing and tossing a leather ball.

Now, a boy begged another to lob the object forward, while enemies attempted to alter its course with jabs of sharp elbows, and kicks at their companions' shins. Sedate strollers looked on with disapproval, occasionally raising an umbrella, or a cane, in protest.

The ball was caught; its new possessor, a ragged, grinning child of eight, looked for a likely accomplice. Instead of risking a throw through jostling arms and feet, he kicked the ball high into the air; it streaked in a surprising arc. Some who watched imagined it would go through an open window and be lost, perhaps forever! Others feared that when it did come down it would splash through the filth in the gutter, endangering them all.

Yet when the leather sphere landed, it went nearly unnoticed. By then, most in the square had seen something else descending, too . . . more slowly, it seemed, and with far greater import. Young and old pointed toward the tall house half a block away, and to something there in the street—something white, lying on the paving stones.

It may have been that others cried out, but what was later recalled was a scream propelled from the throat of the falling body. This still seemed to echo as the boys raced to investigate, pursued by shouting men and staggering, moaning women. Few were uncertain of what they would find. Such an event was far from unheard of in a city that lived with summer heat—where men, and more often women, sat or leaned by open windows.

The boys came to a halt, staring at what they found. One looked away—and then, with wonder, up. In a high frame, he saw a man with fair skin and reddish hair. He, too, wore white, for he leaned out in his shirtsleeves, most likely from a room in his own home. He stood absolutely still, staring at the body below, while the curtains on either side of him fluttered in the breeze. A moment later he turned, and was gone.

Soon many in the street moved away as well, some with looks of pity, others with revulsion written on their slack faces. The boys, shifting from foot to foot and still curious, watched while a handful of knowledgeable gentlemen knelt to be sure. But nothing would ever return life to the young woman who lay there, her dark hair in disarray, her body clad only in a shift. She was still very beautiful, though her head was turned back at an absurd angle. Clearly, the fall had killed her. That much, even the boys could tell.

However, as several others continued to stare up to the fatal window whose curtains still waved almost gaily, some asked themselves the usual question, which came from a greater experience of life.

The fall, certainly. And yet, might there also have been . . . something more?

BUFFETED BY A fierce night's wind and rain, the brig *Swallow* lay over on her side as she churned along through the white-crested Atlantic. Most on board had seen worse weather, but still they clung to their loved ones—at least, those who had them near. Others made do with sacred books or brandy bottles. Yet another group of passengers down in the very bowels of the craft shook in solitary misery, with nothing to cheer them at all.

Above these timid souls, seamen did a good night's work in the rigging, adjusting canvas sail or replacing tatters as they blew out, keeping their vessel alive. Nor was their work in vain, for by the light of a new day it was seen that the ship had run through the storm, and would have little trouble maneuvering the channel into which it now sailed. The wind, yet fresh, in fact gave the captain a chance to steer sharply as he made his way past black rocks and grassy islands, at last gaining a clear view of his destination.

There, finally, was Boston. At last count it was home to seventeen thousand, all owing the several oceans much for their livelihood, and indeed for their oft-envied wealth. At any rate, that was the way it looked to the *Swallow*'s captain who made do with very little, while out upon the sea.

He smiled, noticing some of his liveliest passengers clinging to the side of his vessel, gulping salt air that caused their neck cloths and shirt ruffles to whip as they gazed upon the shore. No doubt after this passage they'd pray never again to leave it! The sight these gentlemen devoured *was* pretty, the captain had to admit—almost like a toy town, quite nicely made. Before them fresh white houses seemed to sit on smooth mounds of green baize, bathed in sparkling sunlight, sung to by circling gulls. Indeed, the province of Massachusetts had much in it to admire . . . if its inhabitants did strike a man from Spithead as overly zealous. Boston, surely, had more than enough church spires pointing up at the Creator, proclaiming the godliness of her citizens!

This citizen of a greater world was glad to be bound for a long, unholy wharf that stretched out to welcome seagoing men and their cargoes. His own load was a mixed one this time, for part of it had come to him unbidden. But he would likely make out well, after all. In a few hours he would get on with his own affairs, while those whose lives he'd preserved went ashore and scattered, giving him precious little thanks for a job fairly done. Some, at least, he would be glad to be rid of! Yet he supposed there was little likelihood of great improvement in the next lot to come aboard, when he began the tedious voyage home to Portsmouth.

This thought caused the captain to shake his head ruefully as he continued to watch the pointing passengers below—until Long Wharf claimed his full attention.

Chapter 2

⟶ *Bracebridge, Massachusetts*
Thursday, August 15

Above the Musketaquid River and the dozing village of Bracebridge, two friends strolled beside an orchard, while a dog with dappled fur wandered ahead through blue-green blades of rye. None of them had any clear direction, but walked to enjoy the quiet afternoon and the ripeness which suffused the hot, humming countryside.

"I believe," Richard Longfellow was advising the young woman at his side, "that you would do well to set out a few others, to take the place of those in decline. I'll be more than happy to supply you with budded stock already in my nursery, Carlotta, for the promise of a warm pie or two. But you seem to be thinking of something other than apples."

"I do have an odd feeling," Charlotte Willett admitted.

"Involving the thumbs, perhaps? A sort of pricking?"

"Oh! Can you feel it too? *Are* we to have a visitor, do you suppose?"

Longfellow brushed an impertinent grasshopper from his snowy sleeve, then replied with an amused smile. "I'm afraid I can't claim an intuition to match your own—something for which I thank Heaven! I did, however, receive a letter yesterday." He pulled a sheet of paper from his pocket as he went on. "This tells me that a visitor will indeed be coming out from Boston tomorrow—yet he's traveled a great deal farther. I must warn you, too, that he's something special. I find myself eager to see just what you make of him! Earlier today, I made it a point to alert the taproom at the inn, telling them they'll soon entertain a wealthy gentleman who comes to us from Italy. This caused something of a stir." Longfellow chuckled at the memory.

Charlotte resettled one of her cider-colored locks with a penchant for freedom under her bonnet's straw brim. "And this mysterious gentleman's name . . . ?"

"Gian Carlo Lahte. We met in Milan two years ago, and we've since exchanged letters on quite a few scientific subjects. Though I hardly know him well, I believe him to be a quick-witted and superior fellow, not many years above my own age, who has traveled extensively. Already, my sister is pleased with him; you see she's added a postscript of her own."

"But how did Diana meet this paragon?"

"As you know I direct my foreign correspondence to Boston, rather than Bracebridge, and it seems Signor Lahte saw Diana and my stepmother drinking tea when he looked for me in town. On the strength of our acquaintance, they asked him to join in." Longfellow refolded his letter and stuffed it back into his loose linen trousers. "I must remember to ask him what he thought of our Madonna."

"If Signor Lahte raised her spirits, I would imagine he found her charming. But I believe her mornings *are* easier to bear, now."

"I pray they are, for poor Montagu's sake! A man suffers greatly, it seems, to become a father."

Charlotte smiled gently as she plucked a burr from her dog's ear. Yet while Orpheus sneezed and shook himself she straightened with a frown, reflecting on the months ahead. Inhaling deeply, she looked off toward gray hills that rose beyond the glittering river. Both were nearly obscured by the fragrant haze of the August afternoon.

Longfellow allowed his own attention to wander, until he found himself gazing at a low rock wall atop the knoll on which they stood. There Eleanor Howard rested, near the grave of Aaron Willett. Sickness and sudden death had left Charlotte nearly alone in the old farmhouse below, where she had been born . . . which she and Orpheus still shared. For a while Lem Wainwright had been a help and a consolation—but now the boy had ridden off to Boston, where he prepared with a cousin to enter Harvard College in September. At least her brother Jeremy had been back in June—though after six weeks he'd embarked on a new life, as well, this time as secretary to a banker in Geneva. Before recrossing the ocean, he had again entrusted the farm he'd inherited to his sister's good care.

Following Jeremy's departure, Longfellow had been glad to see that his frequent companion retained her cheerful outlook. But this hardly surprised him, for he had long known her temper to be an even one. She seemed to perceive a natural harmony beneath the world's turmoil, and to embrace it—something he observed with a degree of skepticism. Yet this happy bent kept her trim vessel (as he sometimes imagined) riding an even keel, its straight mast and plain sails rarely leaning too far, one way or the other. Though just where she set her course was anyone's guess!

Five years had passed since Aaron's death, and still Mrs. Willett showed no inclination to wed again. Nor had she been asked, as far as he knew. Of course, her reputation was hardly a help to her there. Beyond the fact that her first husband had been a Friend from Philadelphia— and how that had shown a lack of sympathy for local prejudice!—she had also developed a well-known curiosity which could not add to her appeal as a woman. At least this seemed the view held by most eligible men about the countryside, if it was not his own. But Diana had managed to marry a respectable man, so was there not hope for Charlotte, as well? And if such a thing did occur, would it not make her a less frequent topic of village gossip? That, surely, would eliminate a great many of his own worries!

Richard Longfellow continued to muse while he accompanied his companion to a wild rose that climbed the arms of one of the orchard's elders, a gnarled tree with only a few small fruits to show for the summer's warmth and rain. As he watched her reach for a cluster of flowers, something else came into his mind.

" 'Gather ye rosebuds while ye may,' " he quoted. She stopped where she was, and her azure eyes sparkled with amusement. She then recited the poem's end: " '. . . And while ye may, go marry; for, having lost but once your prime, you may forever tarry.'

"Richard . . . ?" she asked a moment later, snapping off a fragrant white blossom. "Did Mr. Herrick ever wed?"

He realized his error at once, but it was already too late to retreat.

"I believe not."

"Then doesn't it seem odd . . . ?"

"What, Carlotta?"

"For a man who refuses to take the step himself . . . to recommend it to others."

"To virgins, actually, if you'll recall the title. And women, of course, are quite different from men."

"Do go on!"

Gathering his thoughts, Longfellow turned his face to the sky. A number of sunlit clouds now floated above the haze. Though none was yet the kind of towering presence that might bring a storm, he asked himself if each was as innocent as it appeared.

"For a woman," he finally said, "the strength of a man is commonly held to be a desirable support—and very often, I think, it is a necessary one. As this tree is. We know most women are easily swayed . . . and for this reason they are likely to need some form of guidance, as well. At least, their happiness cannot be complete—it is said—if they lack the care of a husband, or a father. Yet in the case of a male, a good cook in the kitchen may be quite enough to ensure a serene and enjoyable life. Though I suppose I would be happier myself," he concluded darkly, "if I had such a servant in my own."

"We needn't abandon all hope, for Cicero may yet marry. Even if you, like Mr. Herrick, do not."

"You know, there are some who find it difficult to forget—"

His tone was so changed that Charlotte knew he thought again of Eleanor. Impetuous and beautiful, her sister might well have thrived under the guidance of this man, she reflected. Yet had their marriage taken place, she was sure both would have felt its benefits.

Longfellow knelt down and seemed to examine a

length of lichen-covered branch in the grass, until a cloud of thrips tickled his face back to its usual composure.

"But I think that a man who waits overlong," said Charlotte, "may become too old to wed." His vanity responded as she had supposed it would. His hazel eyes snapped as he rose to stand over her once more.

"Too old? I hardly see how, Mrs. Willett! A wise man will wait for maturity, before he chooses a mate for the rest of his days. However, a cursory study of the species will tell you that for a woman, the opposite must be true."

"Do you say, then, that a woman should marry *before* she becomes too wise?" she asked with a smile.

"Before it is too late—for other reasons. As a country-woman, you should realize—you can see that while a man is never past the setting of fruit, he must take care to choose a wife who is sufficiently young, as well as willing—if he desires children. For this purpose, awaiting wisdom in the female is hardly necessary, nor is it advisable. And fruit, after all, is what most agree is Nature's intent in a union. Fruit, foals, or sons. Or perhaps daughters," he added fairly.

Though it seemed as if a thorn had pierced her, Charlotte tried to take no more from these words than she supposed they had been intended to convey. She had attempted, and failed, to produce either sons or daughters. Yet could this be *all* one hoped for, in marriage?

"You give a useful warning, I'm sure," she replied at length. "Though at twenty-five, I believe I still have a year or two left, to decide. But let's return to rosebuds, Richard. A man who waits overlong to gather his own might find himself in more *danger,* I think, than a woman who tarries."

"How so, Carlotta?" her neighbor asked with new interest.

"You see how this rose clings to a much older tree for support, as you recommend. Yet while the rose thrives, her prop appears to falter. I suspect that's why wild roses very often choose mature subjects. The softening crotch of an old limb offers security and a foothold; and with time, the rose will find even greater encouragement to wander—though this may do damage to the tree. Not what one hopes for in an orchard, I think. Nor in a marriage."

"A strange metaphor, Mrs. Willett," Longfellow answered, startled anew by his neighbor's knowledge of life beyond her own simple hearth. "Shall we, then, eliminate this deadly climber?"

"Perhaps not—for it is pretty," she returned, again taking in the blossom's sweet aroma. "But we might agree to put off further talk of marriage . . . until we're both a little wiser."

Longfellow accepted the truce with a nod.

"But Richard, do tell me more about this attractive stranger who has been recommended by Mrs. Montagu—the friend you would have me see tomorrow."

"*There* is a man who has broken a heart or two, I would imagine. I would not be surprised if he even pleases a woman as particular and obstinate as you! Though in Lahte's case—"

Longfellow stopped short. "I only promise, Carlotta," he continued, "that you'll be entertained. As long as you refuse to accompany me to the center of the world's culture—though I've assured you I would care for you as a brother—I'm glad to house a part of it here, to give you a small taste of Italy's many marvels."

"Will this marvel arrive in time for dinner?"

"He proposes to come at two."

"Next I suppose you'll ask me to help with the preparations."

They exchanged smiles of perfect accord. And soon, after both had taken a last, silent look toward the hilltop, Charlotte led them down the grassy slope, bobbing like a pinnace through parting green waves—leaving dog and man to follow, contented, in her wake.

Chapter 3

GIAN CARLO LAHTE did, indeed, arrive as promised the next day.

At two o'clock, a statuesque stranger, exquisitely dressed, was observed by visitors and servants to climb down from a chaise and stand in the rising heat of the Bracebridge Inn's gravel drive. The gentleman even seemed to strike a pose for them—until the lad who had led his horse and conveyance away came back from the stables pushing a hand-cart, and started to move a brass-studded trunk across the road.

Signor Lahte sent the boy off as soon as they reached the maples near Richard Longfellow's front door. Once alone, he removed his calfskin gloves. He opened a hand-kerchief, and flicked a layer of dust from a coat of scarlet silk minutely embroidered in thread of gold, and from a matching waistcoat. While cocking his head to the song of cicadas performing in the whispering leaves above, he dusted lemon-colored breeches and white silk hose, then adjusted a pressed beaver hat over black tresses that fell beautifully about his shoulders. At last, Signor Lahte found time to admire the tall windows and white façade of the house before him. In another moment, its largest door flew open and Richard Longfellow came striding out, his arms held wide with genuine pleasure.

Some time later, as the sun continued to blaze, the two gentlemen sat coatless beneath an arbor of vines above a small flagstone piazza, enjoying an unobstructed view of the village, fields, river, and marshes below. During a pause Longfellow rose and unbuttoned his waistcoat. He casually encouraged Signor Lahte to do the same.

"But what the devil would make you consider settling here?" he finally asked outright, before sitting down again.

"What man could resist such natural beauty?" Gian Carlo Lahte countered. His voice was light and playful, his English quite tolerable. He made a move with his hand, extending his praise from the piazza to the vista before them. "What could be more delightful? Your arbor, full of fruit—the quiet river and dwellings below—the warm sun, and air full of enchanting smells of field and forest pine. How the country soothes one's senses!"

"The months on either side of our summers are somewhat different. Many feet of snow may then fall onto our enchanting fields and forests, not to mention the roads between. I warn you, Gian Carlo—our little world is not always as kind as you find it today."

"I have walked on ice many times," came the guest's proud reply, delivered as if he remembered these occasions as feats of daring—which caused the others at the table to smile.

While the two continued their banter, Charlotte Willett observed them in silence. Though perhaps forty years of age, Signor Lahte still had a figure whose youthful litheness matched his frequent bursts of enthusiasm. And what wonderful eyes! Light gray and quick, their pupils expanded with little warning, giving one the idea of peering through a window into a dark night. He was clearly intelligent. He also sighed easily, as did many an idle gentleman. But she imagined him capable of a great deal. In short, Gian Carlo Lahte seemed a paradox of easy smiles, carriage, and attitudes, yet also a man whose body had been molded by healthy discipline, and perhaps even rigorous training. But to what end?

"I promise you," Longfellow insisted, "that come January, our landscape will resemble Stockholm, rather than Milan."

"Is your blood too thin for this place, my friend?" the Italian then inquired of the venerable figure leaning against the doorway, nearly lost in its shadow.

"As I was born in Boston, sir, I find it just bearable," Cicero answered quietly.

"Ah—then you are not a traveler? I had supposed . . ."

"Cicero once accompanied me to England and the Continent," Longfellow informed his guest. "That was on the occasion of my first tour, but for some unfathomable reason he has since refused to go along. In this, and other things."

"Years ago I had little choice," the older man returned dryly. "At the time I was owned by the father of this man—my current employer."

"*Current* employer?" Longfellow retorted. "Have you decided to pack your bags again, after all? Should you need assistance, be sure to tell me!"

Signor Lahte hurried on. "I believe that I understand,

signor. You serve the aristocracy, much as I have done. At least, we have been asked to use the same doors."

Cicero's glance to Longfellow signaled his approval of this diplomatic guest, for manners pretty enough to match his face. The old man then went inside for a plate of cheese and pears.

"I have also seen more to admire here than the landscape," Lahte added, moving back to his original topic. "Before us, there is a rare calm . . . a gentleness . . . an innocence that is a true delight. I suppose any man must find what I see before me a joy in all seasons!"

"Innocence?" Longfellow responded with a chuckle. For some time he had noticed Charlotte's unusual stillness, though her frequent smiles suggested that she was, as he'd predicted, fascinated. He next observed with interest that she reddened at the compliment, though the crafter had been careful to direct his eyes away during his skillful delivery. The rogue possessed an urbane and honeyed tongue, at least. Learning what else he might be capable of promised to make the week ahead a stimulating one.

"Signora," said Lahte, as he stood and set aside his napkin.

"Yes?" Charlotte replied, her breath quickening.

"I believe I may thank you for engineering our *repas?*"

"We each collected what we could—and, took courage at the thought that the meals during your recent crossing might have left you a little hungry."

"If only you knew! A journey full of such horrors! Yet I can almost forget its savagery, having now tasted your delicate *gambero di fiume fresco*, spiced with *cannella* . . . the *poulet en mayonnaise* . . . the refreshing *insalata*, with fresh *fungo* and *dragoncello* . . . stuffed eggs with bold mustard . . . this peasant bread . . . *magnifico!* How could a man not be overwhelmed, by such pleasures of the *campagna?*"

"While you were in the kitchen with Cicero," said Longfellow, "I explained to Lahte how the local boys trap crayfish in Pigeon Creek. Of course, Gian Carlo," he went on, "we thank India and the Company for our cinnamon, and Madeira for this wine. But our bread flour came from the fields before you, and was ground in the village mill you see there—you can make out the roof over the trees. The wood across the way supplied our mushrooms—and as for the chicken, eggs, and cream, the salad and the tarragon, all came from Mrs. Willett's barnyard, dairy, or kitchen garden."

"You live like a king, Richard, yet you do not have the trouble of a court," Lahte sighed, sitting down again at Cicero's entrance.

"In winter, our tables tell quite another story. If you stay, I promise you'll make the acquaintance of salt cod and beans. Though I do appreciate your good opinion. I'm sure your appetite has long been satisfied by delicacies only the aristocracy commands."

"My talent has allowed me to try . . . many dishes," Lahte replied, as he deftly sliced into a ripe pear that had been put before him.

Longfellow cleared his throat, then leaned forward to divulge to Mrs. Willett something he had kept from her.

"Signor Lahte," he said in a confidential tone, "sings. In fact, for many years he has been a wonder of the operatic world. Did I mention this to you before, Carlotta?"

"No," she whispered back.

"Gian Carlo, will you describe for Mrs. Willett some of your professional ports of call?"

The Italian replied with a flourish of the silver knife he held, before he finished the slice of fruit in his mouth.

"First, madama, Italy; then, the chapel of a duke, in Stuttgart. I moved on to Dresden, while that city drew all of Europe to its bosom, to be nourished by the world's best music. But then, the Emperor Frederick and his Prussians—and your British, Richard—chased the armies of the rest of the world up and down that land, causing many singers and musicians to flee. Those who were born there could not, of course, leave as easily as the rest, and I have since heard that many fell beside the soldiers of Austria, Sweden, France, Russia. . . ."

Lahte paused to savor another bite of fruit, then shrugged his shoulders with a sad smile before continuing.

"At that time, I was given letters of introduction by Maestro Annibali, a very kind man indeed! Since I had learned some English, I went to London. There it was pointed out to me, as it was to all the rest, that I was not *the great god Farinelli*! Still, I did well; not only my voice, but my dramatic powers, too, were called remarkable. I was often asked to sing, for the opera, and the oratorios. I also performed for gentlemen in their clubs, where I met a number of lords. Soon, I was invited into their homes . . . so that I might entertain their ladies, as well. Yet after a time, one wearies of the affections of the great . . . who are rarely constant. One begins to crave a simpler life. However, I did not wish to bury myself, like Farinelli, in a Bolognese villa, waiting for the final curtain to fall."

"Too quiet a life?" asked Longfellow.

"As you say. I, myself, settled in Milano for a time, where there is music far better than the usual fare of the provincial *teatri*."

"But do you expect to hear anything as fine in this place?"

"No, no! You see," Lahte explained, leaning forward eagerly while his voice rose with excitement, "when I left Milano, it was to come to the New World! For many of us, the call of your freedom, your liberty, is so strong it

becomes like a lovely taste upon the tongue! So, I have
come here with great hope, to be far from courts, tyrants,
priests—a long way from the Hanovers, the Habsburgs,
and their laws that destroy one's soul. Coming here, I call
an end to politics, jealousies, intrigues—an end to life
that ignores the ways of Nature. For they are the true
things! I have also come to study Science, like you,
Richard. And in this new land, I hope to build a home
worthy of devotion—even of great love."

While he spoke, Charlotte watched the movement of
Signor Lahte's hands. She had seen his long, delicate fingers stroke a spoon, toy with a bread basket, caress a wineglass. She could not imagine them gripping a scythe or a
hoe, at least ungloved; but then, with wealth enough he
would never need to. Yet it was an odd thing in Bracebridge to take no part in bodily labor.

"Science does, indeed, make an exciting mistress,"
Longfellow assured him. "One I will happily share with
you. But can you give up your previous love altogether? In
Boston, you know, they allow no theaters."

"No music?" Lahte asked, incredulous.

"Oh, we enjoy our music. In fact, the city manages to
gather together an orchestra every few weeks, attended by
the governor and a few hundred invited guests, who come
to dance and otherwise amuse themselves. We also have
chamber groups. And I have been lately told that singing
masters are on the increase. It seems they improve not
only the voices in our choirs, but our singers' opportuni-
ties for courting . . . though this development has caused
some preachers to fear Bacchus himself has come among
us! Still, you might share your own knowledge of vocal
study, for the sake of the art. And, perhaps, our ears."

"Possibly," Lahte replied, his eyes now strangely hooded.

Longfellow relented at last. "Well, then, as a fellow

scientist, I will be glad to assist you in settling. As it is, Mrs. Willett and I have far too few intelligent neighbors."

"Ah, bravo, Richard! What, then, must I do?"

"First, declare your intention to reside to one of our selectmen. Happily, I am one, so that is done. It is we who keep the peace here. We will take your pledge—something most of our villages require of visitors who remain for more than a week or two. I will tell the others that I'll be responsible for your good behavior; you will vow to behave; the village will assure you that should you ever ask for its charity, it will ship you back to wherever you have legal residence. Though I doubt it would extend to paying your passage back to Milan. I rather think we might arrange to have you dropped by one of Boston's wharves—"

"This is hardly a way to welcome a man who comes with his pockets full," Signor Lahte replied with new coolness.

"But there is some sense in it, for it keeps farmers from having to support those who aren't their own. Most here make just enough to keep themselves in sugar. 'Charity begins at home, is the voice of the world.' "

"It is certainly the voice of those who *have* a home."

"You need not feel alone. Even I have been 'warned off,' as the law calls it. Although the good people of Bracebridge have elected me to serve them repeatedly—and at my own expense—they would soon send me back to Boston if I found myself fallen into penury. I believe, however, that we might spare you the usual bond of forty pounds."

"How kind."

"As soon as you find property you wish to buy, we will again appraise your character. Finally, you may sign a petition to settle. At that point, you'll be one of us. More or less. You do know," Longfellow asked sharply, "that the Church of Rome is held in low regard by the province of Massachusetts?"

"That, I think, will be no problem, for I have gladly left the Pope and the Vatican behind. Yet I ask you—can talk of government and religion be fitting on such a day? Instead, will you allow me to give payment for my dinner with a song?"

"We would be delighted!" cried Longfellow, his eyes suddenly charged with new life.

With an air of purpose, Gian Carlo Lahte stood. He raised a hand to his brow while composing his thoughts, and inhaled deeply. He gazed at the leafy vines above them . . . his lips parted . . . his arm stretched upward . . . and he sang.

The notes that flew from his throat were borne on a voice so strong, so brilliant and pure, that Charlotte's lips, too, parted while she watched and listened. She felt her own breast heave as Lahte's voice soared, unbelievably, angelically, higher and higher—as if it would take her heart up with it. Soft, trembling notes were followed in the same breath by piercing leaps; these in turn gave way to bubbling trills not unlike the magnificent song of a woodland thrush. It was glorious—it was astounding! First tender, then commanding, he continued with an unearthly grace, a peculiar ease. She could hardly imagine how—

Across the stone table, Longfellow saw his neighbor blink rapidly. Then he watched her shudder, as the terrible truth became clear. Observing that moment of knowledge, he even felt a pang himself.

> *"Cara ed amabile*
> *ombra mai fù*
> *di vegetabile*

cara ed amabile
soave più,
soave più"*

Signor Lahte finished the brief aria. Having paid tribute to the ripening grapes above them, and perhaps to something more, he lowered his eyes with a look of pride that soon turned to confusion. He was waiting for Charlotte to speak, but she could not.

"Madama," he said finally, "perhaps you do not understand what most of Europe knows. I am a *musico*."

More was exchanged though their eyes, which could hardly have been said with words.

"I have never heard such beauty before," she then replied, "yet I do know—such things are sometimes possible."

"Ah . . . *sì*."

"To Britain and the Continent," said Longfellow, "our famous guest is known as *Il Colombo*, the Dove."

"How kind of you to share with us your gift—" Charlotte stumbled as she again realized its source. "—and your great talent," she finished.

The musico walked to her side. "It is my joy, always, to give what brings pleasure." He reached for her hand and brushed it, surprisingly, with the tip of his nose.

"I should also mention, Carlotta," said Longfellow, "that Xerxes, the gentleman in Handel's opera from whom we've just heard, is a Persian king—though his actions are somewhat less than noble. In fact, he plans to steal his brother's fiancée. First, however, he makes love to a tree in the lady's garden. It would seem he has a rather uncertain nature."

"He sings *to* Nature," returned Lahte, "as do I, Richard.

*Roughly, *"How rare, gentle, and worthy of love, this dear shade."*

But after enjoying your *insalata*, I ask you, madama: Should a love for *vegetabile* be mocked? After all, many things on this earth are worthy of our passion," he said as he released the tips of her fingers.

Both men now turned to face each other again, and Mrs. Willett soon found herself pondering what two such forces might mean for the future, and the safety, of the neighborhood. Before she could decide on an answer, or even make further amends (for what, she hardly knew), an even more jarring chord came to put an end to their unsettling entertainments.

BARELY AN HOUR earlier, Caleb Knox was driving along the nearly deserted Boston-Worcester road, wishing he were home. The farmer gave the reins he held a mild shake, causing them to ripple—but it was not enough to alter the pace of the horse who pulled his wagon. Judy kept plodding, and the rude conveyance rolled on, slow enough to suit the weather, its sleepy driver lulled once more by the creak of heavy wheels.

As they passed a field aflame with tall goldenrod, Knox imagined himself in a chair behind his own house. The smell of hot sun on his shirt reminded him of his old dame's ironing, done outside in summer beneath the kitchen overhang. If only, he thought, he might get up and walk down to the spring for a drink of cold water. The ale he'd consumed at the Blue Boar, after he'd left the mill where he'd exchanged grain for flour, had not helped to quench his thirst at all. Neither the first pint, nor the second, nor even a third.

The horse neighed unexpectedly, as if she, too, longed for refreshment. Then he saw that something else concerned her. Beside the road, next to a long hedge of old hawthorns, stood a lone mount that wore a bridle and saddle while it grazed. It was a curious thing—and yet, on such a warm afternoon, perhaps it was not.

The farmer pulled himself erect as he looked out from under his rime-ringed hat. The horse's rider was no doubt asleep nearby; he could see that a nest of sorts had been made in the grass. But why would he be *there*, when he could have chosen the shade of the hedge? Why would anybody lie out full in the afternoon sun? And what were all those flies doing? Despite the heat, Caleb Knox felt a chill.

While he hardly relished the exercise, it did seem this situation might be worth a closer look. So, when his wagon came even with the saddled horse, the farmer gave a pull that made Judy stop, her large head shaking. He climbed down, giving further instruction for the animal to stay where she was. Precariously, he leaped over the wide ditch at the side of the road, landing on both feet. Then he wound his way through the weeds until he reached the silent rider.

The man was not resting. In fact, it looked as if he would have no further need for rest ever again. Caleb knelt down to make sure he was not wrong. After that, he spent a few minutes in quiet speculation.

Surely the poor devil had been drunk—he could smell it, and it appeared he'd even lost some of his liquor down the front of his old black coat. A sad thing, very sad. One hated to see a man enjoy himself, and then choke for it. Unless—unless he'd been thrown? Maybe he'd directed his horse down from the road, intending to give them both a rest—and then, maybe, it had shied at a viper. He only hoped the snake, if there was one, had taken itself far away! Yet if the man had carried some form of drink with him, could any be left? There was none around the body, he soon saw. But—might there be something else?

Caleb soon came upon several pieces of Spanish and

English silver in one pocket, along with some coppers, and a few smaller coins made of gold in another. All of these he put into his own pocket with a sigh. They would have to be turned over to the authorities, for it wouldn't do to rob the dead. Although right there next to him was something else that had a pretty shine to it, and even a gem or two. Did this belong to the stranger? It lay close, but . . . maybe, and maybe not. Wouldn't it be something wonderful to give to the old dame? She'd long forgiven him a great deal; she would forget even more, he imagined, if he were to offer her such a gift one day. Besides, it looked as though the dead man was a stranger, perhaps far from home. He and his possessions might never be missed. In which case . . .

At last decided, Caleb Knox put the small, glittering object next to the coins in his breeches. After that, he walked around a clump of yellow stalks full of bees and approached the riderless horse. Its head rose with a whinny. Clucking to keep it calm, he crept the last few feet, and grasped at its bridle. Before long, to Judy's surprise, he had the mount tied to the back of his wagon. Leaving the two to become acquainted, he then returned for the corpse.

The farmer felt a little foolish as he pulled off the man's hat, and set it on top of his own. Next he lifted the pair of legs, and held one under each arm as he walked backward, allowing the stranger's coat to drag over a new furrow in the vegetation. At the ditch, Knox hoisted up the dead weight, and grunted as he carried it down and back up again. At last he rolled it into his wagon. In another few moments, when he had arranged the man decently, he climbed forward to his seat. Finally, he turned Judy around on the road, and started the wagon back toward Bracebridge.

Looking both ways, Caleb still saw no one ahead of him, or behind. Soon, many voices would be clamoring to hear his story, for the reward of a tankard or two. He would not be sorry to tell how he'd found the terrible thing now behind him. At least, he would tell most of it . . . if not exactly all.

First, however, he would do his duty and speak to someone else, who would surely know what more needed to be done.

"you do paint an unpleasant picture," said Richard Longfellow. He smoothed his gathered hair further with a callused hand, feeling new moisture on his forehead. He suspected they'd all become more aware of the great heat and stillness of the afternoon, now that Caleb Knox had introduced Death to their party. "And you believe he met his end recently?"

"A few hours ago, it may be," the farmer replied, his eyes drifting toward a man unknown to him, who stood at the edge of the piazza.

Longfellow turned abruptly to Gian Carlo Lahte, to watch him adjust his coat sleeves over lace ruffles. "You saw nothing, I suppose, on your way here?" he asked the musico.

"Not of that sort," Lahte replied easily.

"Where exactly was this, Caleb?"

"By the old hedge of hawthorn, not two miles east of here."

"And you say you recovered his horse as well. A good animal, do you think?"

"For working fields, no, sir. For walking, it could be . . . though he likely has bloat by now."

"Spirited?"

The farmer considered, rubbing at the stubble on his throat into which sweat continued to trickle. "Not something I could tell," he decided.

"Hired in Boston, quite possibly. Such animals learn the Devil's own tricks for getting rid of a rider." Caleb snorted his agreement, though he had never hired a stable horse in his life.

"So," Longfellow continued, "this man appears to have been thrown after leaving the road, and stayed where he landed until you picked him up. You're sure you haven't seen him in the village before?"

"Nor anywhere else. Could be he was a tinker, I thought—yet he had no goods box, nor saddlebags. Clothes like a gentleman's, but too old. Cast-offs, could be, yet still queer, somehow. He did have coins in his pockets. . . ."

Knox reached into his own breeches and carefully brought forth the collection, leaving it in Longfellow's outstretched hand.

"A sad tale, Caleb. But one hardly new these days, with riders having no better sense than to race from hither to yon."

"Amen to that!" exclaimed the farmer, whose plodding Judy had feet the size of firkins.

"You found Reverend Rowe?"

"No. But I heard he went over to Brewster's, so I sent a boy running for him."

"Since this man had no other possessions, I suppose he came from town to visit someone, planning to return by nightfall. A small mystery, but one we'll understand shortly, I'm sure."

The farmer nodded as he put his hat back on. Then he lifted it again, briefly, to Mrs. Willett. Still, he would not go. Instead he turned in the direction of the unknown guest, perhaps hoping to have one stranger's presence, at least, explained that day.

"Ah!" said Longfellow. "Since we may all soon be neighbors—Mr. Caleb Knox, farmer and son of Bracebridge. Caleb, this is Signor Gian Carlo Lahte, a gentleman of Milan."

Lahte stepped forward and graciously offered a hand, which was gingerly taken.

In another few moments, anxious to tell a yeasty story that had risen into a substantial loaf, the farmer disappeared around the corner of the large house, on his way back to the Blue Boar.

"This thing may well have one or two points of interest," Longfellow mused, looking more closely at the moist coins in his hand. "Will you come, Lahte? Good. Cicero? I thought not. Mrs. Willett, will you wait for us here or return to your own chores?"

"If we're to suppose this unfortunate man traveled here to meet someone, as you say," she replied, "then it might be better if I went with you. For what if he came to see me?"

"To buy a pound of butter? Unlikely, but as good a reason as any, I suppose, to examine a corpse. Come along then, Carlotta. But wait a moment. . . ."

Longfellow strode past Cicero into the kitchen. On his return, he carried a small box of coals.

"For fumigation," he explained. "Now I believe we're ready."

With that, the small party started off across the fields, leaving Cicero sitting silhouetted under the cool green vines, finishing the plate of pears.

Chapter 4

It's a convenience built this spring," said Richard Longfellow as they walked between weathered headstones, along a shaded path.

He went on to explain that the subterranean chamber behind the burial ground had seemed a useful idea, when suggested by a pair of men in need of work. The selectmen had gladly approved the digging of a temporary site where they might leave the dead, when circumstances kept the unfortunate souls from being immediately interred in the churchyard. Everyone knew it was no easy thing to take a pick to frozen earth; nor did anyone want to worry about the spread of putrid fever in warmer weather.

"Down these steps, and leave the door open; I'll just touch this scrap of paper to the coals, and light the pair of candles. No, I don't know this man. Do you, Mrs. Willett?"

Charlotte, too, descended into the close, timbered space, where the aroma of damp earth vied with something less wholesome. She saw the body lying on a trestle table, and looked instinctively to the closed eyelids, then at the waxy face. The man's pale features suggested someone of perhaps forty-five, possibly fifty. Clearly, this wasn't a farmer who'd spent his days in the sun. His oily hair had a reddish hue, as did the short curls on the knuckles of his smooth, unbruised, and unadorned hands. The nails were surprisingly clean—a benefit of long gnawing by their owner. She speculated he was a person whose fortunes had fluctuated. Though his apparel was quite worn, it seemed to be made of thin-stranded and tightly woven fabric, surely not home-loomed. It looked as if the cut of the coat was original, and the stitchwork good; yet there was something unfamiliar in the proportions of the garments, as well as their finishing details. Over much of this clothing there was a dark stain—which accounted for the smell.

Looking up, Charlotte at last shook her head to Longfellow's question, while noting that Signor Lahte stared hard into the stranger's face, as she had. He then pulled himself together with a start.

"Can it be," Longfellow asked in surprise, "that *you* know this man, Gian Carlo?" A brief wave dismissed the idea. But Longfellow persisted in his concern.

"You seem unwell. The stench is strong, and the stagnation of the air may have caused it to lose its potency— er—well. Perhaps we should move on."

Lahte now attempted an explanation of his own. "Richard, a man of art . . . of strong feeling . . . he can be—" The musico suddenly fumbled for his handkerchief, and held it tightly over his distressed features.

"Something of a shock, I would agree. I, too, have little stomach for viewing death. Though something tells me Mrs. Willett will linger a while longer."

Charlotte looked up from examining a marred hat she'd found on the beaten dirt of the floor. "Surely, offering a prayer would be appropriate?"

"Hmmm," Longfellow responded as he led Signor Lahte up the wooden steps set into the soil, both of them rising once more toward warmth and light.

When she was alone, Charlotte closed her eyes for a moment. The tallow candles continued to smoke and sputter. Then, she opened her eyes and slipped behind the table, to lift the head of the corpse with her hands. The neck seemed whole, but the top of the skull *was* damaged. Even more strange was the fact that the indented area was not at all swollen. This told her he must have died very soon after his injury occurred. Of course, he might also have died from inhaling what he could not swallow.

Nearly overcome by this horrible thought, and the odor, Charlotte looked away; but soon, she forced herself to examine a patch of the matter on the coat more closely. It was unusually dark, and the observation caused her to feel a new shiver of unease.

In another moment she heard a phantom echo of the angelic voice of Gian Carlo Lahte come into her questioning mind, and she felt a sudden rush of warmth. *Did he know this stranger?* Or had her imagination, too, become overly active? Longfellow had also wondered if his visitor was acquainted with the man—yet why would Signor Lahte not say so, if it was true?

Blowing out both candles, Mrs. Willett climbed the steps and pulled the door closed behind her. At her appearance Longfellow strode forward, while his guest continued to pace slowly among the stones some distance away.

"Are you satisfied, Carlotta? It seems clear to me that he was thrown onto his head."

"Yes, but—"

"You question, too, where he's come from. I'll make a sketch, and send it off to Montagu in Boston. But I believe the signs point to an unsuccessful fellow less than a gentleman, lately arrived from abroad. You will have seen that his hair and skin are similar to those of many Scots and Irishmen . . . yet somehow, the face reminds me more of the Alps. However, as you'll agree, physiognomy is not yet a true science. I would much prefer to see a sample of his hand. It's unfortunate that he carried no papers."

"The clothing—" she began again.

"That, too, is curious, but inconclusive. As to his pockets—these coins could have come from a number of places, if the gold ducats do suggest the Italian trade. Have you an idea of your own?"

"He appears to have lost some wine, which I presume he drank while on the way here."

"I will give you no argument there."

"But when?"

"When?"

"He could hardly have vomited the wine up, I think, after a fall—at least, not if his death was due to the obvious injury. The blow must have come only moments before his heart ceased to beat."

"Do you refer to the lack of fluid within the depression? You're probably right. Well, the man's stomach could have rebelled first. Or he could have gotten off his horse, then lost his stomach, and stumbled. If he next fell back onto a rock . . . ?"

"But how would that explain the great force of the blow? From what I saw, I can hardly believe—"

"All right, he was thrown *after* he regurgitated, which he managed to do while still *on* his horse."

"Perhaps, then, his death was caused by choking, and

not the fall. At least that would remove blame from a poor horse—"

"In either case, it would have been accidental; thus, it is no further concern of ours."

"Still, I wonder. Wouldn't the village rest more easily if a physician examined him?"

"I suppose it might. Nothing, I hope, points to anything more unusual in your mind?"

"Only the face. Didn't it seem to you to be quite haggard? He could have suffered a recent illness—perhaps a mortal one. Richard, if the dark matter I saw—"

"He hardly seems jaundiced, if you next mean to tell me he died of yellow fever! And he would have been ill, indeed, probably in the last stages of the disease, to produce what the Spanish call the *vomito negro*. In that case, I doubt he could have sat a horse all the way from Boston."

"That's true. *But did he look well to you?*"

Longfellow examined her familiar features closely, before he gave his answer.

"It might be best, after all, to post a sign warning others not to enter. Many ills race swiftly through a population . . . especially, as I think of it, in August and September. And, as Boston is a seaport—yes, I'll make a sketch, and when I send off my handiwork I'll enclose a request for Warren to come, just to be safe. It will give him a healthy ride. Now, where has Il Colombo got to? There he is, next to all the Proctors. Shall we take him home? He, too, seems not entirely well; I hope melancholy is all that is wrong with *him* today."

As they joined Signor Lahte, they saw that his spirits had already returned. This was fortunate, for Reverend Rowe approached them along the main road.

"Gian Carlo," his host called. "Are you sufficiently restored to be presented to what passes in Massachusetts for a holy man?"

"I will be delighted," the musico answered.

"I doubt that," said Longfellow, "but we shall see."

"so. I ASSUME you were born a Roman Catholic, signor?"

Christian Rowe, clothed in his usual ill-fitting suit of black broadcloth, pronounced the strange title with great distaste, after receiving what he supposed was a sinfully excessive bow.

"I was raised in the Church, good Father, but I now dispute the many laws of Rome—and I strongly repent of partaking in its superstitious ceremonies."

"Oh?" Rowe brightened a little, while he adjusted his stiff round hat over a halo of golden hair. "Then am I to presume you are now a Protestant?"

"I protest much in this sad life, Father, and pray you will take me into your flock. For like the poor sheep, I must look for guidance. I must tell you that I learned of your wisdom even before coming here."

"Really!" the reverend responded, rising on his toes. He gave a fond sigh for several slim volumes of his sermons, copies printed the previous winter and left in a King Street shop. Perhaps not all of them had languished, after all. "That is gratifying," he allowed, giving the gentleman before him a faint smile. "Although as a minister, rather than a popish priest, I should be addressed as 'Reverend,' or simply 'sir.' We do not see our spiritual leaders as all-powerful, yet make no mistake, sir—ministers *are* well respected here, for their wisdom and learning."

"But of course!"

"You do realize," Rowe interrupted with a new suspicion,

"that there is no question of a Roman mass ever being said in Massachusetts?"

"Who, Reverend sir, would dare to so pollute such a grave and holy place?"

After that, Rowe's face beamed with a beatific mildness . . . until a slight movement drew his attention, and his expression changed once more.

"Madam, have *you, too,* gone down to examine that man's body?"

"I was convinced it was my duty, sir, to examine his face, since no one yet knows who he is."

"Duty! A word one rarely hears on your lips, Mrs. Willett—"

Longfellow caught the preacher's eye; then, he turned to gaze at a new slate roof on the stone manse behind them, a recent, and expensive, gift.

"But you are entirely correct," Christian Rowe continued, "in suggesting it is the duty of us all to help our fellow creatures. Someone, somewhere, must be searching for this man—whose death, I am told, was an accident?" The preacher relaxed only when several nods assured him he would receive no more unsettling news.

"Well, then, that's that," Longfellow concluded with evident satisfaction. Like Rowe, he had no desire to add to their previous experience of crime, and punishment. "It won't be necessary for you to take more than a brief look at the body, Reverend. As it is the height of summer, I have some fear of contagion. In fact, I believe I'll call for a physician to see to him, at the town's expense. I plan to take the likeness of the corpse myself, so that they can ask in town who he was. It seems to me he came here by way of the Boston road, and I suppose Town House will soon hear a complaint; if not, there will be plenty of lodging houses to examine."

"Your friend Captain Montagu might be of some use in that."

"What a good idea, Reverend. I'll be sure to let him know you thought of it. Now we must be off, but I will return shortly with pencil and paper."

As the minister walked back to his parsonage, the others began to climb the long hill that rose to the east of the village.

"A fine piece of flattery," Longfellow soon commented. His Italian guest replied with a slight smile.

"While in the service of others, I have had much practice."

"You did warn us of your dramatic accomplishments. Here, however, you may be called a truth-slayer and a wastrel, if they are ever discovered."

"Ah, yes. If they are discovered . . ."

"It seems I will be busy for a while, so you may as well ask Cicero to help you settle yourself into the house. Then, you might enjoy a siesta."

"An excellent idea."

"Tonight, I hope you will delight us with your voice again, and show us your skill at the pianoforte. After that, we might all go out and take a look at the sky."

"The sky?"

"Astronomy," said Charlotte, "is one of your host's favorite hobbyhorses."

"An excellent breed, capable of taking us into astral realms. Much like your splendid arias," Longfellow concluded.

"Oh, yes."

Il Colombo replied with a weariness Mrs. Willett noticed with new sympathy. She had wondered at his earlier efforts to ingratiate himself with the Reverend Rowe. Now, she asked herself if Signor Lahte might not feel he must pay for his supper—and for their company, as well. Might he tire, too, of being eternally reminded of the singular difference that set him apart from the rest of his sex?

These queries were joined in her mind by others, while the trio moved quietly through the heat of the afternoon. And then, Mrs. Willett recalled something more. Like small feathers, such ideas had a way of floating about and tickling one, which was not always entirely pleasant.

Chapter 5

M ADAM —? Is there an answer?"

The young man who stood before her pulled Charlotte from a new reverie, while Orpheus continued to wag
his tail after receiving a pat on the head for his attentions.

A few minutes before, Thomas Pomeroy, newly employed at the Bracebridge Inn, had come to the front door
rather than the back. In doing so he'd surprised first
Hannah in the kitchen, and then Charlotte, who sat in
her study staring at rippling leaf shadows on blue walls.
Again, she looked to the messenger who had brought the
note she held in her hand.

"Oh—yes—I'll write it down, so Mrs. Pratt will have
something to fall back on once the glass comes in. As she
suggests, a joint purchase of bottles should bring a better
price. How kind of Lydia to ask," Charlotte added. What

she did not add was that her note would also give him protection from the landlady's suspicions that he'd gotten her instructions wrong, when glassware of varying sizes arrived.

While she took up her quill to jot the brief order, Charlotte saw the young man glance around, his gaze falling on Eleanor's drawing of her parents, then a hand-painted screen before the cold hearth, shelves of books with darkened spines, and finally, the drawered desk at which she sat, with its miniature of Aaron Willett in its usual place. When she finished, she folded the sheet of paper and passed it to Pomeroy, studying him in turn.

He was not unlike Lem, she decided, opening a place in her heart still occupied by the boy, though he was gone to school. She missed his quiet, cheerful presence as he devoured a book beside her in the evening, once Hannah, her frequent helper, had left them . . . his acute concentration while he mended a piece of furniture . . . his occasional chortle, while he thought of something she could only guess at. In stages, he had grown from the child she'd taken in to a friend with a pleasing personality, and no little wit. In short, he'd become a true companion.

The lad before her now seemed to share Lem's curiosity, and he was nearly the same age, if Thomas Pomeroy did appear to be more experienced. Of course, he had traveled; his London tongue told her that. There was also a kind of hard-won knowledge in his eyes. That suggested he'd known something beyond life's small strains . . . perhaps even one or two of its calamities.

"Is life in Bracebridge to your liking, Mr. Pomeroy?" she asked gently.

" 'Thomas' will do very well, madam, if you please. Yes, I do find much here to my liking. Though it is not England, it seems better to me, in many ways."

"How did you find us, I wonder?" she continued softly,

giving him the chance to ignore the question if he chose. Her kindness was rewarded with a further confidence.

"Partly by chance, and partly by choice," he told her quite happily. "After I spent several weeks in Boston, I decided to seek a different kind of life. So I asked for rides away from the city with wagoners who were about to leave. I allowed their destinations to take me several miles out, at the price of conversation and a turn at the reins. That way, I was able to learn of, and then see, the towns of Salem, Wakefield, Lexington, and Concord . . . and Roxbury, Dorchester, and Braintree to the south. I next met a man going to Worcester, and we stopped for dinner at the inn here; then, I discovered Bracebridge was the best of all! Mr. Pratt, too, seemed to me a fair and honest man."

"He is that, and more. And I'm sure we are all flattered by your choice! But do you have further plans, beyond your present occupation?"

"Yes, madam, I do. I know I have the whole world yet to discover—but I may decide to do most of my seeking here, if my first impression does not alter. Which I hardly think it can," he finished with a smile. "I hope I may soon become something more than just a stranger," he added.

"There are several ways to join a community. Some you might find quite pleasant. . . ."

"Do you mean I might marry here?" He laughed. "First I wish to establish myself in the eyes of men—before I begin to look deeply into the eyes of any woman."

Somehow, thought Charlotte, though these words had been spoken with conviction, she did not believe Thomas Pomeroy would long restrain his passion for life. Something told her that *this* young soul was not likely to become lost, as others were, in Science, or Politics, as long as there was a chance of something warmer being served up.

Suddenly, she was struck by another idea that held her answer on the tip of her tongue, until she swallowed it thoughtfully. Was she not in a similar situation? This boy had only begun to live his dreams—but she, too, could embark again on a new life, if she chose. She could even leave this farm, though she did love it, and start on an entirely different road . . . if a man were ever to capture her heart again. She had recently denied her interest in such a thing to Richard Longfellow. But had she told him the entire truth? Possibly, the summer's long, warm days and soft, pleasing nights had already begun to encourage something she'd hardly felt since—

Charlotte realized Thomas Pomeroy had spoken to her again, and now regarded her with an expression of amused sufferance. This made her suspect, with a blush, that he would make a kind and gentle lover himself, whenever he might attempt such a thing. With, she hoped, a girl of his own age.

"Nothing else, then?" he repeated.

"Only my thanks to Mrs. Pratt."

"That I will gladly convey."

Thomas Pomeroy then went out of the study and through the front door, escorted as far as the lawn. Orpheus sat down and watched silently, ears cocked, as the young man headed across the yard and out onto the road at a jog.

Finally, dog and mistress turned back to the relative cool of the old farmhouse, where they soon found new occupations.

THAT EVENING, AFTER the last of the twilight had faded, Richard Longfellow carried a telescope out onto the grass beyond his piazza. Here he had a broad view of the dark canopy overhead, which was increasingly dotted with stars. As their twinkling grew brighter, and the eternal White River appeared above, he bent to adjust first one steel knob, then another.

As promised, Gian Carlo Lahte had favored them with several songs after a light supper suitable for a summer's eve. Music from the pianoforte still drifted out through the open windows. But Longfellow forgot this pleasant sound when Saturn, the most remote of the sun's six planets, showed him its rings and a revolving moon. Great distance, he had long ago realized, at first made far bodies seem more exciting than near ones. However, once such excitement waned, he generally went back to studying more closely the well-known surface of the earth's own orbiting companion.

Due to his intense concentration, he was at length startled to sense someone standing at his side.

"Which is it?" she asked.

"Saturn. As you'll see, if you use your own ocular orbs."

"So it is," Charlotte replied, after she'd done so. " 'I saw Eternity the other night, like a great Ring of pure and endless light,' " she quoted, very softly.

"Is there anything else you need my help in discovering tonight?"

"Overhead? Nearly everything, I suppose . . . but I had hoped to discuss something closer."

"I suspected as much."

"Richard—"

"Yes?"

"A musico is the same as a castrato, is he not?"

"Yes, Carlotta. Yet this one is not any castrato. In the world of art, Lahte is special. Even among the hundreds whose voices earn them a living."

"Hundreds!"

"It's said at least a thousand are cut each year. Sadly, most will scarcely benefit from the procedure. But Il Colombo has enjoyed fame and fortune because of it."

Charlotte quietly pondered the little she knew of this, one of Europe's many cruelties.

"I myself," Longfellow went on, "have listened to a few dozen successful castrati during my travels. The entertainment they provide is extremely popular, you know—though in France, there is a prejudice against them. Yet even there, royalty welcomes *musici* at home, when creating their private spectaculars."

"I know Signor Lahte's art has developed through several generations . . . but in our own age, when rights are so often argued, and Reason is highly valued, how can such a thing continue?"

"The audience at an opera, Carlotta, enjoys being part of a prancing, glittering show of wealth and privilege. Yet most I've seen appear to have little concern for the actual artists who please them—or even their music, in many cases, for there's frequently chattering and dining going on throughout a performance." He snorted at his recollection, before going further. "The world that supports such theaters may seem bright, but I am afraid it is darker than our own. Much is hidden from view behind scenery, and much arranged by what we would consider steep bargains—such as Lahte's. True aristocrats might put a stop to it, but they will not. When do they think beyond their pleasures, after all?"

"Edmund Montagu is not far from a title, Richard, and he is hardly a man who would willingly injure others, I think."

"Let's hope not. Edmund seems to have escaped the worst habits of his class. But I will hardly envy my sister when she goes to meet her new relations across the sea! Yet we mustn't forget that such families have long made advancements in Art and Science possible . . . and who will support men like Lahte when the aristocrats are gone, which can only be a matter of time, I can't imagine."

"Then you feel this is something that *should* continue?"

"Well . . . it is the nature of man to excel, and to suffer. And it must have been partly his own choice, Carlotta. Of that I have little doubt, for the level his art has reached requires absolute dedication. Beyond that, if he had not been altered, Lahte would very likely have spent his life in poverty. The beauty of his music does have much to offer the soul, as I suspect you've already decided."

"And yet—"

"And yet, instead of examining the thistles at our feet, let us admire the clockwork of the heavens."

Charlotte quickly sucked in her breath—something unexpected had brushed against her ankle. She then realized that one of Longfellow's cats had come along, with Orpheus close behind. The cat spoke as it threw itself manfully against her knees, to be rewarded by bubbling laughter.

"Can anything be more delightful than the sound of a woman's pleasure?" another new voice inquired sweetly.

Absorbed in their conversation, neither Longfellow nor Mrs. Willett had noticed when the music stopped. Now, each wondered how much of their discussion might have been overheard, as Gian Carlo Lahte continued.

"I have just encountered an enchanting aroma, walking across the grass."

"A piece of chamomile lawn laid this spring," Longfellow told him, adding an edification. "We use it to make a calming tea."

"Of course. How often I have slept with the help of a little flower . . . but tonight, I am quite ready to retire all on my own. That is what I have come to tell you both."

"Do you abandon your new mistress so soon, Gian Carlo?"

The musico sent an inquisitive look to Charlotte, who could not imagine his answer.

"Science," Longfellow reminded him. "At least take a look through the ground glass," he urged further. "It would seem quite rude to ignore her completely!"

"Ah, yes—extraordinary. Such an evening is made for gazing . . . at stars. Still, I must think of my throat. I have already tired myself too much today."

Il Colombo reached for Mrs. Willett's hand and held it briefly. Then he turned and walked toward the house, his shirt a ghostly splash of white which soon disappeared.

Before much longer, Charlotte, with Orpheus, began a journey back across the starlit yard, on a well-worn path that led to her kitchen door.

Longfellow and the cat continued to stare into the darkness, until the beast silently moved off to stalk its prey. Longfellow then sat alone, trying to name a new discontent. Something like a small, chewing rodent seemed to have crept into his own thoughts. There it grew louder, and stronger, as the night wore on.

Chapter 6

WHILE FINISHING A leisurely breakfast, Richard Longfellow watched sparrows drop from the leaves above to devour a scattering of crumbs on the flagstone of his piazza. Across the table, Gian Carlo Lahte poured the last of the coffee from a silver pot, and Cicero continued to absorb himself in the week's *Boston Gazette*.

Shifting his attention, Longfellow surveyed Lahte's new attire. Today his guest had put on a shirt of French cambric, thin enough for comfort even on what promised to be a sultry afternoon. And he had draped a sensible linen frock coat over the back of his chair. It would make him less noticeable in the village than the previous day's scarlet affair. That was regrettable, but Longfellow supposed there would still be some sort of fireworks when Old

World and New converged—a thing that would be good for them all.

Yet a surprise of another sort already occupied Bracebridge that morning. At the moment, it was on its way up from the village, on the fluttering coattails of the Reverend Christian Rowe.

"Do I interrupt a meal of some kind?" the preacher offered in greeting. He pulled a pocket watch from his waistcoat; this was followed by a handkerchief, with which he mopped his brow.

"Signor Lahte," Longfellow replied with mock concern, "has yet to learn that the running of a farm is a terrible struggle, which one must rise early to win. But what has brought you from your own unending toil in support of humanity, Reverend?"

"I have something to say to you which I believe you must find shocking—"

"Nothing *too* horrible, I hope—"

"In vain, I fear! *Someone* in our midst has turned to grave robbery!"

Longfellow sat up abruptly. "Just what valuables has this villain made off with?"

"A pair of boots, and some coat buttons."

"Boots, and buttons. Taken from the unknown man in the cellar, I presume?"

"Of course!"

Longfellow looked off into the gray-green distance, his brain racing, though his face remained placid under the reverend's close scrutiny. While they waited Cicero folded his paper, and Gian Carlo Lahte came around the granite table.

"The boots," Longfellow finally answered, "I can understand. A man finding himself without a decent pair might take what he felt Providence had put into his path. However . . . buttons? Who would take *buttons* from a dead man? I'll admit I didn't pay them much attention yesterday, but I'll swear they weren't gold; nor, I think, were they even gilt."

"You did not include them in your likeness?" Rowe asked accusingly.

"I took only the head. But who would steal buttons, when he could have made off with the whole coat?"

"It was unclean," returned the reverend, disgust written on his face.

"A military man," said Cicero, "sometimes has his buttons removed, when he is disgraced."

"True," said Longfellow, "when they are regimental buttons. But our corpse wasn't in uniform. And if this thing was done to make a point, how then could the same man, apparently moved by honor, have stooped to take the fellow's boots?"

"It is a curious thing," said Gian Carlo Lahte, finally. "But can such a thief be so remarkable in your countryside? In my own, one expects things left unattended to come and go. Especially among those who have little."

Longfellow turned back to Reverend Rowe. "Considering the growing hardships in Boston, I had supposed lawlessness might increase there—"

"It is not a lack of wealth, *but too much of it*, that leads to strife and sin throughout the provinces," Rowe interrupted. "*This* has caused many to turn away from the Almighty, and to forget their places. If He has increased our troubles, it is surely to bring men back to their senses by reminding them of the stealth of the Tempter! We must all continue to root the Devil out, wherever we find him—"

"Buttons," Longfellow muttered. "What did the blessed things look like?"

"Someone else might remember," Cicero reminded him. "Caleb, do you mean?"

"I was thinking of Mrs. Willett."

"Of course, she does have a woman's eye for detail—though little care for the mode. Well . . . on the chance that it could be of some small importance," Longfellow decided, "and, as we must all help the reverend root out Lucifer—let us all go and ask her!"

IN A MATTER of minutes, Christian Rowe knocked on the back door of the house just up the hill. While they waited for an answer, Richard Longfellow nodded to Hannah Sloan, who sat boiling cheesecloth under the ancient white oak next to the barn. He noted with satisfaction that Hannah abandoned her stick and stood to get a better look at the gentleman she'd heard of, though as yet her full, red face showed little of her conclusions.

Mrs. Willett soon invited them into a kitchen fragrant with fresh pot herbs, recently hung to dry among the low rafters. "Have you received word from Dr. Warren?" she asked her neighbor, as the others looked around with interest.

"He sent a note saying he hopes to visit us this evening, after his appointments."

"How much this resembles the place of my birth," Lahte offered. "But in Tuscany, such houses are crowded, and loud with voices. This, I think, feels like a shrine."

"Do you mean a *reliquary*, sir?" came an immediate cry from the reverend. "For bones of the saints, or some of Mary's ubiquitous hairs? We have no need for such nonsense here in Massachusetts!"

"For a few more weeks at least," Charlotte answered, ignoring Christian Rowe, "we'll be less busy than usual."

"And what is it you do today?" asked the musico.

"We'll begin to dry shell beans. But I've set aside most

of the day for making cheeses. Tomorrow, Hannah and I plan to start preserving pears."

"Only you live here, Mrs. Willett, with one servant? There is no man who helps you with these things?"

Undaunted, Reverend Rowe threw out a new reproof. "Some here suppose that a woman can decide her duties for herself, without the guidance of a husband. Yet on the Sabbath, women *must* be led by those of greater learning, so that they will think not on the flesh, but of their souls."

"We do what is necessary, whenever what we can," Charlotte said mildly. "As a widow, I have a right to choose my own occupations. But Hannah is hardly a servant," she added, speaking toward the windows. "She exchanges her labor in return for a portion of what we produce together. Her family, you see, is well supplied with daughters awaiting their own marriages, and homes. Oh, but I do employ Hannah's young Henry, who assists me morning and evening with the milking."

"A skill I, too, learned as a boy," Lahte replied proudly.

"Then would you like to see the dairy?"

"I would be delighted, madama!"

"A good start," said Longfellow, "if you mean to try the country life, Lahte. After that, we might go after a hillside of rye grass—but I recall we've not come to discuss farming or housekeeping this morning, Mrs. Willett. We are here, instead, to ask for your help. We wish to inquire about buttons."

"Buttons?"

"Is it possible for you to recall those worn by the man we saw in the reverend's cellar?"

"Well, I did notice that they were rather large. Molded, I think, and uncovered metal. I supposed the tops were meant to look as if they had filigree on them, though I believe they were nothing so fine. They were the kind whose two halves are made separately, then crimped together over a shank-eye; I'm sure you and Signor Lahte noticed that, too."

"Hmmm."

"But why are his buttons of interest today?"

"Because someone stole them from the corpse last night. Someone who took his boots as well." Though Mrs. Willett made no answer, Longfellow guessed there might be something else she hesitated to ask.

For several minutes, in fact, Charlotte had watched as Gian Carlo Lahte became increasingly uncomfortable. By now, he rubbed the sleeves of his shirt restlessly, almost as if—

"I wonder, sir," she asked him then, "if last night *you* were bothered by something?" Lahte moaned with surprising energy, and began to luxuriate in an orgy of scratching through his sleeves.

"I have been much bitten," he said quite unnecessarily.

"I believe I can help."

"You cannot refer to bedbugs?" asked Longfellow, his eyebrows lifting.

"Mosquitoes, I think," Mrs. Willett reassured him.

"Odd. I wasn't bothered last night, in bed or on the grass. But I suppose you're new to this particular sort, Lahte, and so they find you more attractive than the rest of us."

Charlotte recrossed the room, carrying a bottle of witch hazel and a piece of flannel. After Signor Lahte rolled up his sleeves she began to dab at several red bumps, hearing him sigh with relief as the cooling liquid had its expected effect.

"I would imagine," Longfellow went on, "that you'll soon get used to them, and they to you. At the moment, you're a rare treat for most of our local creatures."

"I have become deaf to the buzzing of many kinds of beings, both large and small," said the musico, not unkindly.

Longfellow observed Hannah Sloan's broad body lean in at the window, and saw that she, too, watched the man being tended. Might she be asking herself if he would do for one of her daughters? For if she had not already heard . . . but there was something else here . . . something curious in the sly way she looked between Lahte and Rowe, and then at Charlotte—

He swiveled abruptly to regard the minister. In Rowe's face, at least, he saw nothing to confirm a new and monstrous suspicion. The man's interest appeared to be held by pieces of pewter and silver arrayed upon the sideboard. Clearly, his thoughts went in another direction. *Or did they . . . ?*

"If there are mosquitoes in your bedroom," said Charlotte, "you might ask for frames to be put into the windows. You remember, Richard, making Diana the gauze screens last summer, after a June bug came in one night?"

"Yes, yes—all too well!" Longfellow again saw his sister running through the hall in her nightgown, clawing at her hair. At least this softened the revolting thought of Reverend Rowe courting his neighbor.

"But I still can't see why I wasn't bitten even once last evening," he continued, seeking further consolation in scientific observation. "North of the bridge where the river slows, down in the marsh grass, one might expect to be bothered. But you wouldn't have been wandering there?"

"Even in Italy," Lahte assured him, "and especially in Rome, we are careful of the *mal aria*, the bad air that hangs over such places on warm nights. Also, I am sure I would find the odor most offensive."

"Presumably. While I recommend the benefits of night air in general—unlike some who would have us suffocated by bed curtains—we mustn't forget that even the ancients feared miasmas that float over water. Especially water that stands or meanders. Do you know, I once stood on the actual Maeander, having gone down to Phrygia from Constantinople to have a look at the land of old Midas—"

"Most edifying, I'm sure," said Reverend Rowe abruptly, "but as our most influential selectman, what will you do about our thief?"

"What *can* I do, Reverend? At the moment, I have duties beyond pilfered boots and buttons. I will admit this affair worries me, and if you discover anything more, I hope you will let me know. But now, perhaps, we should all go about our business."

"If you would care to stay, Signor Lahte, you would be welcome," Charlotte suggested—causing her neighbor to regret the telling of a small lie regarding his own level of occupation.

"I would be delighted," said the musico. His long fingers rolled down his sleeves. "I believe, madamina, that you must be a sorceress. I am cured! And I would gladly learn more of your spells."

Blushing again under the reverend's sharp eye, Charlotte felt she would enjoy learning something more of Signor Lahte's world, as well—clearly a strange one in which poverty and cruelty might join to create rare beauty, though with a melancholy proviso.

IN THE HOUR that followed the departure of Longfellow and Reverend Rowe, Gian Carlo Lahte first explored Mrs. Willett's kitchen, and then wandered her barnyard, acquainting himself with fowl, flora, tools, and utensils, inside and out. The spotted hens under the white oak seemed to give him particular pleasure as he threw them scraps, and it occurred to Charlotte that this worldly man might almost be revisiting his simple boyhood. Pleased by the thought, she turned from the window and again took up a knife, this time to cut into a mass of curd lying in a vat that waited in a water bath by the fire. Crushed rennet, from the stomach of a calf that had provided Easter's dinner, had already done its work, curdling milk from last evening mixed with more gathered that morning.

She cut the curd into small squares, then began the long process of turning the warm pieces gently with her hands, feeling for the mass to lose its moisture. In the meantime, she considered Hannah's choice to work in the yard, even when Signor Lahte came inside to watch her own efforts.

"What is to be done now?" he asked from a low stool, as Charlotte continued to stir.

"In a few minutes I'll ask you to pour more kettle water into the bath, to heat it further. Once it comes to the proper temperature, it has to be kept there for about an hour. Then we'll remove the whey. You might help by lifting and pouring out what's in the vat—just onto the cheesecloth I've stretched over that bowl, there—so the curds can drain. After another half-hour it can go onto the boards, where I'll knead in the salt. Then it all must be pressed into the molds, which I've lined with more cloth."

"And your work will be done?"

"*Then*, we put weights on the top of the molds. In another hour, more weight, and in three hours time the cheese should be almost dry. I'll rub each one with salt, and take them all down to the cellar to ripen. They'll be turned every so often for two months, at least, before the first comes to table."

"How I adore the patience of women! The liquid— this whey—you will make it into *ricotta*?"

"I'm afraid I don't know what that is . . . but the family in Mr. Longfellow's piggery finds whey very enjoyable, and beneficial."

"Your country is indeed a rich one."

"Have you helped to make *ricotta* before?" she asked, after her hand went briefly to a few twists of cider-colored hair that had begun, as usual, to fall.

"I remember only that the liquid was made sour and eaten in my father's house—the rest, he sold to be made into fine cheeses for others. But I did not make *ricotta* myself. As a young boy, my chores were outside. Then, like the cheeses, I was sold to a *conservatorio* in Parma. There I sometimes visited the kitchen to help, and to find something more to eat. But for long hours each day I only studied, and sang. Now I think I will surprise you. Even as a boy I was called Il Colombo, but not for my fine voice; as you know, the dove sings less well than many other birds. No—you see, one feast day, some of us were allowed to eat many *piccioni*—doves, as you say—after a special mass sung at one of the great churches. From that time, I longed to be rich so that I might keep such doves myself. I also hoped to learn the tricks of the bird-catcher—the fowler—by following him into the forest outside the city; in that way I should always have the little roasted song-birds, the ortolans, to eat. I see I do surprise you! But though I was hungry for such things, I was also glad to have more bread to eat than many others, whose voices did not show the promise of my own."

Something made her want to turn away from this picture of a boy hungry for birds, as he himself was taught to sing—but Charlotte found her curiosity too strong. Instead, she asked a daring question.

"I suppose we can never truly understand the ways of Rome here, but didn't your clergy—your priests—didn't they forbid what was done?"

"*Sì,*" he answered simply.

"But then . . . ?"

"At the *conservatorio*, everyone prayed I would be taken to serve Il Papa one day, paid for with good money. Of course this was to be for the glory of God! Yet it is said to be against God's law, to do what is done to so many. The cardinals even say it is enough to condemn such a *dottore* to the *inferno*—but, they also hope we will sing for them like the angels. It is for this reason the Holy Father allows, and pays, and looks the other way. Life, you see, is never without sin, even in Roma."

"But you did not go to Rome?"

"I grew too charming," Lahti admitted with a laugh. "When my voice was ready, my teachers were offered more by the theaters than by the cardinals. In Italy, you know, young men often play the parts of women in the operas; and of course, no women are allowed in the choirs of the Church—this is the order of the Pope. In the theater, it can be unpleasant, even dangerous, for a woman to walk the stage. My own experience has taught me to have sympathy for these brave ladies—indeed, for you all! Especially as I, too, have known the bite of a corset with stays around my chest, and the trouble of painting my face. Perhaps," he ventured with a smile, "I know these things better than you, madamina?"

Charlotte pressed on, soothed by her companion's comforting voice, despite the unusual subjects they pursued. "And the Duke? How did you go from Italy to Germany?"

"When the Duke heard me in a theater in Milano, he

bought my service for two years, so that I might go and sing in his chapel. To him I was able to sell myself, for I had already earned enough to pay the *conservatorio* for my training. That, for me, was the beginning of freedom. But madamina, may I ask something of you?"

Charlotte looked to her hands as she replied. "If you like. But I haven't much of interest to tell."

"I have heard from our friend Longfellow of your husband. He was what is called in England a Quaker, I believe. But there are no other Quakers here?"

"My husband was a Friend—that is what they most often call one another. And he was raised in Philadelphia, where there are many. Here in Massachusetts, I'm afraid Friends are not entirely welcome, but my own parents taught me to value what comes from within, as they do . . . as well as what the world can teach us."

"And, of course, what your good reverend has to say?"

A soft laugh was Charlotte's answer. "I was not raised in Aaron's faith," she added on an impulse, "but I did feel somehow that we were one, from the first." She was unused to hearing herself speak intimately of her husband; it was especially odd to reveal her feelings to someone who was little more than a stranger! But she had quickly found herself drawn to Gian Carlo Lahte in a way that, if not exactly as it had been with Aaron, was not entirely different.

"*Simpatia*," he returned. "This is the best beginning for a marriage. Without it, men soon find passion elsewhere—and women may give back to their husbands a gift of horns." He looked away, as if he feared he'd broken the trust between them—if, in fact, his meaning had been understood.

"Is this why you are here? Do you run from a cuckold?" asked Charlotte, unable to keep what she suspected to herself any longer.

The musico rose gracefully from his low seat. Gaining time, he took two silver tubes from his pocket, and joined them to make a small flute. He tried a few notes before he answered her carefully.

"Why do you suspect this, madamina?"

"Perhaps because you seem remarkably truthful in some things . . . while I suspect you mislead us in others, including your reason for coming here."

Even to her own ears it sounded worse than rude. Would he be insulted? Yet they had already shared much. And what bounds were there, after all, when a man seemed so utterly willing to please?

When it came, his reply, as she'd hoped, was direct.

"I did wish to avoid a certain person by coming here. At least for a time. And it is a woman . . . one who cannot refuse her feelings of love for me. I, too, have feelings—and it is very difficult for a man to refuse, when he is asked to prove himself. Especially when there is little for a lover to fear from such an encounter. Do you, perhaps, understand?"

"I think that I do."

"With you, madamina, I believe I can be honest as I have been with few others. For much of my life, I have run to avoid becoming entangled. It is why I left Milano many weeks ago, when she threatened to leave her home. I tried only to spare an old man—and perhaps to avoid a certain pain myself. Love can bring great danger, and my life has already been . . . full of event. Now, I think I would prefer to live with a woman who is like a sister."

"You have never married?"

He seemed to consider anew before giving her his answer. "In Italy, it is not possible."

"Not possible? How could that be?"

"Do you know what the Church believes to be the first purpose of a union between man and woman?"

"Children." Uneasily, she recalled another recent conversation.

"A musico has no hope of fathering children, and so, there can be no marriage. In my country, this has long been the law." He put the instrument he held to his lips, and produced a few notes, which lingered sweetly.

"But can that be true in this country?" asked Charlotte.

"An interesting question! It is possible your Reverend Rowe will have the answer."

"It is possible," she returned, her face expressing her thoughts in a way that soon caused them both to laugh.

"Madamina! I have been delighted to have a thousand gasp before me; now, I tell you, I only want to play to the vines, and these cheeses, and to a woman who might one day become a sister to me! But tell me," he asked, suddenly in earnest, "could you love a man if you were certain he would never give you a family? Could you . . . could any woman be content, with such a husband?"

Hardly believing she did so, Charlotte replied by telling him a fear of her own.

"You see, I have no children. Yet had I known that would happen, I doubt I would have chosen differently. Even, I think, if I were certain the fault lay with my husband. But I cannot know the fault was not in me. And if *that* is true . . . it would make the two of us, signor, somewhat alike. Would it not?"

He gazed into her azure eyes, which at that moment were sad, as well as beautiful. Gian Carlo Lahte leaned closer, extended his hand, and caught a wisp of her hair that had again fallen from its pins. He gently placed it behind her ear, allowing his fingers to linger.

"*Bella signora*, I salute you!" he exclaimed abruptly, with a deep bow. Then he strolled about the room to the tripping notes of a lively air.

Charlotte looked down with greater concentration to

the task before her. She suspected some might call it scandalous, but she could not help feeling a glow in the sympathetic company of Il Colombo. She had also begun to sense a growing relief deep within her—a thing she found somewhat more difficult to explain.

Chapter 7

WELL BEFORE SUNDOWN and the start of the Sabbath, several regular visitors were again engaged in conversation along rough tables, inside the Blue Boar tavern.

"I heard it with my own ears," Caleb Knox insisted. He lifted a pint of cider brought to him for the latest unwinding of his now familiar story. "Amazing high it was, almost like a trumpet—and then it sawed back and forth like a fiddle for a while, with the tune embroidered in strange ways."

"Not in English, you say?" Samuel Sloan asked pointedly. Hannah's husband had been dismayed when the storyteller sat down beside him minutes earlier, interrupting glum thoughts of the week gone by. Now, his curiosity was stirred.

"No, nor French either. I can't say for sure, but it

seemed to me like the Latin the boys at Harvard College spout out on the green, on Commencement Day."

"There's good times!" returned another farmer at a nearby table. Then he fondly recalled the capers, and the liquor, that followed the great event each year on Cambridge Common, when Harvard sent off another crop.

"He said he was a . . . a music-something-or-other," Caleb said eventually, returning to his tale. "Said most of Europe knows it."

"Not a musico?" asked an old quail who had earlier seated himself by the unlit hearth out of habit, in a broad-backed Windsor chair. His pied eyebrows fluttered while the clay pipe he smoked sent out a series of small puffs.

"Aye, that's it, Mr. Flint," Caleb called over. "I believe that's just the way he said it."

"Oh-ho!" cried a second plump person from a chair by the first—a man generally called Tinder, though Tyndall was his name. "A musico, in a place like this! Who would have dreamed of such a thing?"

His friend Flint wiped his lips and smiled, causing both cheeks to shine more brightly. "I have heard a number of stories myself from a half-brother—the one raised in London, you'll recall. There's flocks of them that come and go all over Europe, these musicos, at the whim of the public, who pays well to see 'em! Like gentlemen, most are . . . though few can claim to come from any kind of good family, of course."

"Well, what are they, then?" asked Jack Pennywort, a small, nearly toothless man who nursed a tankard of ale. "What's so special about him?"

Phineas Wise, the tavern's lean and hawk-nosed proprietor, cleared his throat as he glanced from Jack to the little man's current table companion, burly blacksmith Nathan Browne. The smith, too, seemed puzzled.

"He's a castrato, sons!" said Flint triumphantly, slapping

his knee for emphasis. "Right here in Bracebridge! Probably rich as Croesus! But what on earth would one of them be doing here?"

"One of *what*?" Jack insisted, hoping he was not about to become the butt of yet another tavern jest.

"Do you know, Jack," Phineas Wise asked slowly, "what a gelding is?"

"Certainly I do! A great, good horse for a gentleman to ride, or even a lady. Gentle, they're said to be, after what's done to them."

"Well, that's what's done to a castrato," Wise said, wiping the table before him with a cloth.

"No! How can they do that?"

"I only know it's taken care of while they're boys, to keep the voice from becoming low, like a man's. It will still be loud, of course, as it comes from a large chest. That's *why* they do it."

"Who?" Jack demanded, his club foot scraping on the floor as he shifted uncomfortably.

"Only the Italians, I believe. Though castrati can be found singing in most of the cities of Europe, as Mr. Flint has said."

"He may be a gelding," Flint returned, "but from what I've heard, his sort can still do as other men in most things. For instance, the castrato has been known to fight bravely. And he might be as godly as the next. Or so it says in Scripture."

"Like the Eunuch of Ethiopia—" joined in another, who had a prodigious memory.

"I did take him for a gentleman," said Caleb Knox with growing uncertainty, "though now . . ."

"There's nothing wrong with making a useful horse," Nathan mused, "for many need taming, especially when they're young. But to think of a man—!"

"A man with no seed," replied old Tinder, "is a sad thing to us, surely—but he's something else again to the ladies! Nip to the cat, if you know what I mean." He puffed sagaciously, emitting a Vesuvius of smoke.

"You'd best keep your bride in sight, Nathan, should this fellow decide to go wandering off from Mr. Longfellow's," said Flint with a wheeze.

"Unless he's one of the others," Tinder added, looking about to see who, exactly, was there.

"*What* others?" cried Jack, again fearful that he was about to lose the thread of the conversation.

While several men on the more distant benches began to watch and listen, Tinder seemed to gauge the hour by the light of the fading afternoon. Then, fortifying himself with a few more puffs, he went on.

"Certain gentlemen across the sea, as most of you will know, have long been said to have an *unusually* high regard for other gentlemen, and even for young boys. The Greeks, for instance . . . if you take my meaning."

"You mean buggery?" exclaimed a man who sat against the wall, beneath several barrels of cider.

"To us, a grave error. Yet it is known that in classical times—"

"Then by God, I'll keep Leonard inside, too—and put Dobbin to barn!" shouted a red-faced man who had been in his seat overlong.

A chorus of hoots sounded from a corner, but the original group of speakers frowned at the tendency of the conversation, while a few others clamped their teeth together and thought about going home.

"As you're well aware, sodomy is a grave crime in Massachusetts," Phineas Wise reminded them all, "and the penalty for several of these acts is still death. Though in this century, I am glad to say, we have not gone that far.

But it is still a thing that can bring a place serious trouble. So let us take care! Let us also remember there is a heavy penalty for accusing any man without cause."

"And, for a conviction on the crime of sodomy, you will need at least two witnesses, gentlemen," called a sheep-faced man in traveler's garb, who then went back to giving less startling legal information to a worried farmer.

"If them that sing high lack a certain something," suggested a bull-necked customer in bass tones, "perhaps a man who sings low must have more of it?"

"I'll be sure to ask your wife next time we're alone," came his answer, disguised as a squeak. This caused the large man to rise and stare around the room.

"It is curious, though," Nathan said softly, under new laughter, "when such a man comes here on the very day another finds his way into the reverend's cellar."

"Too damned many strangers come through now," replied Samuel Sloan in a growl. He had turned away from the landlord to pour a bit of rum from a pocket bottle into his ale. "This live one," he added, "will be sure to find real trouble, if he tries anything with my old woman."

Nathan considered an answer, but in the end kept it to himself.

"What is the musico's name?" asked someone stationed by the door. "In case we want to greet him in the road."

"His name's Lahte," said a man just come from leaving a hogshead of salt in Richard Longfellow's kitchen. "Signor Lahte. He's an Italian gentleman, known to Mr. Longfellow from his travels."

"Aye, that's right," said Caleb Knox. "And he says he wishes to settle here!"

"Surely," returned the sentry, "if he's friend to Mr. Longfellow—"

"But shouldn't we have a care, with a man so different in his ways?" Caleb insisted, swaying a bit as he rose to emphasize his point. "For what if he came here to bubble us all, and make his fortune?"

"If he already *has* a fortune," another reasoned coolly, "as Mr. Flint supposes, and he wants to spread a little of it around this sorry place, would any of us be unhappy about *that?*"

The ensuing silence made Phineas Wise smile at the cunning of at least some of his clientele. "Now," the landlord concluded, "if anyone would like to turn these things over with the help of a fresh pint of cider, or something with good barley in it, I'd be happy to accommodate him."

"It is my considered opinion," Samuel Sloan called out a while later, "that as long as we know what to suspect, each may look out for his own pocket—or his morals, come to that—whatever the plans of this castrato be. But what I wonder is, who will be the first brave sprat to run and tell the news to the Reverend Mr. Rowe?"

Another whoop broke out, and congenial laughter soon rolled about the room once more.

It seemed, thought the landlord, that the village had come alive with anticipation—a pleasing thought, for this was a thing he knew did no harm to business.

LATER, ACROSS THE river and up the hill, waning light cast quiet shadows onto the blue walls of Charlotte Willett's study, where she and her neighbor awaited the arrival of Dr. Joseph Warren from Boston. Meanwhile, Richard Longfellow had consumed most of a bowl of gingerbread and clotted cream.

"Was your afternoon with Il Colombo a pleasant one?" he asked between mouthfuls.

"I did find it enjoyable. It's good to have fresh company—especially that of a man who takes an interest in a woman's work."

"Have a care for European flattery, Mrs. Willett. I suspect your new friend is a master of far more than music. Did you learn anything of particular interest?" Longfellow asked further, with the air of one who holds a trump or two.

Charlotte then related much of what she had found curious, if not everything. "One subject, though, did not come up," she finished.

"Oh?"

"That of the operation itself."

"You surprise me."

"Richard, you know I have a keen interest in medicine—"

"An admirable thing in a countrywoman," he conceded, evading her question.

"I'm hardly happy to keep returning to it in my mind . . . especially when I'm not sure I should be asking such a thing in the first place! But won't you tell me?"

Longfellow studied her face carefully, before he spoke again.

"Together, we have felt the worst, Carlotta, that God and Nature can do. As it has affected neither your spirit, nor your virtue, I doubt any new knowledge, even of this sort, will harm you."

"How is it done?"

"Let me tell you a story. It seems a famous musico was visited, one day, by a poor stranger who claimed to be his father. Both had changed greatly since he'd sent the boy to his cruel fate years before; but the old man gave proof, and the musico acknowledged him. At that point, the man asked for money. The singer quickly agreed. However, he insisted that he repay his father with his own coin. So saying, he gave the man a purse that was quite empty, and sent him on his way."

"Empty?"

"Two purses, I suppose, would have been more to the point. But I see that you are after more. Well, as a curious man myself, I requested the details from a fellow student, when I was first in Italy many years ago. It seems when they find a boy with a promising voice who is willing to learn, they first give him poppy juice to drink, and then put him into a hot bath; this promotes sleep, and distends the blood vessels. A skilled physician—for this is not a job entrusted to a fool—makes two small incisions in the groin, severing the passages that lead to the seed organs. In time, this causes both external 'purses' to wither away, as they are of no further use to their owner."

"Oh . . ."

"Here is something else you will find interesting. A castrato is still quite capable of performing the physical act of love, if he wishes to. They are certainly poignant when they sing of it—in fact, it is this, in part, for which they are so highly paid. Yet I have often wondered how much of their noble passion on the stage is feigned. A few quite elegant performers have been notable for flying into tempers offstage and behaving like fishwives . . . at least, until their voices, and their figures, cease to deserve admiration."

Charlotte's eyes were no longer eager, and whatever they saw appeared to be far away. At her feet, Orpheus was considerably more attentive; for this he was rewarded with the last bite of gingerbread.

"You're not the only one to be curious, by the way. I'm sure Cicero longs to ask me what you have. I may repeat it to him one day, once Lahte has gone."

"You don't think he means to stay, then?"

"I doubt it. He may be telling us the truth when he says he would enjoy a quiet life. Still, I think there must be something more to his visit than he has disclosed."

Catching Charlotte's eye, Longfellow held onto it, until she relented and told him the rest of what she had heard.

"Signor Lahte did tell me he was the target of a jealous husband, though I'm not sure he gave the man cause. He said this was the real reason he left Milan."

"Many among the castrati are notorious for amorous exploits, as I've already hinted."

"Yes, you have already warned me."

"Then *here* is something you may not know. One of the missing boots has been found."

"Has it? Where?"

"In the marshes of the river. It was pulled up by a boy out sniggling."

Charlotte sat back thoughtfully.

"In the river marshes," Longfellow repeated. "Where there are the Devil's own mosquitoes at night. The heel appears to have been prised off."

"As if someone hoped to find something inside?"

"Something that might also have been concealed between button halves. From what you've just told me, I think Lahte could have been seeking the hidden message of a lover."

"If we assume the dead man to have been this husband from Milan."

"Quite a distance to come, but possible. And if we suppose Lahte recognized the fellow, it would explain his earlier shock."

"Yes . . ."

"If that is our answer, I don't suppose there is any great hurry to prove it. I'm inclined to allow him time to tell us the whole story, which he seems to have already begun.

He is, after all, a gentleman. More important than that, he's here as my guest. And a host has a certain duty—"

"You're convinced there's no further danger?"

"From Lahte?"

"Or perhaps *to* him?"

"Since this supposed husband has accidentally removed himself, I would imagine Il Colombo is safe enough. Though he might consider himself fortunate to have suffered no more than a fright. We know terrible things are sometimes done by those who love—like the Moor—not wisely, but too well."

Charlotte cocked her head.

It was almost as if, thought Longfellow, she heard something he could not. Then both sat in silence, each absorbed in further speculation, until it was time to light the candles.

"what is it now?" young Dr. Warren asked when he had accepted a glass of sherry. Even by the low light of the tapers, they could see that his color was extraordinarily high as his pale blue eyes scanned his summoners.

"That, of course," replied Longfellow, "is what we are supposing you will tell us. If you are able. As I wrote in my letter, we know very little. However, certain suspicions have been raised."

"Suspicions? I see," Warren replied with an engaging smile, examining Charlotte even more closely. "Are you keeping well, Mrs. Willett? But I will answer this, first, by my own observation. Remarkably well! A fine complexion, indeed. By the way, I have a message for you from a young friend. He begs to be remembered fondly, and is concerned for one of your cows."

"Delilah is much improved," said Charlotte, returning his look of amusement. "But I'm afraid she, too, misses someone who deserted us for a greater world of worthy gentlemen. Is Lem happy in town? Is he lonely, do you think?"

"Lonely? Certainly not! I myself have seen him often lately, and I've presented him to a number of our better citizens. It is my hope that he'll find their acquaintance improving."

"And his studies?"

"Oh, he will do well enough with those. But he's likely to pick up as much of use to him in Boston as in Cambridge. However, let us return to my own small skills. You suspect," Warren now asked Richard Longfellow, "that the deceased may have come here only recently, from abroad?"

"We believe that to be a possibility."

"It may add another dimension to our problem. Still, if he fell from his horse, I don't imagine I'll have much doubt as to the cause of death."

"If you can tell us that is what happened, I'll be glad to hear it."

"Suspicions, you say. At the moment, I am even more interested in what you *don't* say. But let's go and see. Then, I will give you my professional opinion."

Making their way through the warm darkness, they found their lanterns swayed by varying gusts of wind. Soon, trees above leaned down as if inquiring into their mission, until a field's breadth freed them. Seeing the lights of the village below, Charlotte suspected some of her neighbors enjoyed late reading, while others might be sharing a final glass of comfort before going off to bed. None would offer her, or her companions, such a glass tonight. Their visit would be with none of the living.

They passed among the first stones of the church-yard, and walked on beneath waving branches to the cellar's slanted door. Longfellow soon had the door folded back, allowing a current of air to freshen what lay within. Dr. Warren, alone, made his way down the wooden steps. They saw the light of his lantern steady as he positioned it next to the body; then he opened his physician's bag and began his work.

While they waited above, Longfellow and Charlotte peered toward each unseen call from the surrounding graveyard, until at length they were relieved to see a bat hunting cheerfully above in their lantern's light. They enjoyed its clever movements, watching as it wheeled and veered, until at last Joseph Warren emerged. Longfellow quickly closed the cellar door, but the physician showed no sign of being ready to go on. Instead, he sat upon the grass to recover himself.

"Well?"

"Clearly, there was a substantial injury to the head. If he was thrown and fell onto a rock, his death could have been an accident. The smell of wine first convinced me that this was likely, for a drunken man is rarely a careful one. Not a medical opinion; one of personal experience. Then I examined the material that must have come from the stomach, and I began to have other ideas . . . as you did, I gather. The stuff is suspiciously dark, and seems to have caked in a manner that makes it flake even now, if one applies the blade of a knife. I've taken a sample to moisten later. The strength of its color could tell me if blood is indeed present, as well as red wine."

"Do you think there is any danger of contagion?"

"I did, for a few moments. Black vomit may mean yellow fever, particularly in one who has lately visited a southern port. I don't mind telling you I was hardly pleased to suspect it! But as he did not appear to be jaundiced—"

"Something I concluded as well."

"Yes, but he *was* unhealthy, I should say—though without asking a patient for symptoms, it is always difficult to be sure. I did look closely at his mouth. And into it. Have you done so?"

When Richard and Charlotte both shook their heads, Dr. Warren managed a smile. "You should have, for it would have surprised you. What I found there leads me to suppose this man could have been poisoned."

"What!" his listeners exclaimed in unison.

"Of course, there is already considerable decomposition . . ." Warren took a draught of air through his nose, as if to clear away the lingering scent. ". . . and yet, I'm reasonably certain there are burns in the mouth, both on the tongue and inner cheeks. These suggest to me the introduction of a caustic substance. Unless, of course, they're ulcers from an advanced oral malady. If that is the case, then his last days were anything but easy! Yet I suspect there may have been something taken with the wine, which would have caused his stomach to burn and bleed, as well."

"If this is true, Warren, what do you think it was?"

"I can't tell you that, exactly. But I can guess. I've seen similar damage when a patient—a child—accidentally swallowed salts of wood sorrel left carelessly on a table, by someone removing an ink stain. The result, I am sorry to say, was fatal. Salts of lead, too, are extremely corrosive. So is ordinary lye, as we're all warned, for its burn can be both immediate and quite damaging, depending on the strength of the solution. Arsenical preparations usually take a bit more time, but they, too, can lead to accidental death—or an intentional one, on occasion. That, of course, is the interesting question here. If it *was* poison, was it administered by his own hand, or by someone else's?"

Longfellow expelled his breath abruptly. "Can you tell us more, with certainty?"

"Not without a closer examination."

"I see."

"Do you know yet who he was?" the doctor then asked.

"No. But I've sent a sketch of him to our friend Montagu."

"Indeed? At least it might keep your esteemed new brother occupied for a while. I presume you know many of us are displeased by what the captain has been up to lately."

"And what, specifically, is that?"

"He seeks to learn of our private discussions, when they are none of his affair."

"Discussions directed against the Crown, perhaps?"

"*Against* is too strong a word, Richard—and one that is politically unwise to use, just now. Let us say . . . that some of your friends in Boston, who still meet regularly in the Long Room—where you remain welcome, by the way—these men hope to remind the world of the hard-won rights of all Englishmen!"

Longfellow noticed that Charlotte had wandered a little distance away, apparently engrossed in her own thoughts. "Well, Joseph," he said at length, "let us first see what we can do about unraveling the fate of one man, before you go off directing the future of us all. At the moment, I can hardly believe this new theory of yours. And it is the opinion of Mrs. Willett that our corpse might well have choked to death. Can you . . . perhaps . . . look further into the matter?"

Warren gave the selectman a questioning look. "I'll take him with me if you like, and give him a proper burial later—if you will lend me a conveyance and a sheet of canvas. The guard at the Neck does not look kindly on unknown bodies going in or out of town, but at the house of a physician I know in Dorchester . . . I'll see if we can discover something more. In the meanwhile, if you have any true cause to call it murder . . . and if any man you have suspicions of had the chance to meet this fellow alone—"

"I still believe, Joseph, that you're chasing shadows."

"Perhaps. Yet surely you've noticed that they are generally thrown by substantial bodies." Dr. Warren swung his lantern, causing Longfellow's own shadow to sway behind him. "And where," the physician added, "is your constable?"

"In Providence," said Longfellow. "In the morning, I'll see about doing his business for him. I suppose someone should examine the place where the death occurred. I assume you'll send us a report, once you've finished with our stranger? I'd like to have something in hand when we put a name to him."

"With pleasure," Warren replied. "But you may not get it tomorrow. Much of importance goes on at the moment in Boston."

"May I offer you refreshment, at least, before you rush off? I have a guest from Italy staying with me, who has no interest in our politics at all."

"That *would* be refreshing," said the physician, unable to guess the half of what was in store.

Chapter 8

Sunday, August 18

A ROSY SUN lit the moist, green world once more as Richard Longfellow walked out to the barn to saddle his latest acquisition, a dark mare he had decided to call Venus. Both steed and rider, he supposed, would profit from an hour of exercise, before the less fortunate of the two sat down on a hard pew to endure another of Reverend Rowe's numbing sermons. At least, thought Longfellow, he might find something new to ponder while the reverend went on and on.

The air was quiet, the grass thick with fresh dew, and the gaining sun, though it had a distinctly brassy tinge, managed to lift up his spirits as Longfellow led Venus out to the lawn. Still, he was plagued by uncertainty. Could he have been wrong, and Warren right, when a possible crime had been discussed the night before? Was he further wrong this morning in neglecting to stop at Mrs. Willett's door with his chaise, so that she, too, might view the place where Caleb Knox had found the corpse? He decided he would later blame the animal beneath him, who snorted with delight as she picked up her pace along the road. There was also the unseemliness of directing a chaise away from the meeting house on a Sunday morning, when all others would be traveling in the opposite direction. A bit of vigorous exercise was one thing, but an expedition, for whatever reason, would certainly be remarked upon. Once again, he decided that Charlotte would have to rely on what he told her. There would quite probably be little to see, after all.

Yet when Longfellow approached a row of hedge nearly two miles from the village, he saw a figure in plain skirts and a straw hat bend down, and then disappear into the glistening vegetation. That this was the place he sought he had no doubt, and not only because *she* was somehow there before him. Two days earlier, Knox had referred to this planting of hawthorn, all that was left of an old farm that had burned and been abandoned long ago. There, too, was a faint trail leading away from the verge, showing where a body had been dragged.

At Longfellow's urging Venus jumped the ditch, giving a grunt as she landed on the other side.

"Good morning!" his neighbor called, rising when horse and rider were near. Her face seemed like a summer rose unfolding in the soft light, Longfellow suddenly imagined. For some reason, the thought unsettled him.

"I see that you, too, felt the need for exercise this morning," he called back.

"For both mind and body. I scolded myself last night for having wondered exactly what had happened here, without bothering to walk out and look for facts."

"How will one make bricks without straw? A biblical allusion, Mrs. Willett, in honor of the Sabbath. Perhaps one of us will lead the other out of Egypt. Have you succeeded in finding anything?"

"Come see what may have been the rock." She stepped toward him into a circle of grass that had been well trampled. Longfellow dismounted and walked closer.

"Granite," he concluded, when he had picked up the heavy sphere she indicated. It was somewhat larger than one of her orchard's striped apples. He looked at its rough surface more closely. "There are also plates of mica here, and pink feldspar."

"Do you see something else? Something dark, there in the indentations?"

"Possibly," he said, squinting to make the best use of the reddish rays.

"From a felt hat, do you think?"

"You could be right. Well done, Mrs. Willett! We'll know for sure when I've set some strands under my microscope, and compared them with the hat itself."

"So it would seem the man rode this far, and was thrown suddenly, coming to earth one last time?"

"It appears likely," he agreed, relief mingling with renewed admiration for her nimble mind.

"Yet I wonder if it happened just that way," she continued quietly.

"What? Do you fashion a man with your straw, Carlotta, only for the pleasure of bowling him down?"

"I first saw this rock there," she explained, pointing to the spot where he, too, had seen it. "And while it may mean nothing at all, here's something else. . . ."

Taking several steps, she knelt near a patch of mud and gravel which had made a hummock in what was largely undisturbed grass. "I've found a small saucer left in the earth—which I suspect must have held a round object, and quite recently." She took back the rock, and lowered it gently into the depression with a few raised edges of dried mud remaining. It was a perfect fit.

"And—?"

"And yet, as I showed you, I found this rock several feet away."

"By this you mean to suggest—?"

"That if someone had fallen onto it *here*, where it recently was, then it should have been driven further into the ground. But it wasn't. Somehow, it ended up *there*," she finished, pointing to the place they had been standing moments before.

"What if the horse kicked the thing from its original seat, before our man fell? Or do you tell me this rock flew up from the ground to strike and kill the fellow? Assuming, of course, that he was not already the victim of Warren's poison-wielding assassin."

"I'm not completely familiar with Newton's laws; but I would say flight, in this case, seems unlikely."

"There, we agree. Still, for the sake of curiosity, let us spend some time going over the ground together." He held out his hand for the sphere of granite, and placed it into his largest coat pocket. Then, for several minutes, they walked about the damp field until they found themselves many yards apart. It was Longfellow who finally called for a halt. But as Charlotte began to walk toward him, she swooped and again disappeared into the tall grass. She bobbed up with another object.

"An ordinary bottle," he decided when they had come together. "Of inferior glass . . . the kind of thing frequently thrown away by travelers. Although," he added, sniffing at its narrow mouth, "this one does seem to have held wine."

Charlotte took back the bottle, tilting it to better see

the dried lees still adhering to the sides. "But how did it come to fall so far away?"

"Again, Mrs. Willett?" her neighbor asked with a tolerant smile. "Let us suppose, then, that it was carried by the dead man, and not tossed here by any one of a thousand others who have recently passed this way. If our man happened to be violently unseated, possibly by a bucking horse, what then?"

He stopped, waiting for her to draw her own conclusion.

"I suppose you're right," Charlotte conceded, although she also told herself that Science appeared to have its limits, particularly when it came to imagination.

"Well, then, let us go and hear what Reverend Rowe has to say of the week's events."

"I'm afraid I must miss the beginning, for I will walk back." Her face showed that she was not sorry.

"You needn't. Venus will hardly feel your weight, if you would care to come up behind me."

"And cause more comment still?"

"Is it beyond your courage, then, this morning?" He drew his boot from a stirrup, and held down a hand in more insistent invitation.

Charlotte lifted herself with a hop and allowed her waist to be encircled, until she sat to one side of the horse's back, behind the creaking saddle. Then, when he was sure she was settled, her arms around him, Richard Longfellow urged Venus on, taking them back to Bracebridge.

CHRISTIAN ROWE HAD been unusually mild, using one of the Psalms for his text: *The Lord preserveth the stranger; he relieveth the fatherless and the widow: but the way of the wicked he turneth upside down.* In his own way the preacher had thus introduced the once popish Signor Lahte (who sat saved in Longfellow's pew), found a reason to smile pointedly in the direction of Mrs. Willett, and chastised a drunken sot who had fallen from his horse but seemed unworthy of further notice.

When the morning service was finally over, Longfellow and Gian Carlo Lahte walked briskly up the hill ahead of Cicero and Charlotte. Lahte resumed an earlier discussion of Watt's newly patented improvements to the British steam engine, upon which he admitted he'd meditated happily during the sermon.

As usual, thought Richard, the Italian was both lively and attentive, a union rare in mankind—at least, the part of it with which he was most familiar. After Mrs. Willett had gone on to her own home for an afternoon of reading and contemplation, Lahte allowed his host the pleasure of laying out a careful explanation of why a tall structure needed Dr. Franklin's lightning rods; then, Longfellow described the recent installation of several atop his own barn, all attached to an iron tail whose end lay buried in the ground.

Over a simple dinner, the two men discussed improvements in plumbing and illumination; the new hope, dignity, and mobility of the working classes; abuses of lords and churches, old and current; and the growing web of navigation canals in England, which would further reduce prices while greatly facilitating travel in that country.

When their powers of concentration began to flag, the Italian and his host walked across the road in search of a snack and fresh entertainment. The musico then provided Longfellow and Jonathan Pratt with gossip from Milan, as well as news from London's coffee houses which he'd frequented before embarking on his voyage to America. When Cicero joined them, Lahte switched to ribald stories collected in butlers' pantries across the Continent. Even Lydia Pratt seemed to enjoy his company, finding frequent reason to pass by their table, listening to what she could.

It later seemed to Longfellow, as he sat alone in his study at the beginning of a gray evening, that Signor Lahte had a knack for gaining the goodwill of nearly everyone. This sort of charm was something he suspected he himself lacked, especially during his black moods. But then, wouldn't a theatrical performer naturally be more adroit at delivering flattering nonsense? And there was, after all, one man who *had* turned against Il Colombo.

Someone had at last spilled the beans to Reverend Rowe, which had brought the preacher flying up the hill in a royal huff. Once he found them at the inn, Rowe insisted on returning to Longfellow's study for a private talk. There he roundly condemned the musico's imagined proclivity for immoral thought and action, as he had heard such behavior was widely rumored to be shared by his kind. Longfellow had quietly defended his guest but abstained from argument, knowing there was little point. On his high horse, Rowe reasoned about as well as an ass.

Tasting again his swallowed bile, Richard Longfellow walked to a sideboard and filled a glass with port. Upon giving the matter additional consideration, he took both glass and bottle back to his easy chair. Finishing a first glass, he poured himself another.

"From what I have learned," Rowe had insisted, "the castrato is a creature neither fish nor fowl. And how can one even begin to imagine the godless society in which the man was raised—one that brought him to his present state? Even if he only acted on a stage, he would be a thorn in the side of any decent, sober society. And yet, I saw you leave Mrs. Willett alone with this man!"

That, thought Longfellow, was rich, for he and Rowe

had gone out of Charlotte's kitchen at the same time. As if to answer the unspoken charge, Rowe added swiftly, "At the time, *you knew what he was!*"

"But tell me what, exactly, he's done."

"He may have done no direct harm as yet," the preacher admitted, "but think what influence his words might have on such an unprotected female! Have you not seen that they are both the talk of the village? *She* can hardly be expected to have strength of will, or a man's judgment. And Signor Lahte is no fit companion for a headstrong woman!"

"But he has given us his word."

"His word? How can he be trusted to keep it? He holds no faith to swear by—he has even abandoned his Pope! Yet now I'm told his youth was shaped to feed that man's lustful pleasures—and what will happen if he attempts to raise his voice in our own choir? I will not have it!"

"Reverend, I hardly think—"

"His words are as a flow of amber—he tries to trap us like flies! This musico is a danger, Longfellow—and once again, a danger you not only overlook, but bring intentionally among us!"

Finally, it had been a draw. Rowe gathered up his outraged soul and went away, having worn himself down like a clock. Then, left alone, Richard Longfellow was forced to ask himself a serious question. Did he truly believe Gian Carlo Lahte to be entirely harmless?

Admittedly, the Italian had a glib tongue, as well as a rather careless view of the world. He had no family, no prospects for building one. He'd spoken of a new home, a new life—but what, exactly, was his plan, and did it have something to do with his attentions to Mrs. Willett? Could he mean, somehow, to make her part of his new establishment? Did he even mean to marry? Or was he interested in something . . . less?

Longfellow allowed himself another glass, and before it was finished he'd decided his suspicions were unworthy of them all. Instead of fretting further, he turned to study a new painting recently hung next to the even dearer portrait of Eleanor Howard.

Shortly before Diana's wedding he'd commissioned John Copley to paint his sister's likeness, knowing this would please her. And it had—so much that she had allowed her brother to enjoy the picture for a time, until her new home in Boston could be fully furnished. He concluded again that the result was a superior one . . . and poured himself yet another glass of port.

If the English aristocracy could think the artists of America untalented—after seeing something like this!—then they might be shot and stuffed, for all their talk of taste. The auburn locks, the mischievous eyes . . . the small, puzzling smile as she leaned forward, her chin cupped in one hand—all quite lifelike. The young painter had lately done an excellent portrait of Revere, and it would be interesting to see what Copley (whose mother, he recalled, once sold tobacco from her shop on Long Wharf) would make of the town's great popinjay, Hancock! Longfellow had heard Boston's own King John now sat for its busiest brush, when that monarch wasn't off visiting his tailor. Even he must be forced to hold still for ten hours at a time, as other subjects were required to do. How Copley had managed to trap Diana for such periods was a mystery. Though perhaps she had discovered hidden reserves of patience, for one whose business it was to admire and preserve her beauty.

Meanwhile, he sat here in the country while Boston grew impatient in the summer heat. This Stamp situation was so much dry tinder, and secret meetings throughout the town continued to produce flurries of sparks. There was bound to be a conflagration, such as Sam Adams had long dreamed of—something would soon set the place afire. But now Sam, as well as Joseph Warren, might be having second thoughts. For each was newly married, with a wife who would hardly wish to see her husband in serious trouble.

Marriage, he thought sourly. How could any sane man allow even the best of wives to rule him? After all, in most women Reason was no more understood than Greek, or even Latin—and only in its temples could man's salvation be found. Richard Longfellow smiled tightly as he admired a new glass of the same old port.

Still, what did one *do* about women? What, indeed, could he do about Charlotte? Might the reverend's suspicions of Lahte turn out to be true? Or what he himself now suspected of Rowe—!

He had loved Eleanor deeply . . . and so it seemed somewhat peculiar to imagine—though there was no true prohibition, after all. They were surely unrelated, even by marriage. They were simply neighbors, and friends. Good friends! But Mrs. Willett had lately made it clear she had no wish to alter her life. She, too, valued freedom. Let her skate on thin ice if she would, then. It was something he knew to be a fine feeling.

Longfellow also knew where to find comfort of a sort in town, if he chose. But how much better to lead a simple life in the country, he told himself, where one might drink away one's cares hearing only the crickets, whose song he took a moment to enjoy. Far better to avoid the town's many murmurs, including the seductive cooing of its young ladies, all longing to be wed! Lovely young ladies, still . . . like roses . . . like wild roses?

His agile mind was by this time quite fuddled. A new thought caused him to laugh out loud; the next made him scowl. Eventually, he gave them all up to listen to a soft rain fall upon the maple leaves near an open window, while a candle by the sash flickered.

Cicero entered quietly, aware that the man who sat within, once his own young charge, had again entered the mercurial state to which he was prone when his direction became unclear. In one hand the old man carried a board; in the other he held a lacquered box. Without a word he set the painted board on a small table between two cushioned chairs, and sat to arrange familiar chess pieces of ebony and ivory on their proper squares.

Then, both heard a high, musical sound come from the gray twilight. Longfellow immediately unwound his long legs, and leaped out of his chair to investigate. From a tall window he made out Gian Carlo Lahte in the distance, a small flute to his lips. It appeared he was shepherding Mrs. Willett, who walked before him through the meadow grass. And by all appearances, both enjoyed the warm, gentle rain that fell onto their heads.

"What do you make of that?" he asked, staring hard.

"It sounds familiar . . ." Cicero replied hesitantly.

"Of course—it's a tune from the blasted *Beggar's Opera*, which it seems we'll never be free of! 'Over the hills and far away' be damned—what do you say of the *picture?*"

"If it were left to me, I would put a hat on her."

"She might have a care for her health—if nothing else! And it is, indeed, the Sabbath. . . ."

Cicero looked to the level of port left in the decanter before he replied. "There is another thought we might consider. Milking is a something our friend does well."

"Milking? By God, that's true!"

"An excellent talent, I think . . . extracting something useful with patience, and a little pulling."

"Well, let her have her sport. And let us see if your ancient brain is yet capable of strategy. But first, we need more candles—and a bottle of Madeira. I find this port cloying tonight. Bring them here, and though the world about me roars a tempest, I will be as the lamb."

"Asleep, possibly," Cicero muttered, while he made his way toward the pantry where the beeswax tapers were kept. Yet he, too, had asked himself lately just what Mrs. Willett and Signor Lahte were up to. He only hoped that the answer, when it came, would not prove an unpleasant surprise for them all.

Chapter 9

WHILE BRIGHT DEWDROPS still burdened the grass, Longfellow stood in his yard, turning as he surveyed each point of the compass, trying to ignore the tattoo that throbbed in his head.

He turned to the north, and felt a new twinge as he recognized the path where Mrs. Willett had strayed the night before, walking with Il Colombo. His disquiet, he supposed, might only be due to wine and the continuing sultry weather. Yet he suspected that something disastrous lurked just over the rosy horizon.

Before long, Longfellow cheered himself slightly by walking to fill a handkerchief with blackberries for his breakfast. They would taste well on a biscuit, with some top cream. He might pass by Mrs. Willett's dairy for a fresh cup—he supposed he would find her still inside. Or, he might not. Perhaps after he'd consumed a fortifying breakfast and four or five cups of coffee, and had taken a glass of something with Jonathan Pratt while they discussed the latest news from town . . . perhaps then he would go and speak with her.

Signor Lahte slept late, he found on reentering his house. And Cicero had mysteriously decided the pantry needed reorganizing, which caused sufficient fuss to discourage conversation. In the end, after a solitary meal, Longfellow walked out to observe his pigs as they rested in their shady sty. The sight and earthy smell of the contented swine blotted out the last of his unsettled mood, and sent him whistling around a corner some time later.

What Richard Longfellow encountered next caused the happy tune on his lips to die away, for he suddenly saw his sister before him, reaching down from a chaise to take the raised hands of her watchful husband. Even the horses had turned to stare at her, their reins fallen quietly to the ground. Less quietly, Diana came to earth bemoaning her state, continuing her discourse while she adjusted a seersucker bodice over the loose folds of a voluminous skirt.

"Edmund!" Longfellow called out as heartily as he could, walking forward.

"My apologies, Richard," the captain responded, "for sending no word, and for the early hour. But Diana did insist—"

"I am sure," the young woman interrupted, "that my brother will enjoy a visit with his sister who may not last the summer, given the way she feels at this moment! I also imagine that though my husband is called *captain* he might as well be a naval one, for all he knows of horses. I have never had such a jostling. But I'm sure having someone rub my feet will make up for it. Oh, Richard, it is simply dreadful, all that I must endure—"

"Diana, what a joy it is to see you. And Edmund, of course. But as you feel unwell, then why—?"

"Dr. Warren told me I must walk. But the cobbles are too hot, and the air in town is full of such smells! If it isn't the bay at low tide, it's the gutters, and the horse droppings. And the flies! So, I have decided instead to enjoy your country breezes, even if they do frequently choke one with dust. But there is no breeze this morning, is there?" she asked with a look that suggested betrayal, pointing her nose to where she thought a country zephyr ought to be.

"Surely Patty is coming behind to fan you."

"Patty! That lazy thing left me last week, walking off with no warning. One only expects to find such rudeness in a better class of people—but I'll soon replace her, if she won't come back begging! Still, there is another who will come today," she added, with a look to tease him.

"Your mother?" Longfellow asked unhappily.

"She's gone into Connecticut to drink the waters at Stafford—and to bathe in them—for the governor's wife recently returned from a similar *recreation*. My mother plans to stay at the springs for at least two weeks, to see if they will do her any good. Though there is not much I can see wrong with her . . . at least compared to me! Still, it will do *me* some good to have her gone away, for there is only so much advice one can cheerfully take. I'm afraid, Richard, that she is becoming quite unbearable."

Longfellow glanced to Montagu, whose silent reply was clear enough. Had Diana at last become something less than celestial to her new husband? She did seem earthbound today, with her swollen skirts and cheeks. And there was the reported condition of her feet. That was more than he cared to think of, yet he strongly suspected other details would be forthcoming. To avoid them he walked to the back of the chaise; there, he helped Montagu unstrap a rough wooden box, which lay atop a mass of shavings. Taking no chances, Edmund had arrived with his own cellar . . . presumably one whose bottles no one else would feel the need to count.

Once she had lost her audience, Diana seemed to revive, and soon came to watch. When the two men had a firm grip on the wine, she led them toward the door where Cicero stood waiting.

"Go and tell Mrs. Willett I've arrived," Mrs. Montagu ordered after she'd answered his inquiring look with a nod, and a shake of her auburn locks. "For I'm sure I'll need a woman's sympathy to make me feel at home."

"And you might send the inn's stable boy to see to the horses," Longfellow suggested, before leading his guests inside. At last, in the front sitting room, he asked, "If it's not your mother who's coming, then who, exactly, am I to welcome?"

"You'll see," Diana answered, easing herself into a chair. Then she kicked off her slippers and closed her eyes, a smaller smile lingering on her lips.

Montagu followed Longfellow to the kitchen. Together they fed the hearth's coals to heat water for tea, and Longfellow discovered a plate of little cakes from the inn.

"A good trip?" he asked casually.

"As you might expect."

"At the moment, your wife bears remarkably little resemblance to her namesake."

"Probably a healthy thing, for I have heard mortals who marry goddesses rarely fare well. I do rejoice to see Diana become a riper, more maternal woman."

"Hmmm. What does she mean, another visitor?"

"That is a story you started yourself." The captain now seemed to reclaim some of his habitual edge. "By the way, I've brought back the sketch you sent me—for we've learned the identity of the man you found beside the road."

"Have you, by God!"

"You supposed we would not?"

"Well, I thought it might take another day or two, in a place the size of Boston."

"We do what we can to keep a watchful eye on our visitors. And, on our most interesting citizens."

"So I hear," said Longfellow, recalling Dr. Warren's recent warning. "Will you tell me the rest?"

"Shortly. I, too, am curious, and look forward to hearing more of your guest."

"Lahte? Come and meet him. By the sound of it, he's just come down the stairs. I would imagine he's found your wife by now."

Edmund Montagu frowned as he hotted the china pot. "Diana tells me they have already met, while with your stepmother."

"Here's the tin. Do you already know something more of him yourself?"

Montagu tossed out the water, then spooned curled leaves into the teapot before filling it completely with boiled water. "I am aware of the source of his fame, if that's what you mean. He was recognized on the wharves by one of my London acquaintances."

Longfellow put the rest of the tea back on the shelf while he gave a thought to the captain's web of informants, who tracked figures likely to offend the colony's authority—and, more importantly, the Crown's.

Finding a tray, Montagu set onto it the pot, cups and saucers, and silver bowls of milk and sugar. He then rejoiced to see Cicero come in through the back door, bringing Mrs. Willett. She extended her hand, studying his face with curiosity. In another moment she smiled more broadly.

"Ah, Carlotta. But we can see for ourselves, Edmund," Longfellow continued as before, "how Diana and Lahte get on, if we can force ourselves to leave the comforts of the kitchen."

"By all means." Montagu picked up the heavy tray, and murmured a few words of inquiry to Charlotte as they went.

The small front sitting room resounded with a babble of confusion, while introductions, welcomes, and inquiries after health gave way to the search for a comfortable seat, or a spot to stand for best vantage. When the cordial din had lessened, it was again Mrs. Montagu who led the conversation.

"I have said to Signor Lahte that we have an amusing gift for him. Though as yet I have not told him what it is. . . ."

"Tell him now, my dear," her husband said in a commanding tone, as if he had tired of the game.

"Well, then, Edmund had Richard's sketch copied, and it was taken to many establishments in the town, where it was shown to the sort of people who have rooms to let. In one of these lodgings near Long Wharf, the man was finally recognized. And a young boy was found waiting for his master to return . . ." Her glance allowed her husband to pick up the thread.

"A boy," Montagu continued, "who arrived in Boston last week, traveling with a man he calls Sesto Alva. He spoke in French to those who found him, but I have since questioned him further in Italian. He has told us little, however, other than that they both came from Milan."

"*Both* came from Milano?" Though Lahte said the words softly, they were heard by all—for the others had already turned toward him to learn more of this odd coincidence.

"According to the servant. Do you know of this Alva?"

"The name is an old one in that city . . . and I may have met a Sesto Alva. But of course so many claim one's acquaintance. . . ."

"The youth told us he was once your servant, as well—and that he'd come here hoping to return to that position."

"What—what name did he give?"

"Angelo. Nothing more. He has a small mole above his lip, so."

"Ah! Yes, I do know him. He was one of several boys I have employed—but this one, especially, was devoted to me. He is at the moment in Boston?"

"He is on his way to Bracebridge, in a cart that brings our baggage. He should arrive shortly, for we passed them on the road."

"A happy surprise?" Longfellow inquired.

"One of little importance," Lahte answered grandly. "I did not send for Angelo, and he will explain himself when he arrives. Oh, yes, he will explain, or be very sorry!"

IT WAS AFTER one, by Longfellow's frequently consulted pocket watch, when the baggage cart was heard on the drive.

At the sound Gian Carlo Lahte jumped to his feet, only to adjust his clothing with an appearance of unconcern. However, he soon followed Longfellow and Montagu out of doors, where they watched a boy scramble down from a pile of large boxes. At first, Angelo stood, uncertain. Then his eyes found what they sought. He walked stiffly forward, and broke into a run. Lahte, too, advanced, calling out in Italian, which the young man answered.

Il Colombo, for so he suddenly seemed in this master's role, clasped the youth by his shoulders as soon as the two came together on the cropped lawn. They continued to speak in lowered tones while Longfellow and Montagu went to see about the surprising amount of luggage. Once it was deposited in the hall, and the cart's driver had gone off toward the Blue Boar, Angelo was ushered to the door of the sitting room to be presented to the ladies as a temporary member of the household. Again, he made his greeting in Italian, and gave an awkward bow.

"He speaks little English, I am afraid," Lahte explained, "but as we have often traveled together, I believe he will cause no trouble."

Charlotte noticed that this boy still had the high, clear voice of a child; nor was his figure yet that of a man. She wondered with sympathy how he found the strength to support the many burdens of a servant's life. Still, far from appearing oppressed, Angelo showed a bold interest in his new surroundings.

"Where will we put him?" Diana asked Longfellow. Signor Lahte responded.

"There is no need to worry. He can sleep on a blanket at my feet. That is all he will expect."

"But surely," Charlotte objected, "he would be more comfortable in a bed?"

"I think not," Lahte replied in an autocratic manner. This she found greatly surprising, and she resolved to keep further thoughts on the boy to herself. Longfellow now asked another question, as politely as he could.

"This young man . . . does he sing, as well?"

"You have seen it, then. Yes, he sings, after a fashion. Sadly, his voice did not develop as was once hoped. But he has been taught to play the harpsichord; he will play for me when I practice. You see, he has many uses. Truly, Angelo has been something more than a servant to me—almost a ward, if you like. Perhaps that is why he still behaves as a child from time to time. If he misbehaves while he is here, I will find a switch," Lahte finished, taking a few swipes with an imaginary branch, which caused the youth's cheeks to brighten.

"Preferably out of my sight," Longfellow replied. "As

to the sleeping arrangements, do what you wish. Now, what in blazes will we do about dinner?"

This comment, addressed to no one in particular, caused an immediate round of discussion. Soon Cicero went across the road to alert the inn's landlord, and the guests retired to their rooms to settle themselves.

While they waited, Charlotte and Longfellow made their way out onto the piazza.

"What do you think, Richard, of the boy's story?" she asked. "It seems to me a very long way to come . . . especially to serve someone who has not called for you."

"I suspect there's more to it than young Angelo admits. He might have gotten himself into some sort of trouble in Milan, as boys will."

"He says he traveled as a servant to Sesto Alva, yet why did Alva come here? If it was for the reason we supposed—if he was in fact the husband Lahte referred to—then why would he employ Lahte's servant?"

"Perhaps he knew nothing of their past relationship. But we're sure to learn more shortly. Our dinner," Longfellow added pleasantly, "should be an interesting one. As my sketch has returned, I'll post it in the taproom when we arrive. Then we'll see if anyone coming through this week noticed someone speaking or traveling with Alva, on the afternoon of his death. One final precaution, which can't hurt."

Charlotte silently agreed, as she looked up to enjoy the voice of a cicada renewing its strident song in the arbor above them.

Upstairs, listening to what he had decided was a most unsettling clatter coming through the window, Montagu hung the damp cloth Diana had dropped by the china basin onto a chair, at the same time asking himself some of the questions being pondered below.

"The ties, if you would, my sweet," his mate requested.

The captain knelt gallantly to reposition her soft shoes, before fastening their lappets. It was a great pity feet were not often seen, for Diana's were indeed lovely. He listened to her sighs as he stroked her ankles gently. She reached out for a moment to touch his hair, then stretched for the cloth to wipe the talc from her fingers.

"I'm glad you don't ask me to sleep at the foot of *your* bed," she said playfully, watching when he rose to put on the light country coat she'd purchased for him at the summer's start.

"You need have no fear of that, my love," her husband returned. "Although once or twice I have contemplated acquiring a switch, like Signor Lahte." To this, Diana made no reply. Her squint, however, made him put aside the idea, though he believed the practice often did some good.

While she was but a woman, it might just be possible, he supposed, for Diana to summon a thunderbolt to do her bidding, like a goddess—given enough of a goad. And this, the captain told himself, was *one* experience with his changeable wife that he would prefer to avoid.

Chapter 10

"I SUGGEST," SAID Longfellow as they sat down in a familiar room on the second floor of the Bracebridge Inn, "that we have our lobsters without delay."

"Please!" said Diana, from her place at her husband's right hand. "For I'm faint with hunger. Do you have sour cabbage in the kitchen?" She turned to Lydia Pratt, who stood awaiting approval of the day's bill of fare.

"Sour cabbage?" Lydia returned. "There's a crock just started, but it's not far along. I won't recommend it."

"I will have some, anyway." Diana was amused to see the landlady's expression of disapproval deepen, even beyond what it had been when she learned a servant sat next to his master at table. Turning on her heel, Lydia left them.

"How refreshing to be in a neutral tavern . . . and a change from Boston," said Montagu. "More and more,

Richard, that band of renegades makes life uncomfortable at your Green Dragon—where I've found I must often go, of late, in the course of my duties."

"There is a suggestion afloat that they buy the place outright . . . but I hardly see how you, a fellow Freemason, can complain of it."

"Your brothers are not mine! The membership of this newer lodge is very unlike St. John's. That is clear whenever we gather together; yours seems to be largely a collection of volatile and obnoxious riffraff."

"Under the ancient laws, St. Andrew's is perfectly correct."

"So your friend Warren assures me—though for the moment he seems to have left the fold. . . ."

Hearing her physician's name, Diana turned and spoke to Mrs. Willett.

"Dr. Warren has told me, Charlotte, that I must walk every day—which is quite the opposite of the advice given to Lucy by her man. I did tell you Mrs. Cooper, née Devens, is also—? Well, *her* physician tells her to stay indoors as much as possible, and not to go *near* a coach or chaise! Can you imagine her utter boredom? Warren's suggestions are better; I'm sure he's worth the two pounds we'll pay him. At least, I'm more inclined to listen to him than to Lucy. She is rarely sensible, these days."

"I spoke with Dr. Warren the night before last," Longfellow continued to the captain. "When he came out to examine this man you call Sesto Alva. Naturally, your name was mentioned. . . ."

"He took a moment to damn the stamp men as well, I suppose?"

"From what I gather, you'll soon find yourself even less welcome at the Dragon, if Oliver comes to sell any of the wretched things. But mark my words—these stamps will end by costing you far more than you'll ever be able to collect."

"*That* would hardly surprise me. Boston's revenue collection is appalling."

"What are these stamps?" Lahte interrupted. "And why do you so despise them?"

"It is the will of London's Parliament, Gian Carlo," Longfellow slowly explained, "that after the first of November, anything written or printed on paper, parchment, or vellum must have an official stamp affixed to it, if it is to be sold or recorded here. For instance, if a man wishes to buy or sell property, if the local innkeeper wants to renew his liquor license, if a fellow plans to bring suit against his neighbor—all will be required to purchase one or more of these paper stamps. It will be the same to sell a newspaper or a magazine. You have heard, Edmund, of the letter our Assembly is sending to each of the others, calling for a general congress to discuss the issue in two months' time?"

"Who has not! 'To humbly implore relief'—a lie more honest men would choke on. But there's little chance a governor of any colony will approve of this affront."

"That, alone, will hardly deter delegates from going to New York."

"No . . ." Montagu's gaze sharpened. "But have *you* heard of last week's rioting in Boston, when the life of the secretary of the province was threatened?"

"We do get the odd piece of news here. Yet Oliver's troubles sound more like summer amusement than anything worse."

"Amusement! If you believe *that*—!"

"Edmund, I would be grateful if you will not spoil our dinner," Diana broke in curtly. Her husband ignored her.

"Last Wednesday," he went on, beginning to glower,

"Andrew Oliver was hung out on a limb of the new-named Liberty Tree! At any rate, his effigy dangled all day from a great elm at Essex and Newbury—along with a paper-and-paste boot, complete with an ugly little devil climbing out of it."

"A boot?" asked Lahte, clearly confused. "What is the point of a boot?"

"It was meant as a threat to Lord Bute," returned the captain. "However, since he left His Majesty's government over two years ago, it is a message that can do little good! This reeks of politics. And we saw the same devil, by the way, last November in the Pope's Day parade . . . another well-beloved excuse for violence among the rabble! They cry that government is out to steal their souls, when all that is being asked of them is a little of their coin—all meant to stay in these colonies, and much of it to be used to pay soldiers who remain to protect their lives!"

"From—?" Longfellow inquired.

"From further raids on our forts . . . or, quite possibly, some new French mischief even closer than that."

"So the redcoats sit in New York."

"*Would you prefer them here?* That might be arranged, Richard, if things keep on the way they are headed. Your ruffians take no notice of office or birth—unless it is to spit upon them! They even congratulate themselves that Oliver will not have the courage to accept his announced position as collector, for they believe they have frightened him thoroughly. And he is the brother-in-law of your lieutenant governor!"

"There's the rub, Edmund. Even the fools among us see he's an appendage of a far more powerful beast. Some suspect every public office in Boston will soon be in the hands of a Hutchinson, an Oliver, or a Bernard—men already united by marriage many times over. This explains our growing fear not of your aristocracy, but of one of our own, begun by some fine fellows who are ready to sell away their birthrights! And you seem satisfied to help them do it."

"Am I to understand that you, too, excuse the actions of this mob?" Montagu asked hotly. Longfellow set his fingertips together, before calmly clarifying his position.

"I will acknowledge, and pay, what this colony's Assembly asks of me. I also respect Parliament's right to tax men who are directly represented by that august body, as you in Britain are . . . but in Massachusetts, remember, we are not. We have long raised our own revenues for the King—gladly! Sam Adams himself has collected taxes in Boston for years, and is no less loved for it."

"He is loved because, like most of your collectors, he frequently neglects to make people pay what they owe! As for revenues levied upon the rest of us by Parliament, I am sure you will recall our taxes flowed freely to help this place during the late war. Yet can we in Britain be expected to pay for your safety forever?"

"Your generosity, I think, was more than matched by the loss of many colonial lives, while you expanded this new empire run by your own moguls—who do little for us in America! But would you have us believe, Captain, that the proposed stamp revenue is intended only to pay for your redcoats? It is hardly a secret that it would also allow the King to pay the salaries of Crown officials here—even to pay our governors. This would take away any chance of withholding their pay, should the plans of these men go against our interests. That opportunity, you must agree, is a traditional British safeguard—and a useful one. We also hear that under the Act those who object will be tried not by a local jury, but by a vice-admiralty court—where a British judge, *with no jury*, determines the law. Is this not a death knell to the freedom you and I should enjoy equally, as British subjects? And if Parliament and the King's ministers can take these rights from us, *who will guarantee your own?*"

"But get on about the tree," Diana moaned, "so we can have done with it. The ladies here, at least, have lost all patience with your politics—though Signor Lahte may later wish to hear the rest."

"It seems," said Montagu, who returned to his story after a long and considering look at his wife, "that the whole town feared to remove the hung effigy, and for the entire day, all going to market were stopped to have their goods jocularly 'stamped' in the name of the thing swaying over their heads. The same farce was performed on the Neck, at the town gate."

"If you would only allow them to see real drama performed, in real theaters," Diana interrupted again, "as they do in New York, then you would have fewer men and boys wandering the streets looking for mischief, Edmund, as I've told you many times before—"

"Diana!" her husband fairly shouted, while his foot slammed onto the floor. When she only looked out the window, he finished grimly.

"Both boot and Oliver were finally taken down by a group of respectable people, who had seen enough. However, others came and paraded their playthings off for a mock burial, carrying them first before the Council as it sat in Town House. They made quite a row with their jeers and cheering, as you can easily imagine. Then, on they went down King Street—well over a thousand now, with new men and fresh plans. They soon destroyed a building Andrew Oliver lately put up on his dock, where they assumed he would sell stamps. After that these 'Sons of Liberty' paid a visit to Mr. Oliver's home. Through good fortune or sense he was gone; but someone told them to leave, in language they found offensive. So, they broke the man's windows and much of his furniture, and tore up his garden for good measure. The governor was not able to raise the militia, and in the end the sheriff could do little. No one would stand in the way of these damned blackguards! Bernard has since tried to warn the Council, but most seem to believe, as you do, Richard, that this was not serious—or perhaps they fear for their own safety. Hutchinson himself was treated to a hail of bricks and stones in the street, before the mob visited his house, as well. But they had not the courage to attack the home of the lieutenant governor. Finally, they took their wretched symbols to Fort Hill at midnight, where they 'stamped' Oliver's image to death, before throwing it onto a bonfire."

"It is the heat," Diana said to Charlotte, when her husband had finally come to a halt. "That is what causes most of our current distress. Sleep is really impossible until three or four o'clock, and by then, the market carts have begun to rumble in."

"It is worse than that," said Montagu. "At best, it is madness!"

"Certainly, Edmund," said his wife, "men do become overwrought, and unreasonable, for they *will* drink more in the heat than usual—very often more than is good for them." She then watched her husband toss back his glass of wine, and pour himself another.

Fortunately, before either could go on, the cold cooked lobsters arrived on a large platter. Surrounded by lemons, they were accompanied by bottled sauce from the Indies, flavored with hot peppers. Small pots of melted butter, too, were deftly delivered by Thomas Pomeroy, who kept a solemn face while serving. At his side, the small daughter of Elizabeth the cook struggled with two glazed pitchers of iced cider. In another moment the landlord himself came through the dark doorway at the top of the kitchen stairs, bearing an earthen crock.

"My *dear* Mrs. Montagu—what a very great pleasure it is to see you!" Jonathan Pratt exclaimed. "And your friends, as well. I believe this is what you asked for?" At Diana's nod, he took a spoon and transferred some of the cabbage onto a plate for her. "But I see," he continued, "that you have honored us by bringing someone new. A young relation?"

Longfellow gave a brief explanation. "Angelo is the servant and musical accompanist of Signor Lahte. He, too, comes from Milan."

Jonathan looked the boy over, before indicating the somewhat older youth who waited nearby. "Then he should meet another who is currently in service. This is Thomas Pomeroy. If you are given time off from your duties, young man, you might care to join Thomas for a game of cribbage, or bowls."

Pomeroy stepped forward with a hand extended, murmuring a pleasantry.

"I am afraid," Signor Lahte said quickly, "that the boy speaks no English. I must teach him—and he will have little time to spare until he learns. If, that is, he stays with me. Of that, at the moment, I am uncertain."

"Does he understand French, perhaps?" Thomas tried, but Lahte remained silent.

"I see," said the landlord. "Well, I'll go down and look to your next course." He held the door for Pomeroy and the girl; then, his own substantial bulk, too, disappeared into the darkness.

Longfellow lifted a lobster from its bed of seaweed and transferred it to a plate. Eventually, each person at the table was supplied with a bright red crustacean. "As enjoyment is the object of this particular exercise," he stated, "perhaps, Edmund, we should forego politics until we have left the ladies. We may then fill Signor Lahte's head with more of our troubles. Now, I suggest we ask him to fill ours with something more amusing. I believe he might tell us how the excavations near Naples go. They have discovered some peculiar ruins under the earth, it seems, at what was once called Herculaneum."

"Ah, yes!" Lahte exclaimed, "Ercolano! In the tunnels are splendid things! And, there is great sadness there, as well." He went on to describe the statues, frescoes, and other remnants of ancient life that had been found under many feet of ash—which, Longfellow tossed in, had been laid down by the explosion of Vesuvius described by Pliny some seventeen hundred years before.

While he spoke more of what he himself had seen, Lahte's face turned quite often toward Charlotte; for her part, she listened with rapt attention to his detailed and strangely moving description of a town long dead and buried.

But inevitably, the talk did drift back to politics.

"What," asked Longfellow, "do you make of Austrian rule in the northern peninsula, Lahte?"

Mrs. Willett had by then finished most of her lobster, though she still sucked gently at its small, flute-like legs. Diana seemed lost in her own thoughts, perhaps wondering how the meal was being received by the new life she carried. Looking further, Charlotte saw Angelo's eyes meet her own again, from the end of the table. The boy sometimes appeared to be watching her closely, though she could hardly say why. Could she be so different from the women of Italy? Was it something about her dress? Or her manner of eating? His fingers had dealt with the lobster set before him in a knowing way not unlike her own—so fear of social error could hardly be the reason for his study. Angelo returned his attention to his master, as Lahte spoke at length of the joint rule of Maria Theresa and her son Joseph, in the Piedmont and in Austria.

A dish of diced, creamed potatoes with toasted crumbs

was brought in next, with a warm casserole of sliced beets nestled in their greens, nearly covered by curls of fried bacon. Thomas Pomeroy left both dishes by Captain Montagu, who stood and helped the ladies. Thomas then took a spoon and proceeded to serve the boy.

Gian Carlo Lahte stopped in the middle of a sentence, and slowly rose to his feet. His face betrayed no new feeling, yet his stance itself was a warning.

"I think, Mr. Pomeroy, you show my servant *too much* attention. He will take care of his own needs—*after* he sees to mine."

"Very sorry, sir," said Pomeroy, although from his smooth tone it seemed to Mrs. Willett that the young man meant nothing of the sort. In another moment, he retreated to the kitchen.

"Charlotte, I saw Lem two or three days ago," Diana informed her friend, breaking the tension in the room; Lahte lowered himself stiffly into his chair.

"Was he well?"

"He seemed so. He walked by the house with Dr. Warren, and stepped in to speak with me for a moment. He left a letter for you—I have it in my things. I suspect he rather misses life in Bracebridge."

"I believe even Hannah looks for him each evening, when she leaves."

"He'll tire of Boston before long. Countrymen usually do. Unless, of course, he gets caught up in courting a young lady."

Charlotte thought of Martha Sloan, a girl who had seemed nearly ready to give her heart . . . but her answer to Diana was delayed by the arrival of a pair of herbed and roasted chickens, and more wine. Again, Thomas Pomeroy was the platter's bearer. After its delivery he stationed himself in the same corner as before, near Angelo's chair.

He allowed his eyes to wander inquiringly, even insolently, from the boy's face to Lahte's.

A cat may look at a king, Charlotte told herself, but he might also lose a bit of fur for it. For the moment, the dismemberment of one of Longfellow's favorite dishes kept the room at a simmer. Yet Lahte's eyes flashed, while Angelo's upward glances seemed almost intended to spite his master. What, exactly, Charlotte asked herself, did she see here? Jealousy, surely. But what could be the cause—and what might be the outcome? She easily found an answer to the last question: trouble, without a doubt!

Diana began to speak softly again, still savoring a bite of succulent wing.

"He is a remarkably handsome man, is he not?"

"Who?" asked Mrs. Willett, momentarily confused.

"Signor Lahte, of course. He has a gentleness that is rather unusual in a man; but there is also fire underneath, I'm sure! I know a number of ladies who would be happy to serve him dinner, if only for the pleasure of staring into those eyes. As you've been doing, Charlotte. I wonder if you might be a little taken, yourself?"

"What?"

"It does look that way to me. And it would hardly be surprising, for you have had so little good company in the last few years, my dear. Perhaps you forget the many ways a man may be of use."

"I have your brother. . . ."

"Oh, Richard *can* be amusing, but he is often less attentive than he should be—as are certain others! Signor Lahte seems more aware of what a lady likes . . . and indeed needs. Though at the moment he seems occupied by the surprise we've brought him. At least he is not as bad as *some* men, who feel they can leave us to our own devices with no care at all for flattering conversation."

"But I have heard," Captain Montagu was going on, "that Frederick of Prussia even now has thousands in his service, whose only business is to bring him information— one reason he was able to outwit the rest of the world so often during the Great War—"

"You do see," Diana added to Mrs. Willett.

The arrival of a Brown Betty and a jug of cream caused a concerted rising and stretching, before the company's final attack. During the respite, Edmund Montagu went to one of the large windows that overlooked several thick-boughed maples, and the Boston-Worcester road. Long-fellow took the opportunity to sit and talk with his sister, somewhat to her surprise, while Lahte and Angelo put their heads together as well.

Charlotte joined Captain Montagu, and found him glad to share his thoughts.

"Diana seems in good health and spirits, Edmund."

"She is strong; but her emotions run to extremes these days, and it seems I can do little to help. I should tell you that I haven't fully informed her about Signor Lahte's . . . situation."

"You mean . . . that he is famous? And the cause of it?"

"Exactly."

"This isn't known in town?"

"He seems to have left Boston the day after his arrival, without revealing himself. And with my wife's condition, I believe the less she knows of Lahte and theatrical life, the better. Though I realize it may be difficult to keep her long in the dark."

"She already seems to think I might have a particular interest in our new friend."

"You? Is this true?" Edmund Montagu bent a little to look directly into her face.

"He *is* a fascinating man of the world," she replied

honestly. "His experiences promise interesting conversation. And he tells me he can milk a cow."

"All fine recommendations. But I suppose you tease me."

"Perhaps I do. Though do you really think such a man could ever be drawn to a woman from such a place as this?"

"Who knows what draws two souls together? Sometimes, I'm even tempted to wonder about myself, Charlotte. The heart is a thing none will ever fully understand, I fear—even those of us familiar with Natural Law."

The jab at her neighbor, offered between friends, made her smile; but Charlotte added the hope that the two gentlemen might swiftly mend their latest rift.

"Let us go and enjoy our dessert," said the captain, "and be finished! It begins to feel too warm here, and I long to sit in the shade of Richard's arbor and doze. Diana must certainly rest, for none of us will enjoy ourselves should she tire." On this point, Charlotte agreed.

Before long, those by the taproom windows watched the party of six make its way down the walk and across the road. Thomas Pomeroy, especially, followed their progress with particular interest, before turning back to the business of the inn.

Chapter 11

As the midge-filled light waned, a familiar crowd sat in the Blue Boar Tavern, once again lubricating their opinions as well as their dry, wagging tongues.

Near an open door, Jack Pennywort—clearly feeling the effects of ale—called out for another pint, intending to pay with winnings coaxed from a pack of greasy cards.

As he watched the smaller man across the table, Nathan Browne smiled behind the lip of his own tankard. Hours earlier he had realized it was too hot to be striking red metal in a smithy. No sense asking for your legs to throb, or your head to ring as loud as your anvil. And by spending the afternoon helping Jack keep his few coins in his pocket, he'd managed to put himself into a better mood. Soon, he would amble home to Sabina, whose curiosity that morning about *a certain gentleman* had made her husband feel less than charitable.

All of the women were twittering like so many linnets at this Italian, whose strange voice could be heard singing clear across the road, when he exercised it. Not that the visitor seemed a bad sort when he came into the forge, to take a look at the dead man's horse. He was hoping for a quiet mount, he'd said—but he gave up on that after viewing the wily beast up close. It was just as well, for the signor didn't look like much of a rider, Nathan thought with a grimace. More likely he was used to being ferried about the countryside in carriages, never asking so much as the name of a four-footed animal. Still, Mrs. Willett seemed to enjoy his company. Or so he'd heard from several gossips. He thought he might ask her about this himself in a day or two, when she next stopped by for a chat.

Another idler at the table finished his third pint of sharp cider. During the game of cards between his old friend Jack and the smith, Dick Craft had been more attuned to a voice in his own head. Now, as the landlord walked by, Craft asked a careful question.

"Mr. Wise—"

"Another, Dick, already? I should say—"

"Uh, no, Mr. Wise. On Saturday, someone said that this gentleman, the one staying with Mr. Longfellow, came to us from Italy."

"He did, indeed."

"And is that place not the center of the world's du—dup—duplicity?"

"Who told you that?" asked the landlord with a new look of suspicion.

"Someone—on the Sabbath. It is even said," Dick continued slyly, "that their Pope may be the Devil himself, come to lead us from the Truth!"

"I doubt that. But it would seem to make no difference in this case, for Signor Lahte intends to follow Roman ways no longer."

"But can he be trusted?" asked Dick, his eyes protruding a bit more.

"Many's the man with friends in Québec, who don't seem the worse for their religion—unless it is in their pockets. For they do love grand churches, it would seem."

"Down in Baltimore," put in a genial lad who'd wandered over with an empty tankard, "only last year, someone pointed out to me a new church built for Catholics, who now attend with no penalty. Though I also heard many have long practiced their rites in private in that colony."

"May it never be so in this one!" cried Dick Craft. "Or some of us will know what to do about it!"

"What is wrong with the Catholics, Dick, in your opinion?" asked the landlord, taking the tankard and moving to fill it.

"For one thing, they dress in women's skirts, don't they! Pope and cardinals—who must be queer birds, indeed. But men may do even worse where this musico comes from. Unnatural things . . . as I believe others have mentioned here in recent days."

"What's that?" demanded another.

"I was also told . . ." Dick went on, pausing for a belch, "that in Italy, which is a country not far from our old enemy France—"

"I think," someone else offered, "the Boot is no *real* country, but more like a lot of towns all lumped together—"

"—in Italy," Dick continued, sweeping the table with a red eye, "and worst of all in a town called Venice— which I don't suppose is far from Hades—"

"Ahh!" came a receptive chorus, as others moved closer.

"—there, they often gather covered by cloaks, and masks—"

"Dominoes, they call 'em," old Mr. Flint weighed in wisely, from his customary seat by the fire.

"—and both ladies and gentlemen dance and carry on any way they please, all night long! I doubt the results of *that* are harmless! Masks, to keep from knowing who's who—"

"And what's what, maybe?" piped a new voice.

"It would keep down the cost of clothing . . ." muttered a man on his way home to his wife in Boston.

"From what I've learned," said the younger traveler who had been to Baltimore, "on some days in most of Europe's cities, any man is allowed to dress in women's clothes—or even those of a king if he wishes—and wander about the streets at all hours. Carnivals, I think these festivities are called. Something to do with Lent, I believe," he added, accepting his recharged tankard from Phineas Wise.

"A Christian holiday, kept in such a manner?" asked a man by the windows with a shake of his graying head.

"Well, now," replied Flint, "you know there's plenty of Harvard lads who like to put on a skirt now and again, for their dramatics. And is there anything wrong with them?" Several wits ventured answers to this, but Flint soon went on. "I remember a time—"

He stopped to consult Mr. Tyndall, who had earlier suffered from dyspepsia, and had dozed off in his chair. Meanwhile, respect for an elder (or it may have been the anticipation of a promising tidbit) made the others wait quietly.

"Back in '19, was it not, Mr. Tyndall? The old Exeter writ business?" Tinder awoke with a start, and Flint repeated the question.

"Aye, it was, as I recall."

"Yes, I believe that was the year I saw your grandfather, Dick Craft, put on a petticoat himself one evening— along with the sires of some others here. And all of them went out onto the streets . . ."

"No!" came a chorus of excited voices. Dick flushed furiously. He might once have joined their amusement, but in the last two years, since the death of the village miller, he had gravitated to religion in an effort to replace the man who had led his thoughts for years.

"All in a good cause," Flint assured them. "All in a good cause."

"What might that have been, sir?" called a callow voice, which made the elder smile.

"I always like a lad who is interested in history, and polite about it," Mr. Flint said. "A fine thing, and let none forget it! Well, boys, it seems that up in Exeter there lived a sheriff, who one day was sent to take a man to jail, his excuse being a particularly nasty writ. For what I can't easily say now, but I do know the town would have none of it. First, there was a great deal of talk, of course—and some of us here rode up there to see what would happen next. What happened was, a crowd of good women came and kept the sheriff at bay, while a few others set the man free. The most peculiar thing was, not a dame there that evening didn't pull on his pants the morning after, and go out to plow!"

Laughter rose and rang between the walls so loudly that some chatting outside stuck their heads in through doors and windows, to see what had occurred.

"Maybe we should call on such women to come and join us now, in rising up against the damned Stamp men!" someone suggested in a piercing voice. Though largely ignored, this thought caused a few to change their seats, and begin to speak together in lowered voices.

Phineas Wise moved off to distribute further libations. Then, Nathan quietly addressed Dick Craft with a concern of his own. "I don't see how this Lahte has shown he wants to bother any here, man or boy, or even the ladies who find him such a marvel! I do know I would blush to see them follow me with their eyes, the way they watch *him*—"

"Nathan, just tell me how it is that he came from the same town in Italy as the dead man on the road," Dick insisted. "Just what are we to make of that?"

For this, the smith could think of no answer.

"About your dead man," said a Worcester merchant who had walked in a few minutes before. A glass of restorative rum now in hand, he sat down. "Is it known yet who he was, Nathan?"

"Captain Montagu came from Boston this morning, and gave Mr. Longfellow the name of Sesto Alva . . . according to Mr. Pratt."

"Oh. Well, then there's no reason to tell them what I saw last week, I suppose. I happened into Pratt's house an hour ago, and I saw a drawing put there by your Mr. Longfellow. I didn't know right away who the fellow was, but I thought I'd seen him somewhere; now, I recall where it was. Last week in Boston, at the Green Dragon, where he sat over his dinner. At the time I remarked he seemed unwell."

"You're sure it was the same man?" Nathan inquired, leaning closer.

"Fair certain," replied the merchant. "But that's not the most curious part of it."

"No?" asked Jack, swallowing a new story, and his replenished supply of ale, with equal pleasure.

"As I got up to leave the place, *damme* if I didn't see what appeared to be the very same man, coming in through the door! Same clothing, same face, more or less, same reddish hair—but this new one a good deal more lively, I'd say. One to steer clear of, I thought, for the long scar below his eye most likely came from a knife fight. In fact, the first appeared almost to be the ghost of the second," he concluded.

"A *doppelgänger!*" cried a customer near the cider barrels.

"A what?" Jack sat up with alarm at another new and foreign word.

"A spirit double," came his answer. "Everyone's said to have one, somewhere. At least, that's the theory of the Dutchmen down the Hudson. It's death, they say, to meet your own, face to face."

"I'd hate to see another of me, then," said Jack with a shiver.

"No more than we," Dick Craft returned.

"It's quite true neither of these fellows seemed happy to see the other," said the merchant, getting up. Then he drifted off to join another group a little distance away.

Nathan thumbed an ear, pondering what he'd heard. At last, he drained his tankard. Tomorrow morning, he thought, while he pounded hot metal, he would have time to consider whether this long afternoon had provided anything beyond the usual tavern nonsense, after all.

THAT EVENING, WHEN Charlotte tired of reading alone in her study, she took up her candle and went to make herself ready for bed.

In her chamber she flung loose the bed's coverlet and the uppermost of two sheets, creating satisfying puffs of air. Then, with her bare feet dangling above the floor, she sat and gazed longingly at the dark window, hoping for some sign of a real breeze. Weeks ago she'd abandoned her usual shift; she now wore one of Aaron's nearly transparent summer shirts of fine Holland. It was short, and its shoulders drooped well beneath her own. It was also cool, and wearing it was a remarkably enjoyable sensation.

After she had rolled up the shirt's sleeves, she took the combs from her hair. When it had all tumbled down she picked up a brush, smoothed her light tresses, and tied them back with a ribbon. That done, she walked across the room past the looking glass. What she saw reflected in its dark surface caused her to stop and stare.

Again, the song of the Persian king came back to her with the image of Gian Carlo Lahte standing on Longfellow's piazza in his own shirtsleeves. *Simpatia*, he had called it, the first time they were alone. She had to admit there was something in this unusual man that moved her—in his voice, his words, even the fingertips that had brushed against her ear—something that made her wish to give him her trust, as he'd suggested. And yet—

And yet, she barely knew him! How *could* she have spoken as she did, and so quickly? Was it because, through his art, he was able to put himself into a woman's place—into a woman's heart—to feel what other men could not? She knew the women of Bracebridge were whispering romantic possibilities to one another, their interest piqued by his strangeness, as well as by his handsome features. She also knew from talking with Hannah that some of their men supposed the taste in love of a castrato might be of quite another sort.

But that could not be true! Longfellow had told her that the company of Il Colombo had long been sought by women. And yet—

She hardly expected every man to surrender to her own modest charms, but why had he spoken to her of wanting only a sister for a companion? Had he grown tired of the chase, and lost interest? Or was Italy an even odder place than she had been led to believe? Curious things were apparently condoned there—even encouraged—for look what had already happened to Gian Carlo Lahte! Could this be true of love, as well?

The Bible, she knew, recorded a peculiar passion shared by David and Jonathan—one which surpassed the love of women. And Shakespeare had written of the Duke of Illyria's lust for a young soldier . . . who had also been loved by the Lady Olivia! She had heard that even today in London, noblemen, at least, might be allowed to choose as they wished. But was such a thing likely to occur in Bracebridge?

Perhaps it was the rising summer moon, or even the *mal aria* from the marshes, that caused her to have such thoughts, she decided as she crossed to the bed she'd once shared with Aaron. She threw herself upon it, and vowed to go back to what she knew.

Only that afternoon, she had seen the musico warn Thomas Pomeroy to keep his distance. But Pomeroy had done no more than approach Angelo, and perhaps admire him with questioning eyes. Earlier, Lahte had been less than overjoyed to see the child; yet he did take him back into his service. He must have felt sympathy for one to whom the future promised little.

But *why*, she asked herself again, had Angelo, unsummoned, crossed the sea? Was it because what she would not suppose of the master was, in fact, true of the servant? Did Angelo look for more than a master in Signor Lahte— more even than a friend? As for the musico, would he not know from his own experience what might befall such a child—one with no protector, who had already grown used to the idea that his body could be bought and sold? Should not this make one feel a tender concern? And would not he then wish to keep others away, to protect the boy?

She next had to ask herself if Gian Carlo Lahte saw in Thomas Pomeroy, late of London, what she could not. Was Thomas truly a threat to young Angelo? And how, if at all, did the dead man, Sesto Alva, fit into this complicated scheme?

By now feeling somewhat dizzy, she lay back and allowed the entire web to dissolve from her mind. Perhaps it was only the heat that suggested these things, and made the details of the situation building around her seem impossible to untangle, or to judge.

One thing was certain. So many ambiguities could hardly encourage sleep. For that reason, Charlotte was not surprised to find herself lying awake in the darkness hours later, while she considered the ways of men, and women, and children . . . and the obvious virtues of solitude.

Chapter 12

AGAIN CLAD IN proper attire for her sex, and somewhat chastened by her flight of fancy in the night, Mrs. Willett walked beside her cows from barn to dairy on another humid morning.

At the doorway, she turned to see Hannah's son running for all he was worth, his face aflame, his feet occasionally slipping on the damp grass. Puffing and flailing his arms like a windmill, Henry managed to stop himself. Then, his chest still heaving, he took the pail held out to him.

"A letter was brought to me yesterday, by Mrs. Montagu," said Charlotte, once the milk had begun to splash rhythmically. "From Lem."

"I hope he still says his prayers, for he'll need them in a

place like Boston," the boy replied. Now thirteen, Henry had decided that he'd nearly reached the estate of manhood; Charlotte recognized the fact that his ears, at least, had grown large.

"He studies, mostly, with his cousin and a tutor," she replied, "though he does find some time for a more social life." Diana's comment about a possible courtship returned to her now, and cost her a small frown.

"Has he trained with the militia yet?" Henry inquired.

"Why would he do that?"

"Because *all* young men long to join. You carry a musket, and march up and down the Common. Will says that's what he does in Concord, on Training Day; and then they all drink ale before going home. I wish I could march about with our militia, on our green."

"I hope Lem is more eager to bring in a turkey with his musket than to assist Governor Bernard. Besides, Henry, you know he has time before he's expected to go."

"They let some practice early, though. Will says boys often follow the rest, and hear some fine talk too! And Lem's sixteen, after all."

"But he's still a part of Bracebridge, even if he has gone off to Boston. Which I begin to wish he had not," she added to herself.

"Martha would like to see him come home," Henry said as if it were a secret, ducking his blond head to speak to her from under a cow.

"Did she tell you so?"

"She can say what she likes . . . even, sometimes, that she doesn't ever want to see *Mr. Wainwright* again! That is usually after she receives a letter, but I know it's not what she means. I think she is really very fond of him. She says she's afraid, though, that he'll be swept away—which I hope he is not! But I don't see how he could be, unless there is a worse flood there than was ever seen here, on the Musketaquid."

Martha's older sister would naturally hear her dreams and fears, thought Charlotte, just as she herself had once heard Eleanor's. She imagined they might do well to be more careful of Henry. But he was a late child, and there was no one else his age at home. No doubt he heard and saw a great deal that he didn't fully understand. "In his letter to me," she told the boy, "Lem asks of you, and he hopes your family is well."

"Maybe I will write to him. Mrs. Willett . . . do you know anything of the new boy who came from Boston yesterday? I wanted to ask you before, but when I came too late for milking . . ."

"No harm done. Though I can't tell you much, Henry. It seems he knows little English, and since few of us here understand the Italian language, it may be a while before he is able to make new friends."

"His master seems happy to have him here." Henry got up and moved his stool and pail to another cow. "I saw them sporting together last evening in a far field, wrestling in the grass. I was watching a snake pull a small rabbit out of its burrow, and then he ate it."

"Oh!"

"It was down by the creek—but only an old milk snake, really. I found it hard to leave, though, until it finished, for I'd never seen such a thing before."

"I see! But you also saw—?"

"The new gentleman, Mr. Lahte, with a boy I didn't know. Though I heard about him later from my sisters. He's a little taller than I am, but he was *weeping*!"

"Was he?"

"Yes, and he was too big for that, I thought."

For the remainder of their milking they spoke of other things, until they set down covered pails at the dairy's door, and Henry prepared to lead the cows to pasture. Suddenly the two turned their heads, to find the source of a sweet sound coming from the near meadow. Charlotte recognized the high, musical strains at once, and felt herself blush. Then she explained that it was Signor Lahte's flute, though she couldn't quite make out the player, given the distance. Henry, it seemed, could.

"Look—there they are again!" he said, pointing. "He's given the flute to the boy now, and . . . and he's twirling him around!" The novelty of this behavior clearly appealed to Henry, who urged the cows forward for a closer look, using a smooth stick he had taken from behind the door.

"Take care!" Mrs. Willett called as the herd swung away, the bell on the lead animal clanking loudly.

For several minutes she stood there, watching. Lem, too, had shown her some of a young man's joys and troubles, she recalled as she walked back to the house alone. Richard must have been right to send their young friend off to Harvard; here, he would have only a small share of his father's few poor plots of land, one day. But how could the village prosper with its most promising sons going off to the college, and remaining in Boston to earn their livelihood? Henry would have to decide before long whether he should go, or stay. And then she imagined another choice—one made by a boy barely older than Henry, to cross a broad ocean in search of his own dream. What sort had it been?

She knew she could hardly ask Angelo, even if they had spoken the same language. But there was still Thomas Pomeroy. Exactly how much, she wondered, did Jonathan know of him?

At least that was one question to which she knew she might easily find an answer.

· · ·

A FEW MINUTES later, Charlotte arrived at the Bracebridge Inn to find Elizabeth busy, as usual, in the kitchen. Tim, the message boy, was there as well, eating scraps of pastry crust. He hauled the milk pails she'd brought in her hand wagon down into the cellar to cool, while Charlotte selected yeasty griddle muffins and fatter soda biscuits for herself, then more to take across the road to Longfellow's household. Both women agreed the visitors might appreciate these for their breakfast, with a basket of berries and Charlotte's gift of a pot of sweet cheese.

Meanwhile, Thomas Pomeroy loped down the servants' stairs from the upper rooms, to encounter Tim coming up from below. Together they leaned against a door frame, speaking softly, sharing chuckles and jabs.

"Madam, good morning," Thomas suddenly called, as he straightened and gave her a quick bow. "Is there something I can do . . . ?"

Searching for an answer, Charlotte took in his neat, glossy hair, clean face with its hint of a beard, pressed apron tied over his clothing, well-developed calves under unexpectedly fine stockings, and finally, shoes of soft, almost unblemished leather. Nearly all of his apparel seemed new. She looked up to see that he scrutinized her own appearance, possibly with an even more interested eye.

How, she wondered, could she ever have thought—! And yet, given what little she knew . . .

"Do you wish, possibly, to change your order for the glass?" asked Thomas. "I can easily tell Mrs. Pratt what you require—"

Before she could answer, Charlotte heard skirts whipping through a passage, and then saw Lydia Pratt herself.

"If you young gentlemen," she cried, "have nothing better to do with yourselves, then I—oh! Mrs. Willett."

As Lydia's demeanor changed abruptly, Charlotte saw

that she had done something else to alter her appearance. Her black hair, though still in its bun, was not as tightly drawn as usual, and a few forced waves rode atop the woman's thin forehead. Her cheeks, frequently almost gray, were alive with a suffusion of well-being—or perhaps something more easily obtained. And could that be perfume coming from a newly drawn lace handkerchief? The indolent summer air had surely whispered into Lydia's ear; possibly, it had even refreshed something languishing deep within her soul. Though not an unpleasant change, thought Charlotte, it was a startling one. Especially as it came on the heels of her own ponderings, during the previous week, over love . . . and death.

"Mrs. Willett?" the landlady repeated. "Are you taking some of our goods to Mr. Longfellow? Or have you news from there already?"

"News? No, I have not seen them today, but my intention is to stop there, to add to their breakfast. Is there something you would like me to say?"

"No, no . . . unless you would ask if they will come again to dine, as they did yesterday. Of course, it is always good to see Miss—er—Mrs. Montagu, and her charming husband, the captain. Now, this other gentleman . . ."

"Signor Lahte?"

"He, too, is a welcome addition to our little village, as I'm sure you'll agree. You have spoken with him at length, I believe, in your own home?"

Although Charlotte had learned long ago that few things in Bracebridge went unobserved, she felt herself bristle.

"For part of a morning, with Hannah. He watched as I made several cheeses."

"I'm sure he found *that* fascinating."

"He seemed to. If you like, I could encourage him

to come and see how you run your own establishment, which must have a great deal more to offer his natural curiosity."

Lydia seemed to agree. "If Signor Lahte would visit us again," she simpered, "I know he would be satisfied! I would be only too glad to give him a tour of the inn's parts." Saying this, she again fluttered her handkerchief.

"But I'm also sure," said Charlotte, "that this morning he and the others will be hungry for your warm biscuits and muffins. Tim has taken the milk downstairs," she added.

"I will note that in the book," said Lydia, her smile vanishing as a matter of trade overcame her mind's other calculations.

Making her escape, Charlotte pulled her wagon around the corner of the inn; in another moment she stood before the open window of Jonathan Pratt's small office. She was pleased to see a round head pop out of it.

"Mrs. Willett! Won't you come in and join me?"

"I would rather you join me in the delightful air," she answered, giving Jonathan a look of such innocence that he answered at once with a conspirator's smile.

"Then I will have to leave off work, despite the fact that I am in the midst of tallying."

"Might we not discuss my account?"

"Certainly! And I will inspect what you have made off with this time. Scones, is it? Oh, muffins—I did sample some of them earlier, but perhaps another one or two will do no harm."

When the landlord had come out into the yard, the two old friends made their way to a rustic seat of logs that sat in a copse of trees not far away. Hidden from most things, it was a place appreciated by those with imagination.

"So, my dear," Jonathan began as he chose a muffin. "How do you like having a stylish European next door? I believe it's nearly all some women now think of. Have you, too, come under his exotic spell?"

"I think," she said, feeling herself redden, "that it is entirely possible I am like other women, Jonathan. He is a pleasing man, with quite a good carriage, face, and manner."

"He is far too handsome for his own good!" the landlord rejoined, patting a waistcoat that rode uneasily over an impressive stomach. "Something I am sure he knows."

"He seems intelligent . . ."

"Yes, he does. That's why I wonder at his being here at all."

"Has our village no exotic charms of its own, in your opinion?" asked Charlotte with a light laugh.

"Charms? In certain young ladies, here and there, quite possibly. Yet I cannot believe any of them would make a proper match for Signor Lahte."

"He could offer one of them a fortune . . ."

"But not a houseful of children to work a farm, or to marry land."

"It's rumored there is another reason he might not marry a young lady." She watched as he eyed her warily.

"If, Mrs. Willett, you suppose I will speak with you of what I suspect you mean, then you are mistaken!"

"But Jonathan, I've been a wife—and have some idea . . . of many things. Besides, if others speak of it, why can we not, only between ourselves?"

"Talk of forbidden love? I don't see that a wife should know much of this subject. After all, women will not find its equal among *their* sex." Though he refused to make further comment, her look of disappointment soon softened him. "However, I do recall that your father allowed you to explore his library, which includes many of the classical authors . . . so I suppose I may in good conscience answer a question or two. If I can."

"Is it possible, that here—? Have *you* known a man to devote himself whole-heartedly, passionately, to another? To the exclusion of my own sex?"

"Possible? Most things are possible, my dear. That is something I've learned while operating an inn. Even with sleeping arrangements—although such things are not supposed to happen. But they do, even here, despite warnings from the pulpit, and penalties occasionally sent down from the bench."

"It is not something one often reads of, though, in our own time— even in Pope, or Fielding. So I wonder—"

"Reads about? Do you actually suppose that novels represent life, Mrs. Willett? Great Heaven! Who would care to *write* of such things? What would others say of such an author? Or *to* him? No, my dear, some things are best spoken of softly, between sensible friends, rather than broadcast in the newspapers, or put into novels! This is hardly a subject even for one's own journal. Think of what might happen, should one's children read—or their children, one day!" Jonathan closed his eyes, then gave a chuckle before opening them again. "Yet there are some of the highest rank and fashion in England who are not afraid of such talk about themselves—as I presume you have heard. And I can assure you that we, too, have such neighbors . . . although they do not proclaim what they do, or feel, to the world. For instance, we both know one pair of pleasant old gentlemen who live a little out of the village . . . but I ask you, Mrs. Willett, who would tell *me* their secrets? Especially as everyone can see that I have another sort of problem for my own."

Charlotte smiled at this reference to Lydia Pratt, before going on. "Jonathan, to change the subject entirely—"

"Yes?" he replied with new suspicion, watcing her blue eyes widen. Now, it appeared, she went for the meat of the nut she had come to crack.

"Your servant, Thomas Pomeroy—"

"What's this? Don't tell me you think—!"

"As you say, I know so little . . . as a woman, especially . . . but I did wonder, when I saw him here at dinner yesterday."

"Pomeroy?" The landlord gave an explosive laugh. "Hah! *That*, I think, is hardly likely to be young Tom's style! No, I would suppose he is quite the opposite. From the way I've seen him watch the various females who come and go, I believe he might behave, if he could, like the infamous Don Juan. Or perhaps your Signor Lahte. Now, there is a life that must give one much to think on. I only hope, if Lahte stays, that he will tell some of his better stories to me! Confidentially, and only between gentlemen, my dear. For I'm afraid I've missed a good deal of what the world offers."

"But where has he come from?"

"Pomeroy? He's English, of course . . . from London. Last week he arrived here from Boston with another traveler."

"That much I know."

"Well, then—after that, he asked to speak with me in private, and he made me an offer. What do you say to this, Mrs. Willett?"

Reaching into a pocket, Jonathan Pratt pulled out a fragment of cloth. He carefully unrolled it to reveal something small that gleamed even in the shade.

"A diamond?" Charlotte asked with surprise.

"It seems Pomeroy's parents were French—forced to leave that Catholic country in order to marry, for as Protestants, they were not permitted the rite. This is the last of a pair of heirloom stones they gave him, with which he was to make his way in the world. He told me the first one paid for his passage here in May. This, he hopes, will help to set him up in a trade, after a suitable apprenticeship. He also asked me to take him on until he could find a proper master—or at least until I might turn this into gold for him, for a small commission. He tells me he hopes to bring his parents from London one day, to share our better life. That seemed to me to indicate a very good sort of lad."

"It is a heartwarming story," Mrs. Willett said softly.

"There is more, and I warn you it's of an even more exciting nature. I overheard Thomas telling Tim that while headed here from London, he barely survived a wild storm at sea which nearly sent his ship to the bottom! Though finally, it only drove them far off their course. By God's grace they anchored safely, and the captain was able to obtain a new mainmast in Funchal. But when he sailed again, it was with three fewer hands, for they had been swept overboard one howling night! Quite an adventure, don't you think?"

"Nearly as exciting as something from Mr. Defoe. Or perhaps Dean Swift?"

To this, Jonathan nodded soberly.

"It might be," he returned, "that Thomas Pomeroy could make himself into a fine novelist, one day. But I would hope, first, that he proves his intelligence by finding more useful employment, or learning a trade. Meanwhile, he does well enough here, which is something I generally expect but rarely find in those I hire. The most promising of people, I am sorry to tell you, are often a disappointment. I do know of one night when young Thomas 'borrowed' a field nag and came in at dawn . . . but then, we cannot all be middle-aged, sedentary, and reasonable, can we? Now, why do *you* ask about him, Mrs. Willett?"

"I have no real excuse. But if he is to stay with us, I thought . . ."

"That you should inquire into his pedigree? Quite sensible, for you will now have something extra to trade, on your next visit to the shop of Mrs. Bowers. At the moment, I can assure you Pomeroy is without other fortune, but I think he'll soon remedy that. He seems to me a clever lad who might easily win a Bracebridge daughter. Though I suppose any young person who comes to us without references could, conceivably, bring trouble. Speaking of trouble, how fares Mrs. Montagu this morning?"

"I haven't seen her. She keeps town hours, you know. But I am going that way. May I deliver your compliments, as well as your muffins?"

"You may."

"Then I'll be going," said Charlotte, rising and taking up her wagon's handle.

As she went on her way, Jonathan Pratt watched her fondly, though he asked himself why she had just set off in entirely the wrong direction.

SOON AFTER MENTIONING Mrs. Montagu to Jonathan, Charlotte had realized there was little chance Diana would yet be dressed, for it was still no more than eight o'clock. But that left time for a chat with Nathan, who should be at work on the other side of the inn's rear yard. She walked past the stables toward his small forge, and saw by the smoke drifting from its chimney that he was, indeed, nearby.

As it turned out, Nathan Browne was just inside the enclosure, working today as a farrier. With a roan's forefoot crooked between his knees, he ran a metal file over the animal's horn. Then he lowered the leg to the ground and stepped back to flex his back and arms, before turning and noticing Charlotte standing there.

"Do you sell door to door today, madam?" he jested, eyeing the cloth packets in the wagon with interest. She offered a muffin, which he took once he'd wiped his hands on his sleeves. Savoring a bite, he stepped forward and squatted to examine her wagon's wheels.

"They're holding well," he commented, checking both sides before lifting his placid gaze.

"A good advertisement for your skills."

"As if I needed work! This is my fourth horse this morning. It seems everyone travels before harvest, but few take enough care of their mounts or carriage horses to have them ready."

"But you were busy all last month, as well."

"Then perhaps the average owner is not as bad as I imagine. Why is it in our nature to think the worst of our fellows, do you suppose? Now, what can I do for you this morning? Are your own feet quite well?" he asked, leaning back to sit in more comfort on the ground.

"They'll do," she replied as she sank to the wagon's bed.

"Still, they might benefit from a short rest." Nathan spread his large, rough hands on the grass. "Some speculate they've taken you too far of late, walking out with Mr. Longfellow's guest." Seeing her frown, he gave an apologetic shrug of his broad shoulders. "Though that is not something I've repeated. Will he stay with us long, do you think? And what does he intend to do here?"

"I doubt he'll attempt to shoe horses, if that's your concern."

"Now I've annoyed you. For that I'm truly sorry!"

"The fault is mostly mine, Nathan. But you're not the only one to warn me lately. Why, I wonder, is no one else willing to make a stranger welcome?"

"I agree that it's a wise precaution—for it's said any traveler might be an angel in disguise. But I would add, not too welcome, or too soon. If he makes his home with us, I'll be glad to offer him my assistance. In fact I already have, on the very afternoon he came from Boston."

Thinking back, Charlotte recalled Longfellow's suggestion of a siesta, on their way home from viewing the body in the cellar—a suggestion to which Lahte had immediately agreed. "What did he want here?" she asked the smith.

"He asked about his horse and chaise—the one he'd rented to drive here—and made sure we would send it back quickly. And then he wanted to know about the mount ridden by the poor devil found on the road. He asked to see the saddle as well, but neither suited him."

He could have been seeking a message, she supposed, as he seemed to have done with the boots and buttons. Though why, exactly, she still could not say.

"I understand what it is to be new to a village, you know," Nathan went on. "When I arrived here, I greatly valued the loan of one particular pair of ears. I still do. Here, let me regale you with a story I ran across only last evening. As you have an interest in things of a mysterious nature, I think you'll find this worth pondering. It seems a merchant in the Blue Boar yesterday was in Boston last week, where he saw our dead man—while still living, of course—in another tavern. The Green Dragon, to be precise."

"Oh?"

"But when the fellow got up to leave, he saw this Sesto Alva, who still sat at a table, walk in at the door!"

Imagining the scene, Charlotte replied with pointed curiosity.

"There were two?"

"There were, though some suggest that the first man was, in truth, what our Dutch friends call—er—"

"A doppelgänger?"

"That's it. Do you suppose such a thing could exist?"

"Do you?"

"I've never seen one. Nor do I want to! I have, however, now that I think of it, seen a man who closely resembles his brother."

"That does seem more likely."

"So I suppose it is not much of a story, after all."

"On the contrary," Charlotte replied seriously. "Is there any more?"

Nathan stood up, and added the few details he'd previously omitted.

"Have you heard," Mrs. Willett then asked the smith, after taking a little time to think, "that Captain Montagu also found Signor Lahte's servant in Boston?"

"The boy called Angelo."

"Who traveled to Boston with Sesto Alva. But as far as I know, Angelo has made no mention of this 'brother.' Surely, he'd think a relation would be interested in claiming the body? And wouldn't it be surprising enough, if Alva did meet a family member here unexpectedly, for him to share the story with his servant? Especially as he had no one else to tell?"

"There could have been bad blood between them. But I've a new suspicion, Mrs. Willett. There may be more to this Alva's death than has yet been told to the village. Do you think so?" Her eyes told him he'd hit on a truth. "It does seem," the smith went on, "that their meeting was less than pleasant. Perhaps, too, Alva saw his business as none of a servant's concern—especially one so young."

"That may be true, as well. I only hope we'll meet this second man, whoever he is, when he learns Sesto Alva has died here. Unless he already knows—"

She stopped short, considering.

"Or, he could have been unaware of Alva's visit to us," said Nathan, "and might well have moved on. If that is so, he may never hear what has happened."

"It's an interesting puzzle," she said, attempting to hide her growing suspicion that it was something far worse.

The blacksmith only smiled, glad to have been of service.

Chapter 13

WHEN SHE HAD reached the road, Charlotte was not
at all sure what made her suddenly change her plan and
continue up the hill in the direction of her farmhouse.
Once inside, she passed Hannah with barely a word. The
rest of the beans would have to wait, and the pears could
be hanged! She went into her study, closed the door, and
sat in its deepest chair, slouching in defiance.

Was it only the heat that made her feel as if her skin
had just come into contact with a patch of nettles? She
did not think so.

First, Signor Lahte had said he had no idea of the
identity of the man found dead beside the road, or how
he came to be there. Then, he remembered that he *might*
know the man, but barely; in fact, he admitted no con-

nection, though he and Sesto Alva, and Angelo, had all came to Bracebridge from Milan. Still, she had attempted to believe him. And now, it seemed there was yet another visitor from Milan—the *double* of Alva. It was too much!

On top of that, Lahte was jealous of a younger man's attention to his servant, though he held the eye of nearly every woman in the village! Not that she, herself, hoped to gain his further approval. She hoped for nothing from him at all . . . except, perhaps, the honesty he had promised. Honesty? *Pffff!* Mrs. Willett blew a strand of hair away from her face. Did he suppose her a complete fool? Someone to whom he could talk sweetly, while adding another link onto his absurd story?

The boy now had a thing or two to explain, as well. Although in his case, she suspected, sympathy would soon make her regret her anger. For Henry had seen the child in tears. . . .

Quite honestly, she reconsidered, could it be Lahte's fault that she had been wrong about Thomas Pomeroy? But could she then be wrong about Gian Carlo Lahte, and Angelo, too? There was *something* curious about the young man, who seemed to bear her an unspoken ill-will. Why?

All of her uncertainties of the night before reappeared. She had guessed Il Colombo had been chased from Milan by a husband. But perhaps . . . perhaps he had not lied to her, exactly, after all? Might he only have held something back? She tried to recall Lahte's exact words.

I did wish to avoid a certain person, at least for a time . . . it is a woman who cannot refuse her feelings . . . she threatened to leave her home . . . I tried only to spare an old man. . . .

Then, as if the season had changed in an instant, she saw the truth leap through a highly colored forest—one which she, herself, had fashioned.

He *could* have told her more. She had believed in him—in fact, had only refused to believe after his attentions to her had stopped. The shame of this now struck her with some force. But if what she suddenly sensed—no, *knew*—was true, then surely, there was something far worse to worry about!

Charlotte rose and went into the kitchen, where she left a quiet word with Hannah. She took a cloth, and went into the cellar to chip pieces from a square of pond ice buried in sawdust. Then she wrapped the chips in the cloth and applied it to her neck, her shoulders, under her thin muslin bodice.

Feeling cooler, she left the cellar with a new plan. When one wanted to verify a suspicion, the simplest thing to do was ask. As a strategy, it was less interesting than most. But sometimes, it did work.

WHEN SHE ENTERED Richard Longfellow's back door, Mrs. Willett heard the pianoforte ringing out from the study. She paused at the entryway to gaze inside. Angelo, she saw, played reasonably well, while Il Colombo stood ready to turn a page. There seemed no doubt today that Lahte delighted in Angelo's company, bending even now to touch a dark curl. It was done with what appeared to be the gentleness of a fond father, yet now that she knew. . . .

Here, in America, things were scarcely as they were in Italy. For here, possibly—yes, here, surely, the musico must have thought he would find peace, one day. But in fact he might well find eternal rest instead, and soon, if what she had finally seen became evident to another. Had one life already been claimed by vengeance? This seemed to her increasingly likely. For if Sesto Alva had come to Bracebridge with a warning. . . .

The thought chilled her further; yet it was with a clear, uplifted spirit that Charlotte hurried on in search of Richard Longfellow. She found Cicero reading in the front parlor, his feet propped by a low stool, a glass of cold tea at his side. He began to rise, but she motioned him to stay still.

"Have you, too, rouged yourself, Mrs. Willett?" he asked as he stared. "Or is it only the heat? Would you care for something?"

"Perhaps when we can sit and talk. At the moment, I need to speak with Mr. Longfellow."

"In that case, he is in the cellar . . . and I wish you well."

Arriving at the cellar door, she heard several clanks, and then an oath. She took the top steps carefully, squinting down to see what might be the matter. A musty, earthy smell grew until she stood on packed dirt, next to a rainwater cistern under the kitchen floorboards. The rest of the room flared out to hold shelves and bins; a further door, she knew, led to a closet by the chimney's base, where glasses of preserved fruits and vegetables were annually saved from frost. Along one wall, lit by a handful of candles melted into brick shelves, were racks of wine bottles that came from several nations. In addition, a pair of hogsheads held a lesser Madeira that was given out whenever the village held an ox roast, or celebrated the King's birthday.

Longfellow rose swiftly, and cracked his head again on a wooden shelf. This brought forth another oath. When Charlotte offered to examine the damage to his skull he declined, but suggested they try a bottle which he chose after a moment's rummage.

"When the rest of the world is an oven, this place becomes a useful refuge. Though few are wise enough to see it," he declared to a nest of spiders above his head.

"I have seen Lahte and Angelo in your study." To this, Longfellow offered no reply. "Where are the others?"

"Montagu, to the best of my knowledge, is writing in his room—roasting like a chicken, no doubt. My sister has gone out for a walk. It is rare to find her more clever than Edmund, but she is under orders, after all. Mrs. Montagu had no taste for breakfast this morning, and hopes to gain an appetite for dinner."

Charlotte felt a momentary regret for having left the contents of her wagon at home, but decided Diana would soon have something far better to distract her.

"You look pensive as well as warm, Carlotta. This wine will help. It comes from the countryside near Paris; I believe many find it supremely refreshing." With some difficulty he removed an unusual cork, creating a pop before he quickly poured a sparkling wine into two glasses.

Charlotte sipped, and smiled.

"Now, you may ask your questions."

Abruptly, her mood changed. "Do I always come to you with questions, Richard? Am I never only civil, and good company?"

He looked at her more closely, seeing that he had stumbled onto a concern whose existence he had not suspected.

"Of course, Mrs. Willett, you are superior company, at any time! I thought you knew that. You must realize I would hardly thrive here as I do without your assistance. Though I'll wager you have at least one question for me. What shall I forfeit, if I'm wrong? A bottle of this champagne for your cellar? A glass house orchid for your study, until winter comes? But what will you give me if I'm correct? What about a cold basket, under the trees along Pigeon Creek?"

"Richard, there is one thing—"

"Ha! Cold chicken, then, I think—and a small cake, too. Perhaps salad of some sort . . ."

"Is that all?"

"And a cheese. That is all."

"Good. Now, I have an idea that will make you somewhat less pleased. I suspect Angelo was not Il Colombo's servant in Italy, nor anywhere else."

"Just what do you suppose he was, then?"

"That, I would like to hear from Signor Lahte, himself. I think you had better come with me, as his host and sponsor. I imagine what the two of them have been doing secretly will surprise you." Charlotte turned and set down her empty glass. In another moment, she began to climb the steps.

"Are you certain?" Longfellow asked plaintively.

"Come, if you value what little peace you have left."

He corked the bottle, and went up after her.

WALKING BACK INTO the heat of the hall, Charlotte reached into her pocket and produced a small folding fan. This she began to wield as she gathered her courage. The pianoforte had stopped, and a discussion seemed to be taking place within the study. When they entered, Gian Carlo Lahte dropped Angelo's hand, and came to bend over Mrs. Willett's. Angelo turned away and gave a kick to the innocent leg of the instrument that had lately fallen silent. It was Longfellow who began.

"Mrs. Willett and I have been chatting, Lahte, and it seems she has some new concern."

"Sì, madamina?" asked the Italian. Angelo dropped a stack of sheets with musical notations into an ornate traveling box, and slammed down its lid.

"Sì," said Charlotte. "I know things are done differently in Europe, or even in England."

"Things? I am afraid . . ."

"Well, what is allowed. In certain cases."

"Certain—cases?" He stared, which caused the two spots on Mrs. Willett's cheeks to burn more brightly.

"I believe," she said, "that I should start at the beginning. Or as close to it as I am able, and still be sure of my footing. Signor Lahte, you once told me, perhaps in confidence, that you came here fleeing from someone."

"Ah, yes," Lahte admitted, glancing at Angelo's back.

"You also said, at first, that you did not know Sesto Alva—though you did seem uncomfortable when you saw him lying dead."

"I am sure that I did! But I barely knew the man, Mrs. Willett. This is quite true."

"Do you, then, know another member of his family more intimately?"

Lahte's lips parted; strangely, no sound was forthcoming.

"It also seems," she continued, "that you were the one who took the buttons, and the boots." A nod was her reward, but still, no explanation was advanced. "You went to examine his saddle too, when you guessed Sesto Alva came here with a message. Perhaps from your servant, whose reason for coming is still unclear to the rest of us. Unless—could it be that Angelo, too, has fled? Perhaps from a father?"

"I beg of you, ask me no more! The boots, the buttons—these cannot matter. But speak further of Angelo, and you force us both to leave this place . . . for your safety, as well as our own."

"Yet if you stay, and if what is already rumored were to be discovered—" said Longfellow balefully, reaching a conclusion of sorts at last.

Lahte drew a long breath. "Yes—I have admitted to you that Angelo is not like most *musici*. This is quite true. He has declared his love for me, was in pain without me, and so he asked Sesto Alva to bring him here. This was against his father's wishes—and mine. Now, I fear, he is unhappy for what he has done. Of course I could send him away again. But would it not be better to help him, to find for him some employment, while time heals the wound I gave when I did not intend it? He serves me well, after all. He is even something like a small brother, in my eyes. Surely, there can be nothing wrong with this?"

A groan escaped Charlotte's lips. "Is that *all* of the truth you care to tell us?" she asked, watching Angelo turn smoldering eyes upon them both, realizing that a good deal of what they said was, in fact, understood.

"I beg of you, Mrs. Willett, keep whatever you suspect secret, only for a little longer!"

Charlotte was about to reply, but stopped as Angelo rushed through the open door, where he jostled another figure attempting to enter. Signor Lahte leaped up, but with enormous effort forced himself to remain where he was.

To everyone's surprise, Lydia Pratt came in. With the help of a curling iron she had now coaxed several black screws of hair to hang beside her brightened cheeks, further softening her usual bun. Beyond that, she had tucked her neck scarf well down, to reveal a red poppy nestled between semicircles of blue-veined flesh.

"Signor Lahte? I have come at the request of the ladies of Bracebridge," Lydia nearly sang. "We ask you the favor of listening to our unanimous decision, and our *sincere* desire . . ." She paused in her pleasure to gasp for breath.

"Signora?"

"We *hope*, as long as you plan to stay, that you will consent to become the maestro of our little choir! You might assist us in our singing—and possibly show us a few courtly dances. The youngest among us could learn from you, too, the manners practiced by the best society. Although it would appear your servant could benefit from learning these first, for he has almost run me down in the doorway." With this last, disapproval took its customary place upon her features.

Now it was Richard Longfellow's turn to groan softly, while he asked again a question that occurred to him lately with increasing frequency. Had the overheated world about him gone completely mad? Still, he rose to the occasion as a host and a gentleman.

"Mrs. Pratt? Lydia. Would you care, I wonder, for a cup of tea?"

Chapter 14

Diana Montagu stopped to examine the few treasures gathered during half an hour's wandering through the fields; she held some lacelike flowers, a small, shiny rock, and a stick with a round swelling in the stem. Her brother, she thought, would enlighten her as to what the last was. It might make him less irritable if she showed some interest in his many dull acres. And after all, what was life, she asked herself as yet another mood overtook her, if one could not bring a little happiness to others?

Though the air was stifling, she felt better as she remembered her recent city walks, and the trials to which they'd subjected her. Here, at least, one did not expect to be bothered—not out in great expanses of green, brown, and silver, where pretty butterflies swooped and rose over weeds and a few bright blossoms. There even appeared to be faint stirrings of a breeze, for something ruffled the topmost leaves and branches of the trees winding their way along Pigeon Creek.

Inhaling sweet smells, Diana walked with renewed purpose toward the green ribbon before her, hoping to sit and bathe her feet. She then noticed a streaking object of white and tan, which looked like someone in shirt and breeches running along a stone wall, before disappearing into the creek's hollow. She presumed it was young Angelo. At least, he would be unlikely to stop and babble at her.

Once among the trees, she found a path made by some sort of animal—or possibly Indians, she imagined with a thrill. How good it would be to sit amidst the cool, thick grass! But she decided against this for the sake of her skirts. Then, when she realized they were hardly her best, Diana again changed her mind and sat.

Overhead, a woodpecker began a rapid tapping that made her more aware of quieter birdsong, once its echoing knock had ceased. So soothing was the whole scene that she removed her hat and lay back, disappearing from the world's view. She allowed her cares to fly away—as far, perhaps, as the distant blue visible through a tracery of leaves. Then, she heard a sharp chattering. A squirrel above her, a large gray one, seemed perturbed. A new sound came from the water—probably the boy splashing as he walked toward her through the creek bed. Would she be discovered? If she stayed where she was, she thought, the grass would hide her. A much larger splash made her suspect the child had fallen into one of the holes where, according to her brother, men and boys sometimes came to bathe. She laughed softly, listening to his irritated mutter.

Carefully, Diana rolled onto her side, and raised her

head—just, she supposed, as an Algonquin princess might have done. As if to oblige her curiosity the boy stopped, turning to look behind him. He pulled off his wet shirt, and she had a clear view of his back. No marks there, she was glad to see. At least Lahte had not beaten him yet. He had smooth, lovely skin. If he continued, she thought wickedly, she might yet see more of it.

Suddenly the boy ducked, and rose up like a harbor seal. As she watched the water flow from his dark hair, Diana got to her knees quietly; grasping a branch, she pulled herself upright. Feeling she committed a pleasant indiscretion, she took several steps toward the bank, holding on to some foliage for balance and cover. She would have taken one step more if the loose, moist grass at the edge of the creek had not given way. Instead, she pitched forward; only the branch in her hand slowed her descent into the water, while her feet slid helplessly down the muddy bank. Finally she lost her grip entirely and sat down in the creek, wet to the waist, while the boy faced her with a look of amazement.

Diana's next discovery only caused her shock to increase—for she saw that the child was not as he should be. How, she asked herself, would the handsome Signor Lahte explain *this* development?

"Signora!" Angelo cried. Though he seemed about to bolt, he stayed and helped the less fortunate Mrs. Montagu in her plight. After a period of tugging and tussling together, both collapsed safely into the grass. A string of rapid words followed, which Diana could not understand—yet their import was unmistakable. Someone would soon feel the brunt of a raging temper—no doubt, she decided, for good reason!

Waiting no longer, Angelo snatched up his shirt and set off for the house at a run.

Diana gathered her skirts in her hands, and lifted them well above her sodden slippers. Then, walking as quickly as she supposed Dr. Warren would allow, she hurried forward, hot on the trail of Angelo's flying heels.

"OF COURSE, WE have no *intention* of inquiring into your plans," Lydia Pratt insisted, as Charlotte poured a cup of tea from the pot Cicero had just provided. "It is only that we hope to become better acquainted. *Will* you remain with us for long, signor? And is your little boy to stay, as well?"

Charlotte shrank into a chair behind the tea service, feeling Lahte's embarrassment, as well as Lydia's apparent lack of anything like it. Of course they had been unable to continue their original discussion; that still hung like a threatening cloud over three of the four present. Suddenly, as if the long-awaited storm had arrived, a door at the back of the house flew open with a bang, causing them all to jump. A moment later a pair of feet thundered through the passage, and they had a glimpse of Angelo as he ran toward the stairs to the rooms above. Soon a door above them slammed. Another in the upper hall opened with an oath; a further set of steps marked the progress of Edmund Montagu coming down.

Gian Carlo Lahte sat back with apparent relief. He seemed about to speak, when a noise similar to those abovestairs came from the kitchen. This time, it led to the sudden appearance of Mrs. Montagu.

The bedraggled state of his sister's dress was enough to bring Longfellow to his feet. She hissed and motioned for him to sit, while she caught her breath.

"My dear!" cried Captain Montagu, entering the room behind her. He, too, was shushed. Diana created a dramatic pause by raising a hand, making sure of her hold over the assemblage.

"Where," she demanded, "is Angelo?"

"Angelo?" asked Montagu. He whipped around to face Lahte. "What has the boy to do with this?"

"I believe," said Longfellow, "that he's gone upstairs. What has happened, Diana? You look surprisingly unkempt."

"I'm sure I do! For I was almost drowned in that filthy stream of water behind your house. As it is, my gown is ruined—and several other expensive articles of clothing, I have no doubt!"

"As you are a poor swimmer, I would advise you to choose a tin tub, the next time you wish to bathe," her brother replied dryly.

"Yet had I done so, I would hardly have seen—"

Observing Lydia Pratt for the first time, Diana narrowed her eyes as if her own home had been invaded by something small, and less than welcome.

"Well, what *did* you see?" Longfellow prodded. "A moose, perhaps, wandering up from the marshes?"

"What I *saw* was Angelo in the water, disrobing—"

"Well, my dear, that hardly constitutes a crisis, for you have come upon a brother, and presumably a husband, in the bath before."

"What has frightened you, my lady?" Lahte asked with a frown.

"I will tell you! I saw, signor, what looked very much like . . . how shall I put it? *Like a feminine bosom!*"

"Aah!" Lydia Pratt gasped, at once shocked and satisfied.

"I understand," Lahte returned calmly, while he extended a hand. "And I am most sorry if it has alarmed you, madama."

"I am sure you are! For what must it say of *you*, sir?" Diana countered.

"Is this a frequent occurrence?" Longfellow asked hesitantly. "Perhaps a further result of the procedure that causes the castrato to lose his—"

"Castrato! Where? *Angelo*?" Diana blurted out, looking about in hopes of seeing for herself.

"Angelo, yes," her brother replied. "And, of course, Signor Lahte."

"You!" The lady gaped as she turned to the Italian. "You, a—a—! And . . . and the child, too?"

While Gian Carlo Lahte sought a reply, they again heard a stamping of small feet on the stairs, followed by Angelo himself. He had quickly thrown on dry clothing, but now wore skirts, while his hair was pulled up into a dark, wet knot; a few strands still fell about his delicate ears. Rapidly, he crossed the room, spitting emphatic words as his eyes bore into his master's face. Upon reaching Signor Lahte, he began to shout in angry sobs, his voice high and strident.

There was little else Gian Carlo Lahte could do. Reaching out, he brought the child into his arms and bestowed a firm kiss on rosy, upturned lips beneath his own. It was meant to stop, to prevent—but it also had the effect of calming, until the two stood quietly, twining as only lovers will.

Most in the room were spellbound. Only Mrs. Willett sighed softly, a smile on her own lips at last.

"Carlotta?" Longfellow asked, when he realized that her mildness was quite unlike his own warring emotions. "Did *you* know of this?"

"For an hour, at most. But Richard, let Signor Lahte speak. He might now tell us a great deal more."

When their mouths had parted, Lahte kept a protective arm around his young servant, who looked increasingly pleased. "Ladies . . . gentlemen," he began, "I would like to present to you my wife, Elena Lahte." Then, he murmured softly to his companion, *"Cara sposa. . . ."*

"Grazie, caro," she responded, looking up at him with shining eyes.

"Cicero," Longfellow remarked, speaking to the door where he knew the ever-curious old man lurked. "Port, please. My sister, who has brought us yet another surprise, will now require reviving."

Chapter 15

ALTHOUGH DIANA HAD not fainted entirely away, she had in fact swooned and fallen into a convenient chair. As Charlotte went to offer her assistance, Lydia Pratt, barely disguising her malicious joy, sidled toward Richard Longfellow. But he had already made his way toward Captain Montagu, hoping to share the burden of council.

It seemed that Gian Carlo Lahte and his bride were the only ones in no hurry to improve the situation; Lahte silently fingered the gold ring that again graced Elena's hand, while she purred with contentment.

"Well," said Edmund Montagu to the rest, after he had spoken for several moments with their host. "It seems that some of the truth, at least, has come out. But I, for one, am at a loss to understand why this charade was necessary. Signor Lahte, what could justify treating a wife in such a manner? And how, sir, did you ever manage to get her to go along with you?"

"I hardly know where to begin," replied the musico. "But you are right, Captain. You must now hear the whole truth. It is the fault, first, of the Holy Father in Rome."

"An interesting idea," Longfellow countered, "but hardly an explanation." He watched his guest summon strength and wit, before starting out on what proved to be a long and involved story.

"The Pope," Lahte said finally, "does not allow *castrati* to marry. However, that is what I have done. For many years, I cared nothing for this ban for I, too, saw no point in marriage . . . for myself, or for a woman I might choose. But then, I turned away from the stage to seek a better life. In Milano I hoped only to share my knowledge of music. And then, one day, a friend presented me to Don Arturo Alva—a man of old family and fortune, who had also a daughter. His daughter and I had already met, in the city's cathedral. After a mass there, Elena found a reason to speak to me, when her father went to light the candles. She later asked someone known to her to call on Don Arturo, to ask him to engage me, so that I might teach her more of music. This was done. But I soon found Elena believed she was in love with me. She was not yet fifteen—but in many noble families, even children are given in marriage. Elena then told me her father had made his choice for her. For a nearly a year, they had argued over a gentleman who was well beyond the age of her father—a man Elena did not like. Finally, Don Arturo told her she must accept this man, or enter a convent to live with the sisters."

"How terrible!" breathed Diana, alert once more.

"I knew I could not give Elena all that she deserved, and what most women desire. But what could I do? I, too, now longed for another to share my life." Lahte stopped as his throat closed over words that might further express his hopes.

"She had," he soon continued, "no longer a mother to advise her, and few others to guide her. Don Arturo often treated his daughter cruelly, keeping her from the governess who defended her, until that lady died tragically. She was kept even from her maid, if she would still not obey. Without love, Elena was without hope, and I was saddened to see her so. At first I did not intend . . . but in the end, I found an English parson who toured the cathedral, as many do. I paid him to meet us both there one day, to perform the ceremony that would make her my wife— at least, in the world that does not bow to our own religion."

"Yet you stopped short of carrying her away?" Longfellow asked delicately.

"Elena was my wife, but only in name. I could not bring myself . . . with one still a child. Then we spoke of my wish to go to America, and I promised I would return for her. If pressed further, I told her she must go to the sisters, as her father required—for in a convent, I knew she would find not only a refuge, but learning. After a year or two, I hoped she might still wish to join me in a new life— if she then felt it would bring her contentment. But, if she had by then come to consider our marriage a mistake, Elena could forget what she had promised, for it was not a true oath in the eyes of the Church. She would be free to marry again, if she chose. I would not hold her to her vows."

"But she chose to be with you," Diana returned, pleased by the romance of his story. "Even though you had not yet made her *entirely* your own?"

"*Sì*, signora."

"I do begin to understand your wife's recent irritation with you," she added thoughtfully.

"But the father?" asked Longfellow, eager to hear the rest.

"After I left Milano, Elena again argued with her father, telling him against my advice that she would never agree to marry the man he chose, for she was already married to me! At this, he laughed—yet he had the gates of his house doubly guarded, so that no one who did not belong could enter."

"But Sesto Alva . . . he was your wife's uncle?" Charlotte guessed.

"Nearly—a cousin to Don Arturo, and a man I met only once. Of course, his position in the family allowed him to come into the house. But he was only a poor man who did small things in life, for small reward. I have learned from Elena that he spent the little his family provided—then, he lived by his wits, as you say. Often he would pledge or sell plate or jewels, for those who needed funds quickly. Elena had a little left to her on the death of her mother, and this she urged Sesto to take, to bring her to America—where, she told him, he might also improve his own life. Sesto agreed to do this. Yet I am sure he hoped to receive more from me when he brought Elena, to keep our new home a secret from her father. Unfortunately, there are always whispers—and Don Arturo himself learned that I had come here. I had not kept my interest in this place a secret, after all."

"And then, when you saw Sesto—?" asked Longfellow.

"When I looked down at him, there in your cellar, I saw only Arturo Alva! For they were much alike—except for Don Arturo's scar. I imagined Elena's father had come for revenge. But very soon, I realized it must be Sesto.

Then, I suspected Elena might have sent him to me as a messenger."

"Thus, the business of the boots and buttons?"

"In my country, those who travel alone often conceal valuable objects, for they know they could be robbed. Sometimes they also hide messages, so that their families might hear what has become of them, if they are unable to return. I hoped Elena had somehow hidden such a message for me."

Following her own thoughts for a moment, Charlotte recalled Thomas Pomeroy's diamond, which she supposed might have been similarly concealed in his clothing, while he traveled. Had Sesto done the same? Gems were, after all, a part of his business. But there was something else she felt she must ask.

"Did you know," she inquired, "that a man who may be Elena's father was seen last week in Boston?"

"You knew of this as well, madama? Yes, Elena has told me Sesto came face to face with her father, soon after they left their ship. Sesto denied to Don Arturo that Elena was with him; then he slipped away, hoping he was not followed to the place where they stayed. Sesto swore he was in Boston on another mission; he pretended I had left Elena in London, and arranged with him to bring me a young boy I was fond of, to take her place. It was foolish, perhaps—but he had little time to fashion a story. He also brought to Elena the clothing of a serving boy. My wife was amused, at first, to imitate those women in the operas who sing their roles in trousers. But later, when Sesto did not return from his ride to find me, she knew she must keep up the masquerade, to remain safe from harm until she found me. Then, I asked her to remain disguised for her safety, and for that of my new friends. I thought, if word reached Don Arturo that I was here with a boy, then he might believe Sesto had told him the truth. In doing this, he would only assume what others quite easily suspect, after hearing stories of *musici*."

"There may be a good side to this, after all," Captain Montagu pointed out to Longfellow, when Lahte had finally finished. "Once your neighbors hear your guest has a wife—one whose father refuses to acknowledge a Protestant ceremony—and that the cruelty of the Church of Rome was responsible for their flight from Milan, then they will take Lahte's side. At any rate, they will surely keep their eyes open for Don Arturo."

He paused to look pointedly at Lydia Pratt, who nodded for herself, and for the ladies in her circle.

"I do not suppose," the captain continued, "that it will be easy for yet another foreign gentleman to make his way, unnoticed, to your door. Is the father," he now asked the musico, "able to speak English?"

"I have never heard him attempt it."

"Perhaps, then, we are in little danger after all," said Longfellow with relief.

"Though I think," Lahte added, "that Don Arturo could make one think he is a Frenchman—as we are far from Paris here."

Montagu now addressed the happy couple sternly. "One day soon, you must confront him. Of that, there can be no doubt. But I would like to find him first. Where was Don Arturo last seen in Boston?"

"Elena could not say," said her husband. "Sesto never named the place to her, for they did not know the town well."

"I believe," said Charlotte, "it was in the Green Dragon."

"How did you learn this, Mrs. Willett?" the captain asked with a bemused expression.

"Nathan Browne met a merchant here at the Blue Boar, who saw both men together there last week."

"Then it seems I have yet another reason to visit that infernal place. You're sure it wasn't Cromwell's Head, or the Bunch of Grapes?"

"The Green Dragon," she repeated with a look of sympathy that pulled a small smile from him.

"Then he may still be a patron. When he's found, we'll keep a close eye on him. However, if he succeeded in following his cousin from the tavern, then Don Arturo may have followed him here, as well. But how is it, sir, that you and he arrived in Boston at nearly the same time, as did your wife and Sesto Alva?"

"Though I set out before the others," Lahte answered, "I traveled slowly, by land, as far as Calais. Then I stopped in London, to settle some accounts. Elena tells me she and Sesto left Milano three weeks after my departure; thinking to avoid discovery, they went by carriage to Marseilles. From there, a French ship took them on. I think it likely that Don Arturo came directly by water, perhaps from Genova—Genoa, you call it. If that is so, he might even have been the first of us to arrive."

Charlotte shifted in her chair. Though she had little personal knowledge of ocean travel, she knew it could be a dangerous undertaking. Another question that had occurred to her was unsettled by a sudden wish to know if her brother Jeremy had arrived safely after his own crossing, for she had not heard from him since his departure.

"I am sorry," Lahte continued, looking to Mrs. Willett and noting her unhappy expression, "that I have had to play a part before you. If there had been a different way— but until I could speak with Don Arturo, I thought it best to hide Elena from the world's eyes. And then, madama, you guessed the truth."

Signor Lahte had, in fact, given a grand performance, Charlotte decided. She would long remember some of its more pleasant moments. But she also knew that truth was better, and safer, than illusion. It would soothe the inflamed village to know he was a husband, after all . . . if that knowledge did disappoint a few hearts. Now, Gian Carlo Lahte and his young wife could simply be themselves. And yet, she had to suppose their troubles were scarcely over.

"Edmund," Richard Longfellow said quietly, taking the captain aside. "There is something else . . . something Mrs. Willett and I have discussed. I think you should seek out Dr. Warren, too, when you return to town."

"He, at least, won't be difficult to find. But why?"

Longfellow outlined Warren's reasons for suspecting Sesto Alva's death to have been unnatural—as well as Mrs. Willett's more recent suspicions, founded on a sphere of granite.

"I will keep all of this in mind," the captain finally answered. "But Richard, remember one thing more. Often, a hireling can be found to do a man's bidding, whether it is lawful or not. A false Frenchman haunting Bracebridge may not be all you now have to fear. Quite possibly, one of Boston's own ruffians has found a new employer. . . ."

At this, Richard Longfellow looked increasingly uneasy—a thing for which Edmund Montagu was thankful.

Chapter 16

LATER, MRS. WILLETT walked out to find the Huntress, nearly full, climbing the blue sky to the east of Bracebridge, as Apollo and his golden chariot raced toward the opposite horizon. Despite this fine setting, she thought, her neighbor would have to make do with bread and bacon for his picnic, along with oiled, herbed greens. For his part, Longfellow had promised to dip into a jar of olives and to cut a slice from a wheel of cheese from Parma—both lately ordered from a Boston storehouse to make his foreign guest feel at home.

As she moved through her own garden, Charlotte listened to the distant calling of a mother to her child from a house down by the bridge. The air, still and clear, carried sound a long way tonight, she noted. She heard someone far off repeatedly striking metal on metal. When that stopped, there was only a dim murmur she knew to be the movement of water among reeds, and the voice of crickets as they awoke from the torpor of the afternoon, to warn of the coming autumn.

She found it odd that Nature appeared as usual, after the drama of the day. Now, thanks to Lydia Pratt, wives surely told husbands what they'd learned earlier of the castrato and his marital arrangement. By the bridge where younger women frequently lingered, hoping to speak with youths on evening errands, news of Signor Lahte's bride must also be a popular subject. Even the children would be buzzing with twisted tales of a dark, foreign man about to come and take them away, if their behavior did not improve.

Charlotte hoped the usual peace of the village would soon be recovered. But what if Don Arturo Alva did come, intending to retrieve his daughter—or to do even worse? Could Dr. Warren's suspicions have been correct? Or even, perhaps, her own? The physician had still sent them no word.

When she reached Longfellow's flowers, Mrs. Willett inhaled their heady scent, and found her neighbor cutting a pink specimen with a pocket knife. "Madam," he called to her as she approached. "May I take the basket, and give you this rose as a compliment? You have been instrumental, once again, in bringing consternation to our lives, to occupy us all for days! Do I smell fried bacon?" When she had accepted the rose, he lifted the cloth from the basket with one hand, taking its handle with the other. "I am in very good humor tonight, Carlotta, for some reason. Possibly it's because I cannot think of a better supper companion. I've left my own supplies on the patch of chamomile. Will you take my arm?"

"With pleasure, sir," she replied formally. "I hope you won't mind to hear I've invited one more. . . ."

Longfellow's face fell and he looked in each direction, until he noticed her smile. When her whistle had brought Orpheus from his exploration of a rock ledge, the three made their way to a flat and fragrant spot near a line of long shadows.

"You know," Longfellow told her, negotiating a screw into the neck of a bottle, "some will think our rendezvous a romantic one, rather than a simple outing to enjoy the air."

"I suppose it's possible," Charlotte replied as she set out two plates.

"You're not even a little pleased with the idea?"

"Tonight, I would imagine Bracebridge has other things to talk about," she said, her tone sober.

"Of course. I only thought—"

"You supposed my feelings bruised, and believed I needed courage. You could even suspect me to be unhappy enough to enjoy revenge." Her look assured him it was not so.

"Pass me the bread, and I will enjoy some of this bacon," he said with an answering grin.

"Where have you left the others?"

"Cicero," he said, finishing a bite and reaching for his wineglass, "is serving something or other to Lahte and Elena on the piazza. We all decided they would enjoy a few hours alone. As the old man knows no Italian, their secrets will be safe—if they have further secrets," he added, his brow suddenly furrowed. "However, I believe for tonight they will put intrigue aside. They must be ready to fulfill one final promise of their marriage vows."

"I think that's already accomplished. Or do you imagine 'Angelo' slept at Lahte's feet last evening, as he proposed?"

"Hmmm!"

"Though she's young, I hardly think Elena lacks a woman's natural feelings, or charming wiles."

"Or the usual jealousies," her companion added, his look to her more thoughtful than before.

"But where are Diana and Edmund?" Charlotte inquired, turning the topic away from her discomfort.

"They've gone to the inn, where they're no doubt enjoying an intimate supper upstairs. They, too, have some private matters to discuss."

"Does Edmund still plan to leave this evening?"

"When it cools. Now, he's quite sensibly giving my sister more time to scold him. Diana is displeased to have been left in the dark with regard to our guest's colorful history. She said as much when you left us earlier—in a voice none in the house could fail to hear."

"Do you believe he'll be able to find Elena's father in Boston?"

"For Edmund, such a thing should not be too difficult—if the man is still there. But now, let us forget the others, Carlotta, and concentrate on the joys of our own supper. Tomorrow will be soon enough to think of this jumble again."

Thus bidden, pleasure finally came, and remained with them for nearly two hours. Then, while a softer light embraced the earth and an owl began to call, Charlotte and Longfellow walked back toward the house. They paused to listen to Gian Carlo Lahte, they supposed, again playing the pianoforte, this time for his wife.

However, soon after, on her way up the hill to her own home, Charlotte saw something that told her they'd been wrong to presume the girl indoors. Elena Lahte, or at least a remarkably similar figure, stood not far from the garden path ahead of her, talking with someone under the vast web of moonlight.

Charlotte stood still. She also signaled Orpheus to sit, which he did readily, though his nose continued to seek out new information. At first, she had no wish to intrude on the pair who stood in her way. She even thought of reversing herself and taking the broad road to her front door. But hearing harsh words, she changed her mind. They were not Italian, nor English, but French words—some of them, at least, fluently spoken.

Had either been less intent in their argument, they might have spied her through the light foliage of the tall roses. But at the moment, neither one seemed to have eyes for the world. Abruptly, the tenor of their confrontation changed from that of a difference of opinion to something stronger. Suddenly it appeared that the girl had been grasped, and was held close.

"*Misero!*" Elena cried out the single word as she twisted free; then, she lowered her voice while backing away from Thomas Pomeroy. In another moment she turned, lifted her skirts, and ran toward the protection of her husband.

Mrs. Willett was prepared to clear her throat, so that Pomeroy might know further interference with Signora Lahte's desires would be witnessed. But there was no need. Instead of following, Thomas Pomeroy spat on the dirt before him, and then stomped away. Careless of his clothing, he made his own path through the roses, taking a direct line back to the Bracebridge Inn.

Charlotte felt several things other than relief, as she and Orpheus continued home. What she had seen baffled her, and she now wondered all the more about Jonathan's new servant. Had he waited for Elena to wander out into the garden for a breath of air, so that he might try his hand at seduction? Surely, the village had been full of such thoughts lately! And Jonathan had already assured her he supposed the young man possessed an amorous temper.

And yet, the real significance of what she had seen continued to elude her, even when she lay her head onto a feather pillow, and began another long, hot night of troubled tossing.

· · · ·

ALMOST AT MIDNIGHT, a man in casual attire walked along Boston's Union Street, until he saw the familiar sign of a green copper dragon.

When he went through the open door, the brick tavern seemed not unlike an oven slowly cooking an assortment of pungent humanity. Inside, the air was redolent of tobacco smoke and sweat, with a few less pleasant odors of a hot night; fortunately, these were sweetened by rum fumes, the aroma of citrus and spice rising from punch pots, and a prevailing smell of ale. All in all, this thick air welcomed city men long used to worse, if it did come as a contrast to that which Captain Montagu had lately enjoyed, riding in from the country.

He looked around at the collection of men, and assorted women—serving maids, two traveling ladies who had arrived late to avoid the day's heat, and a few hearty local women, seemingly unmarried friends of other drinkers. Some ate, some drank, many read newspapers, a few played at whist and tiles. There were also, he saw with no surprise, some whose pastimes were arguably less innocent—men he knew, crowded into a corner around a collection of small tables.

There was Revere, the silversmith, red-cheeked and wide, with a sharp eye for all that went on around him. Tonight, he sat at the side of Joseph Warren. The physician's light blue eyes continued to leap about as he leaned toward a friend as yet unknown to Montagu, his lips near the fellow's ear. Next to Warren, with his back turned . . . that had to be the elder Adams, the ringleader himself. There was no mistaking his palsy as he raised a hand in assent to something said at the next table, then brought it down hard, causing his cup to dance. The heat had made the poor fellow's hair and coat even less tidy than usual, Edmund decided before his eyes moved on.

At another table hunched Will Molineux, the Irishman at the center of much of what had lately been reported to Town House. It seemed a bad omen for him to be here among many men of St. Andrew's Lodge, for by habit he should have been with his Liberty Boys at the nearby distillery, instructing them in how to brew sedition. And quite possibly, how to make off with someone's purse. Molineux sat with a strange smile, listening to a man who appeared, by his garb, to be newly arrived from London. This tender soul had dressed himself up as a macaroni complete with velvet suit, and lengths of loose curls under a feathered hat. The effect was rather like Signor Lahte's, the captain supposed, though it was somehow less successful in such a callow version. Ah, well. At least it was a relief from the more dangerous sort now all too common in London—those of Clive's pack glittering in gold lace, with the gems of India sewn onto their clothing, often followed by a pack of tinseled, pinchbeck imitators. Yet was there something more to be seen here . . . ?

Montagu walked around for a better view of the man's face, and was rewarded with a blank look. It was Ian Whately, by God! The captain forced a cruel smile, causing the other to look away in disgust, after he'd raised a small looking lens to an arrogant eye.

Whately again spoke loudly of the libertine John Wilkes, a gaming friend of days gone by—before that firebrand's expulsion from Parliament, and from England. Certainly an acquaintance with a well-known enemy of the King's party would please the local nabobs, who would no doubt grow to enjoy this fop, after they'd had their fun with his costume and manner. Let them laugh, as they persuaded him to become more like themselves—something he would be glad to do, by degrees. Eventually, they might even ask him to join their lodge. And then, Ian could relay conversations of great interest, when he slipped away to join his true friends at Town House. All in all, the disguise seemed well done—if the 'peeper' was a bit much.

But what was happening tonight to draw such a collection of men not usually seen this late together, at least in public? Something the Crown should know about, surely. Was more trouble in the works? Montagu was again thankful that Diana, and their future child, were safely tucked away in the country.

One face the captain did not see in the crowd was that of Don Arturo Alva. He would have to seek out the landlord and again show him the sketch—a close copy of the one Longfellow had made. But first, Montagu decided to spend a moment on more subversive matters. Give them their Liberty, he thought as he moved closer to the knot of seated men. Give them enough rope—

To the captain's surprise, he now recognized a youth sitting at Dr. Warren's table. He hoped this one would not be overcome, one day, by their studied madness! Such company could only prove a goad and a threat to a boy unfamiliar with the town. And should the worst happen to Lem Wainwright, what would he ever say to Mrs. Willett?

By moving a little, Montagu was able to stare Lem full in the face, which brought their eyes together. Did the boy seem upset to see him? Was he guilty for what he had done, or planned to do, with these men? No! Happily, it seemed to him that Lem's honest face showed only pleasure. In another moment, both had begun to smile.

"Ho, Captain!" called Paul Revere, raising an engraved pewter tankard from his own shop in greeting. "What has brought you away from your bride at this hour? And is Mrs. Montagu well, sir?"

"Exceedingly well, thank you," Montagu returned, walking closer. "She enjoys the country air."

"A good thing! Is the silver frame I made for your miniature still to her liking?"

"It is as good a one as she has ever seen, she tells me. It is also her constant companion, whenever I am unable to be with her."

"Let us hope that will not be for long," said Sam Adams, "for family is the glue that holds the world together . . . as my own wife now tells me."

"Indeed, sir. I hear you've recently gained a surprising number of Sons, who follow in your footsteps."

"Of many mothers, I do admit—but all joined by a similar desire," Adams replied seriously, to chuckles from those around them.

The captain changed his focus. "Mr. Wainwright, have you yet mastered your Latin and your Greek?"

"I confess I haven't, Captain," Lem replied, standing. "And I'm now told I have more to learn than I'd supposed. In fact, several gentlemen have offered to tutor me."

"Though I believe it is Mr. Longfellow who paid your bond to the college, and he who sponsors you?"

"Yes, sir. For which I often praise him."

"We only wish, Captain, that Mr. Longfellow were less busy in the country, so that he might visit us as often as do *you*," said Sam Adams, with a gentle smile that hid well-known steel.

"I suppose you have already heard, Mr. Adams, that our friend has a subject of unusual interest to study at the moment. Dr. Warren must have told you of his own visit to Bracebridge last week?"

Several heads turned Warren's way, but on that matter, apparently, the physician had held his tongue.

"In fact, Dr. Warren is one of two men I've come here

to find tonight. Might I ask you, sir, a few questions concerning your recent medical observations?"

Nodding, Dr. Warren rose quickly and led Captain Montagu to an alcove away from the rest.

"I will only keep you a moment, Doctor, as I'm aware that I intrude on something . . . but tell me, if you will, what you've made of this fellow Mr. Longfellow says you carted off to Dorchester, now known to us as an Italian named Sesto Alva. Please hold nothing back, for I believe your information may well affect the safety of our friends in Bracebridge."

Warren looked closely into the face of his inquisitor. What he saw convinced him to speak freely.

"As a physician, I will tell you that one idea, at least, can be discounted. The man's lungs were clear; he did not choke. Instead, inside this Alva, as you name him, I found several bleeding ulcerations. Some others seemed to have hardened into scars. His stomach was surely affected by a malady, and for some time. What that was, I cannot be sure—a chronic illness, perhaps. All I can say with certainty is that his death was not the result of a moment's evil on an entirely healthy body. Still, he *could* have consumed poison that day, as I suggested to Longfellow—for the sores in his mouth were severe, and may well have increased as a caustic material sat in it, after death. . . ."

"You cannot rule out murder, then."

"I cannot. There was also a blow to the skull, as I suppose you've heard."

"Made in anger, do you think?"

"Possibly; perhaps only the result of a fall. But this in itself seems unlikely to have killed the man, given the circumstances. Still, it *is* there."

"So. Medical science can help us little . . . and we are forced to renew our search among the living."

"Which takes us from my strength, back to yours."

Neither spoke for a moment; the discussion seemed concluded.

"What is your feeling about the new revenue stamps, Doctor?" the captain asked abruptly. This time, Warren was quick with an impassioned answer.

"While we agree that the death of one man must be counted as a thing of importance, your stamps threaten the *rights, liberty, and property of many thousands*—most of whom see these possessions as more precious, more worth guarding, than life itself!"

"Will you then encourage the mob to hang not an effigy but a man, when it next feels a need to protect such things?"

Warren smiled and bowed slightly, backing away. "In Boston," he replied, "I know only citizens who wish to keep their homes and families from harm."

"To do this, Doctor, they begin by destroying the peace and security, even the homes, of Crown officials. But let us hope a taste was enough to warn all men of the poisonous effect of such actions!"

There seemed little more to say, and with a swift acknowledgment, they parted.

After that, Edmund Montagu made his way to the tavern keeper to inquire about the sighting of a doppelgänger the week before. The busy man pointed out a girl who had served that evening; tonight, too, she was occupied with fetching orders. This time Montagu took a protesting subject by an arm, and led her into the alcove he'd earlier occupied with Dr. Warren.

"This man," he said, again taking the drawing from his coat. "Do you remember seeing him?"

"Yes, sir, I do," the pert and pretty girl replied, standing still at last. "I remember *both* of them. Very alike they were, when I saw them together."

"What day was this?"

"Wednesday last," the girl replied.

"I've already heard they had much the same appearance . . . but can you recall anything *different* about one or the other?"

"Different? Well, sir, apart from quite a nasty scar on the side of his face, the one who came in second that night did seem better cared for . . . and he tried to order in French, on the first day I saw him. *Biftek*, as they say, and *vin* for wine. I thought he must be down from Québec. The other, who may have been a poorer brother, spoke queerly too, though his few words to me were in English. He asked for a bowl of bread and milk with his ale. That was on the night the two of them met, before the second gentleman arrived."

"But you say you saw both men before last Wednesday?"

"The one I called the poor brother came in a day or two earlier, had a little soup and some cheese, and then took more off with him. It seemed to me he had an attack of indigestion, but when I asked if he was ill, he only waved me away. I worried he might have a touch of the summer complaint. But he certainly did not come by it from eating our food, sir!"

"And the other? He came to eat?"

"He sat and had his dinner another day, as well."

"So each came in alone, before; but this time, they met by accident?"

"It seemed so—yes, sir. Both did look quite surprised!"

"Did they appear to be on friendly terms?"

"No," the girl answered, "they did not, though for a few moments they sat together, talking quietly."

"And how did they leave?"

"I saw the one who was ill go out the back, toward the little house behind. Then, I heard the other exclaim. He rose as well, threw a coin onto the table, and rushed off in the same direction. That was the last I saw of either one. Was there some trouble, sir, between them?"

"It looks that way. . . ." Captain Montagu replied. He then let the girl go to see to her customers, watching as she melted into the welcoming crowd. He thought again of what Dr. Warren had told him, and of the lingering illness of a man soon to die. Then, to no one in particular, Montagu added, "but the real question is, for how long . . . ?"

Chapter 17

W
ITHIN THE GLASS house built onto the side of
Longfellow's stone barn, Cicero spent the morning gar-
dening, while he also cultivated a philosophical mood.
Holding a clump of potted cactus from Mexico in
his hands, he observed a web deep within its golden,
curving spines. Here a spider had found safe haven, covering the smooth green skin with a circular tunnel the
size of an old man's thumb—though it seemed to do no
harm. The spider might even assist the plant, he imagined, by devouring smaller visitors who came with a more
destructive hunger.

He had seen more than one such cactus, though carefully watered and given good soil and sun, become host to
cottony mites, and finally turn to brown mush. This particular specimen seemed to thrive on little water, with its

roots in gravel and a guest upon its back. As it did well, he would leave plant and animal as they were, he decided; he would not apply the yellow dust he'd already puffed onto the others.

Heat, sun, water, soil—it wasn't easy to tell how much of a thing a plant might need. What suited one sort could cause another to sicken, and eventually to die. They were not unlike people, Cicero concluded, each born with a certain bent—a particular humor—which a wise man made little attempt to alter.

Cicero's meditation beneath the lightly whitewashed panes was interrupted by a swish of skirts, as Mrs. Willett and Signor Lahte's young wife entered the glass house. Signora Lahte, he presumed, must now be dressed in her own usual apparel; a previously secreted trunk had come earlier that morning from Boston. Today, she wore an open robe of bright, thin silk, with a beaded sash to accentuate her slight figure. Her eyes resembled smoky pearls, between lids and lashes carefully darkened with what he guessed was lamp soot. She had also reddened her lips somehow, and wore ruby drops at each ear. Amazingly, yesterday's sulking child had been reborn a beauty—whose equal, as far as he knew, Bracebridge had not seen before.

It seemed to Cicero, too, that Elena quickly felt the mysteries of his sanctuary. And why not? Full of the incense of flowers, sulfur, and moist soil, with its raised tiers here and there aglow with deep color, it was not unlike a Roman cathedral—though the latter, he recalled, did tend more to darkness.

"Richard is away?" asked Charlotte, her voice subdued as her feet crunched across the gravel, while her skirt of plain linen whispered its own familiar greeting.

"This morning, Mrs. Montagu decided that he needed to take her out riding, in the chaise."

"Oh. When I met Signora Lahte in the garden, I hoped we could all walk together, so we would be able to talk. My French speaking, as you know, is hardly—" She stopped as they watched Elena bend herself far back to marvel at the tree fern that nearly touched the roof.

"You may find, though, that you have another language in common," Cicero replied. "One I expect we all share."

"Which is . . . ?"

"That spoken by the palate."

Her look of puzzlement soon turned to amusement. "As well as the tongue? Of course!" she laughed. "Secluded here among rare vegetables, your wit is sadly wasted, sir. But we will respect your quiet worship of the beautiful. We will go out instead into Mr. Longfellow's kitchen garden, where we will speak of sprouts."

Pleased by her good humor and sense, the old man continued to smile long after Mrs. Willett had gone. He then decided that his neighbor possessed a beauty quite equal to that of Il Colombo's young lady, after all.

WHAT CICERO HAD told her was true. As Charlotte walked about the garden with Elena, the girl recognized much, repeating new names as her companion gave them—then giving back her own.

Basil, Elena informed her, was *basilico*; the mint, *menta*; thyme, *timo*; lavender, *lavanda*. On the other hand, the *salvia* she pointed to was not the cardinal flower, but ordinary sage; *prezzemolo*, plain parsley; the onion was *cipólla*, while French tarragon, as Charlotte recalled hearing before, was called *dragoncello*.

The greater world of vegetables seemed even less familiar. Although here, according to Elena, grew the familiar *carota* and *patata*, there was also the hot, red-bottomed *ravanèllo*, larger purple *rapa*, leafy fringed *lattuga*, larger heads of green *cavolo*, and pimply green *cetrioli*. Yellow corn, it seemed, was *granoturco*, putting Charlotte in mind of turban-topped gentlemen in curling slippers. As she repeated the word she mimicked such a man, twisting the ends of long, invisible moustaches—causing Elena to cry *"Turco!"* and pretend to be a whirling dervish . . . until a blue butterfly floated by. Then she stopped and gazed with longing at its delicate beauty, as it played freely above their heads.

This lady was very different, thought Charlotte, from the petulant boy who had been jealous of her on the previous morning. Now, it appeared, Elena was happy in the knowledge that her place with her husband was secure.

And yet, *what of the previous evening?* How could she manage to ask of that? It still seemed to her that Elena had been threatened. What if it were to happen again?

Seeing Charlotte's concern, the spirited girl appeared to encourage further conversation—perhaps, thought Charlotte, because she sensed an ally, and one who understood the world they shared as women.

At first the going was difficult but gradually, a flow of understanding grew between them. Soon, using words taken from French, Latin, and English, as well as movements of hand and eye, they abandoned their embarrassment and charged on like children designing a language of their own.

That Charlotte wondered about Thomas Pomeroy was made clear the moment she spoke his name. It took another moment for Elena to realize she and Pomeroy had been observed in the garden. Then, the girl let out a dramatic moan and produced a flood of words, which did little good. Halting, she began again, her dark eyes intense. She soon made it plain that Pomeroy had spoken to her of a drawing—the sketch of Sesto Alva that Richard

Longfellow had lately put up at the inn across the road. This Thomas Pomeroy had seen. He had also, apparently, seen Sesto Alva before, out on the Boston-Worcester road. And he had seen not only Sesto, but Gian Carlo Lahte—for the two had been together!

When this was understood, Elena vigorously shook her head, calling it a lie, asking, as did Charlotte, why Lahte would not have said so before, even to his wife. As for Thomas Pomeroy, Elena suspected he thought himself in love with her. Charlotte showed that she had supposed much the same—even while the girl masqueraded as a boy. And yet, she asked herself, what could Thomas Pomeroy have hoped to gain by his lie? Had he actually believed Elena would go with him, thinking her husband had murdered her kinsman? That seemed unlikely—until Mrs. Willett realized there might be a further explanation.

She drew a sharp breath as she recalled Captain Montagu's warning of the previous afternoon. Praying the girl would understand, she continued with as much speed as both could manage.

"Elena, could your father . . . pay someone—pay a man . . . to harm . . . to injure . . . *faire du mal, à ton époux?*"

"My husband?" Elena looked at her with amazement.

Charlotte abruptly remembered Jonathan Pratt's jewel—given to him by Thomas Pomeroy! What if Don Arturo met the boy in Boston, and gave him the diamond as a partial payment? Could Pomeroy then have come to Bracebridge *to await the arrival of Gian Carlo Lahte*? He might have hoped to steal Elena away—perhaps even to avenge her father. And, if such a thing *could* be bought, might Elena's father also have paid for the death of Sesto Alva?

Elena suddenly rose to the tips of her toes and pointed

toward the house, while her other hand flew to her lips. Below them, someone crossed the road, making for Richard Longfellow's front door. Even at a distance, both knew it could be only one man.

In the same instant, Charlotte realized Lahte was alone in the house. He might have arranged for something to be brought to him from the inn . . . or Lydia might have sent her servant with something—it did seem Pomeroy carried something on a tray—something hidden beneath a cloth—!

Choosing to trust her instinct, Charlotte bolted. While she ran, she lost sight of Thomas Pomeroy as he went behind the house. Then she heard a sharp scream; Elena had joined her on the path that led to the kitchen door.

Once inside, both stopped . . . but they could hear nothing more than their own breathing. Clutching a handful of Elena's skirt, Charlotte motioned for her to follow, down the passage that led to Longfellow's study. The two women stepped silently over carpets and boards until they came to the open door, and peered through into the familiar room.

Gian Carlo Lahte looked up at them from a book, smiling a question at their sudden appearance.

"You could be in grave danger," Charlotte warned. Something in her face convinced him at once. Lahte leaped to his feet, looking around for a weapon, finding one in the hearth's metal poker.

Wielding this, he inquired further. "Where?"

Again, they stood frozen in silence. But there was still no sound, until Elena gave a small, helpless gasp.

"We have just seen Thomas Pomeroy," Charlotte explained, "coming to the front door. I can't say for sure—but I think he may carry a pistol. Did you summon him?"

"No." Lahte shepherded the women into a corner. He

then went out into the hall. In a few moments he returned, perplexed.

"No one is there. But why do you—"

"If he heard us come from the back to warn you, he may have gone," said Charlotte, hoping this was true. As his wife sank into a chair, Lahte went to her side.

"*Cara?*" he asked, only to see her shrink back in horror. Once more Elena screamed, but this time the sound came from her very soul. In another instant they heard the sharp report of a pistol fired from outside the study's open window. Next came a crash as a metal round exploded a large enameled vase that had stood only inches from Elena's raised hand.

Had Lahte not been in the act of kneeling to his wife, it could easily have been his head that received the impact, Charlotte realized with a sickening jolt. Wanting to approach the window, she held back, asking herself if Pomeroy might not have a second weapon ready to discharge. Then Lahte leaped toward the casement himself. She lunged to pull him away, while he shouted a barrage of abuse.

After that, both watched Thomas Pomeroy run off across the fields toward the river, twisting back grotesquely from time to time, as if he were a dog whose tail had been caught in the jaws of a cruel trap.

"THE SCOUNDREL MUST have hidden a boat in the marshes," declared Richard Longfellow. He had heard the terrible story; now, the great affront he felt to both himself and to his guests was apparent in the rippling of his cheeks. He took a glass from Cicero, who brought wine for them all.

"The young wretch," he concluded, "would have had no motive of his own, being little known to any of us. So

you could be correct, Mrs. Willett, in assuming Thomas
Pomeroy to be in the pay of Don Arturo."

Charlotte saw that Elena's eyes swam with the pain of
new awareness, while her fear ebbed away. She hardly
wished to add to this anguish, but had little choice.

"Richard, what if the boy was sent not only to kill
Signor Lahte . . ."

"What else?"

"He may have been paid to take Elena, too, and bring
her back to Boston." She could not make herself say a
second possibility that had occurred to her. The proud father might also have wished to destroy a daughter who
had brought him shame.

"Hmmm. It would seem, then, that Montagu was correct. We must confront the father; and we may all be safer
in Boston, than here."

"I assume so," Diana readily agreed. "We have locked
our doors for years against villains who would prey on us,
or take our silver—at least in the evening. Besides, after
what I have seen happen in this place, Richard, I ask
myself if your village is not more dangerous than most
of Massachusetts."

Lahte had been listening to Elena as the girl, who had
taken him aside, spoke rapid Italian. Finally, with a look
of sadness, he turned back to the others.

"In Boston, Richard, we will wait for a ship to take us
away. Even in the beginning you seemed to know this
would be so. Elena and I will return to a place where I
have more power to protect her—where I have greater influence in society. We will go to London."

"But first," said Diana, "you must rest with us in
Boston, for a few days at least. At Richard's house, I think,
for it is larger. Charlotte, do come, too. I should like to
have your company. And yours?" she tried, giving Elena a
look the girl seemed not to understand. But when Diana

held out a hand to her, it was accepted. This, thought Charlotte, was a kindness which gave both women a renewed sense of safety, though it was something she found herself unable to share.

Longfellow now made a suggestion.

"We might arrange for a musical evening, Gian Carlo, to encourage Boston's support, as well—in case you should again change your mind . . . or, should you need further help while you wait for passage."

"I shall be happy to meet the people of Boston," Lahte began in reply, until a sharp rap came on the front door. He and the others seemed to stiffen, as Cicero went out of the room. In a few moments, Christian Rowe was ushered in, trailed by a woman in the throes of her own agitation.

"We have here a thing that must, by law, be returned," Rowe began officiously. "For I fear it has been stolen! Mrs. Knox came to me as soon as she suspected it was wrongfully taken." He gave a nod, and the small, trembling woman held out an object she'd brought curled tight in her sun-browned hand.

"Ooh! How lovely," Diana cooed with surprise. She leaned forward to examine several bright loops of gold fashioned into a coiled serpent, whose sparkling green eyes were not unlike her own. "Are those emeralds?" she asked, a moment before Gian Carlo Lahte gave a startled exclamation.

"What is it?" Longfellow asked his guest.

"I believe—it is only a cloak pin."

"I guessed as much, though it's not mine. But was this stolen from you? *From my own house?*"

"It is not unlike one I once owned while living in Milano," Signor Lahte replied. He turned away, as if the object was of no further interest. Again Elena spoke to him, but she received only the briefest of answers.

"Where, exactly, was this found?" Longfellow then asked the reverend.

"It was taken up by Caleb Knox, from the body of Sesto Alva as it lay beside the road."

Now Elena, too, gave a small gasp, before she and her husband traded looks once more. It appeared hers expressed something more than wonder. It also seemed, to Charlotte at least, that Lahte's eyes held a hard command.

"Only nearby," Mrs. Knox insisted. "For I'm sure my husband would never think to rob a dead man . . . but when he gave me such a treasure, I did feel uneasy, and worried whose it *might* have been."

"But you say it was once yours, Gian Carlo?" asked Longfellow, striving to be perfectly clear.

"Perhaps. Yes, I think that it may have been lost before I left Italy—when, exactly, I did not notice. But now, I suspect Sesto found it in the home of Don Arturo. One does leave cloaks with servants—and Sesto was not always honest, as I have already told you."

"Well," Longfellow began, glancing at Elena, only to find that the girl seemed unnerved once more.

To Charlotte, it appeared that her neighbor was carefully weighing Gian Carlo Lahte's answers, balancing them against other information he recollected, until something in his face changed. At the same time, she asked herself if there might not be another explanation for the stolen pin's reappearance.

Longfellow reached out and took the gold clasp from Mrs. Knox, who seemed glad to be rid of it. "As an official of the village," he kindly informed her, "I will take this into my own keeping, with my thanks. And I will do what I should have done several days ago," he told the others. "We'll go to Boston tonight, in the cool of the evening, with the moon to light our way. I will speak with a justice of the peace on Friday—Judge Trowbridge in Cambridge,

I think. After he hears what we know, I believe he'll call for a coroner's inquest. He might also sign writs for the arrest of Thomas Pomeroy and Don Arturo Alva. The truth must soon come out, as it generally does. But for the good of all, we will help it along."

Yet as Richard Longfellow studied the faces of those before him, he felt a doubt that the whole truth would be likely to please each and every one.

Chapter 18

Early the next morning, Longfellow rode the ferry from Boston to Charlestown, where, upon landing, he took a road that led past wasteland and clay pits to Cambridge.

He found Edmund Trowbridge sitting in an office near the courthouse. Attorney General of the colony for the past fifteen years, Judge Trowbridge no longer represented Cambridge in the Assembly, though he was, currently, a member of the Governor's Council. But Longfellow knew he might still find time to listen to an old family friend, and to attend certain cases that were to a scholar's liking.

Trowbridge did agree to hear their evidence the next day, when Longfellow promised to bring back with him several other witnesses: Signor Lahte, his young wife, Captain Montagu, and Joseph Warren—assuming the physician could leave Boston and his practice. While he heard the story, the judge recognized the name of Caleb Knox, known to him from an earlier case concerning a purloined cow. He also smiled at the mention of Jonathan Pratt, for while riding circuit, he'd made many stops for refreshment at the Bracebridge Inn. He even chuckled as he anticipated a fit challenge for his disciplined brain—something beyond the pecuniary squabblings on which he was most often asked to focus his attention.

And so, Longfellow returned victorious across the broad mouth of the Charles. Once the ferry had docked on the Boston side, he remounted and rode up to his house on Sudbury Street.

The place looked well, he thought as he examined its brick front by day—except for a few cracks left by the memorable shaking of the earth ten years before, which could hardly be helped. Situated between the Mill Pond and Beacon Hill, the comfortable structure his widowed stepmother continued to inhabit had the advantage of a large garden behind, part of an enclosed triangle completed by Hannover Street and Cold Lane; there was also a livery stable handy at the far side. And it was only a short walk to the Green Dragon . . . a matter of further convenience. All in all, the property was sensibly placed, neither across Mill Creek in the crowded North End, nor too close by the center of Crown activity between Long Wharf and the Common. One could do far worse, choosing from the town's two thousand assorted dwellings these days.

He left Venus at the stable, and walked across sod and garden to the back of his house. Inside, he was met by the two servants who remained in the absence of their mistress. They had long ago learned to expect odd things from friends of Miss Longfellow—now, Mrs. Montagu—but this foreign couple that came with her brother was something else again, their anxious faces seemed to complain.

"How are the ladies?" Longfellow asked. Hephzibah and Rachel exchanged knowing glances, before the elder answered.

"We made a bath for them each in their rooms, from the outside kettle," said Hephzibah.

The dumbwaiter he'd fashioned the previous year would have made their work less difficult, he supposed. Still, it would have been no pleasure, in this sultry weather, to fetch water from the central well, heat it, and haul it to the side of the house. He greatly preferred the system he'd designed for his own home in Bracebridge, where a hand pump moved water from an enclosed boiler next to the cellar's cistern, sending it to each of the upper floors.

"They are now on the high porch with the gentleman," Rachel added, "where there is a breeze. Would you want some refreshment brought up, sir?"

"Not just yet. I may find something else to do before long."

"Captain Montagu has called and gone away again, but said to tell you he will soon return," said Hephzibah.

"Then bring up a bottle of currant wine from the cellar after all," Longfellow decided.

"Do you know, sir, that your own servant has left us this morning, to attend to some private business in the town?"

"I suggested it." Longfellow knew Cicero was in an awkward position; the old man was now only a sort of valet in a house where he'd once reigned nearly supreme. It had been a small act of mercy to send him off.

Hephzibah gave a sad smile, shook her head at life in general, and took herself after Rachel down the kitchen stairs.

Longfellow climbed to the floor above to find Gian Carlo Lahte seated with Elena, Diana, and Charlotte, all of them lounging comfortably on the large open porch, propped by pillows as they watched the slow movements of ships in the harbor.

"I see you've organized something like a seraglio," Longfellow commented to Lahte, meaning it in jest. He then reddened, as he recalled the traditional protectors of such places. "Yet not quite a paradise, after all. Don't trust the water in town, Lahte, no matter where it comes from—my own well not excepted. We all know the reason they sometimes stink, but it's beyond our powers to keep them perfectly clean. Wine is safer. Or perhaps you might care to walk out for a tankard of ale?"

"I am sure I would enjoy it later," the musico returned, "but now, I am hearing of the ladies and gentlemen of Boston from your sister, who kindly instructs me."

"No doubt you'll both be glad to hear I've sent a message to the lieutenant governor. You and I have an audience with him this afternoon."

"Richard," asked Charlotte, "will you tell Lem we've arrived, as well? I hope he can find time to call."

"He will, if I have anything to do with it," Longfellow assured her. "We can see what knowledge he's picked up in the metropolis—which I suppose will need knocking out of him again, as soon as he goes home."

It was then that Hephzibah reappeared with a welcome message.

"Sir, Captain Montagu is below."

"WHOSE PISTOL WAS it?" Edmund Montagu asked, cautiously sipping a glass of currant wine as he sat with Richard Longfellow.

"According to Jonathan, Pomeroy took it from a guest who left it in his room. Though how Pomeroy knew of it no one can say, for the man swears he left it deep in a trunk."

"That does suggest—" The captain paused to speculate. "At any rate," he soon continued, "Thomas Pomeroy will now be fleeing from his former friends, on shank's mare if he has no other. Has he funds of his own, do you know?"

"Jonathan gave him a purse of gold coins only yesterday morning, in exchange for a diamond Pomeroy claims he brought with him from England." Longfellow went on with the story until Montagu held up a hand.

"I'll look into this further, Richard, before we see Trowbridge tomorrow. I had one of the sketches of Sesto Alva shown about again, with the addition of his cousin's scar—but so far it has not yielded any results."

"Did you see Dr. Warren?"

Montagu then revealed most of what he had learned two nights before, while at the Green Dragon.

"Then it's still uncertain how Sesto Alva died. That is irritating."

"I agree. But was murder ever simply done, or discovered?"

"Cain was easily found. . . ."

"Unfortunately, neither of us is omniscient, Richard. Although I do have a pair of new assistants who may be better at this job than you, or even I." Captain Montagu then described the recent arrival of two 'thief-takers' from London, whose business it was to apprehend accused criminals for the law. "These men," Montagu concluded, "can think as a low, criminal mind will . . . and one day, I suppose, they will be hung for crimes of their own. Unfortunately, those of good character are rarely welcome in their ranks. Still, we may as well benefit from such talents when we can."

"Perhaps now that they are out of London, our more pious ways will improve them."

"I see your mood is playful today."

"If it is, it's because I'm avoiding my responsibility. I have yet to tell Lahte he may choose to have an attorney present, when he's examined," said Longfellow, his face clouding.

"Do you think one is necessary?" returned the captain.

"Perhaps not, yet. But it does begin to look as if Lahte is something more than a victim in this affair. If he himself dropped his clasp at the scene, and if someone else should come forward who saw them together on the road—then I wonder what the law will say. It may be forced to try him."

"If Lahte repeats under oath that he is innocent, he should be believed. After all, he's a man of some standing."

"But if we believe Lahte—if we believe Sesto Alva took the clasp from him while they were both still in Milan—then why would Alva wear the thing on his way to meet the very man from whom he stole it? That makes little sense to me."

"Possibly he'd decided to give it back. I have learned," the captain continued on another front, "that you and Il Colombo propose to visit Hutchinson this afternoon."

"At any rate," said Longfellow, as he began to wonder how closely his movements would be watched in town, "we will draw Tommy's mind away from his recent troubles."

"Let us hope so."

Captain Montagu then sat back to sip the last of his sweet wine, while he began to ponder a new suspicion of his own.

IT WAS NEARLY three by the church bells when Richard Longfellow and Gian Carlo Lahte left the house, after a

dinner of cold vegetables and haddock pie. Following
Hannover until it turned to Middle Street, they walked
on for half a dozen blocks, past Cockerel Church, then
around the corner to a pilastered mansion that stood on
one side of North Square.

Built only two blocks from the sea, the large brick
home of the Hutchinson family had clean lines in the
classical style, and was, as Boston's citizens often declared
with pride, magnificent. The business of its current owner
was obvious; each window, flanked by tall columns, was
topped with a bright crown. Longfellow explained to his
foreign guest that the place in a very real way belonged
to the town, for its current furnishing had been largely
financed from the rewards of numerous public offices,
which came from taxes paid by the city's lesser mortals.

After a liveried footman admitted them, they were left
standing in an impressively large hall.

"Who, I wonder, is that?" asked Signor Lahte, once
they were alone. He pointed his gold-handled walking
stick at a statue across the vaulted room, lit ethereally, it
seemed, by light from above.

"One of your own countrymen—and, coincidentally,
one of mine."

Lahte walked toward the carved alcove that held this
work of art and read with a smile the name of Cicero on its
pedestal. Strolling further, he looked into a room whose
long walls held tapestries, and paintings surrounded by
gilded wood—where fresh flowers stood in cut crystal
vases, perfuming the air. Everywhere, it seemed, were the
trappings of wealth.

"Richard," asked the musico, "how did this great man
come to be here?"

"Thomas Hutchinson is a Harvard man, of course,
and one of Boston's own. Though this house was inherited, he began his political career over thirty years ago as

nothing more than a simple committeeman. Now he sits at the side of our royal governor, and perhaps enjoys even greater influence than Bernard, as the holder of several reins of power. He'll be governor himself one day," Longfellow speculated. "When Sir Francis has had his fill of Massachusetts. After last week, I suppose that day may not be far off."

"What are these other reins you speak of?"

"Mr. Hutchinson also became a simple judge years ago. Today, he is our Chief Justice. And he is a member of the General Court, which drafts our laws and decides on governmental salaries."

"I begin to think he is a Medici!"

"There's more. He's written a volume of this colony's history; in fact, I hear he's nearly finished with a second, built, too, upon the documents of our ancestors."

"He finds time for all of this?"

"And, when a large part of the college burned last winter, the lieutenant governor came up with the plan for a new Harvard Hall. He also designed much of his summer home in Milton. You see, there is ample reason for him to be admired as a man of artistic sense, as well as a wielder of power."

Lahte concealed a yawn as he waited to hear more of the man's perfection. Longfellow gave a sidelong glance, and a brief smile.

"The heat, and our haddock pie, have fatigued us both. But I believe I've said enough."

"You have certainly sharpened my desire to see this fellow. If life is just, he will be horribly bent and ugly, and possess, perhaps, a cough like a rattle."

Longfellow's lips curled further. The next moment, almost as if he had been waiting in the wings, Thomas Hutchinson himself walked into the entry hall.

Gian Carlo Lahte's surprise was obvious, as he took in

the striking similarity between the lieutenant governor and his host—something the latter had not mentioned. Both, he saw, had the same hazel eyes, penetrating, though far from cold. Both were tall and spare—each was well supplied with a gentleman's grace and charm. If the lieutenant governor was his fellow townsman's elder by a score of years, the only obvious difference between them was that where Longfellow was dark, Hutchinson was fair. And either one, the world could see, would make a formidable adversary.

"I apologize for having kept you waiting, gentlemen. I have been speaking to my brother-in-law Mr. Oliver. Andrew is distressed by his recent adventure, when he was singled out by the Liberty Boys—and others of the community who should know better! He is afraid, he tells me, that there may be worse to come. And indeed, who can predict what a few scoundrels might like to do to any of us with privilege? How rarely they realize this carries with it a vast obligation. But how is it, Mr. Longfellow, that you are in town today?"

"I have come, Your Excellency, to present a visitor," Longfellow replied to the man often referred to as 'Tommy Skin-and-Bones'.

"The gentleman from Milan, is it not?"

"Sir, I am your servant." Lahte bowed low and extended a leg in courtly salute, as each admired the other's rich and careful attire.

"I am yours, sir! I have heard of your talent, which I am aware reflects many years of training and devotion. It is my great pleasure to have one of such discipline, and such accomplishment, in my home. Have you come here with friends?"

"I am with my wife."

"Your wife!" Hutchinson exclaimed, before catching his tongue. "Well, then, I would be pleased if you would both honor us by coming to dine, when it is convenient. As a newcomer, you cannot know that I lost my own dear wife some years ago; but I am certain my sister-in-law, and my children, can entertain you. Possibly, you will be good enough to entertain us, as well? What Bracebridge has made of your music, I only wonder; but I hope you might sing for us—perhaps as soon as we are blessed with some relief from this oppressive heat, and you are comfortably settled."

"Signor Lahte may be gone before long," Longfellow broke in. "It seems his safety is threatened, and his marriage is in question."

"Who dares to threaten him?"

"The young lady's father."

"Indeed . . . indeed."

"It seems Signora Lahte left her home abruptly, and we now believe her father, Don Arturo Alva, has come after her—and that he may have engaged a man to shoot at Lahte. Happily, he was no marksman."

"In Boston?"

"In Bracebridge."

"Ah, well. I am glad to see, sir, that you have escaped injury. But it seems we frequently hear of curious things taking place in your adopted village, Richard—especially when Mrs. Montagu visits with my daughters. Do you know, listening to their chatter, I've lately begun to wonder if there is not a new caucus growing among the young ladies, which will one day rule us all. They now tell me silk will shortly be spurned, and replaced with woolen stuff prepared entirely by their own tender hands. Where do you suppose they learn these strange ideas?"

"From their London magazines, no doubt," said Longfellow, returning the lieutenant governor's cool smile. "But look here, Hutchinson, can you legally record Signor Lahte's marriage in this colony, on the strength of a parson's letter which he has brought with him from Italy? It seems the actual ceremony was a quiet affair."

"I suppose I might do something. But what about this father? Where is he now? We can't have such men running about, attempting murder!"

"At the moment, he appears to be in hiding."

"Gone to ground, eh? Where was Don Arturo Alva last spotted?"

"At the Green Dragon."

"A well-known den for foxes," came the chilly reply. "But, I will take your letter, signor, and find a place for a copy in our own records. As a judge, I do see some benefit in proving a young woman has left her home at a husband's command, instead of simply fleeing a father's control. Though I suppose there is still the question of whether she *could* marry, legally, without his consent. Speaking as a father myself, I believe we had better not encourage young girls to try such things. They most often end badly. But when the deed is already done, and has involved both clergy and . . . consummation? . . . then there is little even a governor can do to restore things to what they were. I will give you another piece of legal advice, Signor Lahte. You should be married again, by one of our own clergymen. That, none here would question. And of course, if the father is guilty of soliciting your own death—! But what of this hired assassin, Longfellow?"

"I imagine the young man is already far away."

Hutchinson gave the matter another moment's thought. "If," he concluded, "after all, you wish to leave in secret, Signor Lahte, I'm sure we'll be able to find you room in one of our departing ships. Perhaps in a bark leaving Clark's Wharf for the Canaries next week? Once there, you can surely find another to take you farther. If you choose to go, sir, for your own safety and that of your wife, I will see to it that you are not listed as passengers."

"I would be most grateful to Your Excellency," Lahte replied, though he still appeared undecided.

"I would also," said Longfellow, "invite you, sir, to join many of our friends on Monday evening. I plan to gather several musicians whom you know, and Il Colombo has agreed to sing."

"That would be delightful, I'm sure," said Thomas Hutchinson. "And let me know if I may do anything more," he added, signaling that the interview had ended. After shaking each man by the hand he moved to go, then turned back.

"You must realize that I, too, disagree with this stamp business, Longfellow—and I've long told them so in London. But I can do no more to put a stop to it than I have already tried, through official channels. Last week I was stoned in our own streets, as I believe Captain Montagu has told you. Our fellow citizens should indeed practice to improve their aim, if they intend to do any real harm. Nonetheless, I did not enjoy the experience. Ah, well. Tonight, I will put on my surtout and slippers, sit down with my family, and wonder what the rest of the town is up to. I pray it is not much, in such appalling weather."

"I have every intention of emulating your own peaceful pursuits, I assure you," came Longfellow's quiet reply.

"Perhaps," Hutchinson returned with an uncertain smile, before he walked briskly away.

Chapter 19

⌐ *Saturday, August 24*

O N A MILD morning two days later, Richard Longfellow set off in a rented coach seated next to Mrs.
Willett and Edmund Montagu; Signor Lahte shared a
side with two young wives. As the roads were still dry,
the party had decided to take the long way around to the
coroner's inquest.

From Sudbury Street, four horses pulled them along
the base of Beacon Hill and on past King's Chapel, along
Treamount. From there, they skirted the Common until a
jog took them to Newbury, and eventually across Hannover Square. The great oak at the corner of Essex caused
them all to look up as each imagined or recalled events of
the week before, which had taken place beneath the
newly named Liberty Tree.

Leaving town, the coachman drove down Orange onto the narrow Neck, where they were surrounded by stinking mud flats—as luck would have it, they crossed over at low tide. Once past the old fortifications and the town sentries, the coach continued west toward Roxbury. There, it turned north, soon moving over Great Bridge and the Charles below; minutes later, they saw a church steeple and then the golden cupola of the Cambridge County courthouse, near Harvard College.

Longfellow remembered as he rode that Judge Trowbridge had been both troubled and intrigued by what they had told him on the previous afternoon. He had examined the witnesses and in the end did, indeed, sign warrants for the arrest of Thomas Pomeroy and Don Arturo Alva. Trowbridge had also been given a brief statement written by Joseph Warren, who promised to testify more fully when he answered in person. Although the judge raised his curling brows at the information that the body in question had been buried in a churchyard in Dorchester, a hint from Longfellow that it might carry the contagion of fever was enough to settle the matter. Dr. Warren was well respected in his profession, Trowbridge had maintained with a squint, and was a man whose medical observations, at least, could be safely taken.

Today promised developments of considerable interest, for the sheriff had been ordered to send a summons to the farmer Caleb Knox in Bracebridge, as well as one to Jonathan Pratt. Longfellow supposed both would bring their spouses.

They finally arrived at the courthouse to find the Pratts, the Knoxes, and Reverend Rowe all waiting in the entry, while another case was considered in the large room on the first floor. In the weighty atmosphere, few words passed between them. Fortunately for the nerves of all, onlookers and participants soon spilled out, and those newly arrived from Boston and Bracebridge made their way inside.

When they had taken places at the front, Mrs. Willett lost herself in childhood memories, thinking back to the several times the Howard family had come to view suits between their neighbors. Though the raised platform before her held only empty chairs, she knew twelve men would return to hear the second or perhaps the third case of a long day. A small box nearby would see a series of witnesses. Farther along, in armed chairs, judges would sit with a high bench before them. Between bench and spectators stood a rectangular table topped with baize, set with ink pots and quills; there, lawyers acting in a case, dressed in robes, generally sat by with others in plain clothing, who came to observe and to learn. At the moment, two such young men bent over pages of notes with their satchels at their sides, waiting.

The jury soon returned from its brief withdrawing, and many more spectators crowded in through the rear door. At last, through a doorway behind the judges' chairs came Justice Trowbridge, robed in black and bewigged, followed by a smaller man in street attire. Each settled himself. Then, at the clerk's call for silence, Trowbridge looked with a scrutinizing eye over the party surrounding Richard Longfellow, before nodding to the jury and beginning new business.

"This, ladies and gentlemen," he started, addressing the room in a well-tempered voice, "will be a Coroner's Inquest. It is not yet a trial. The court's duty today is to hear evidence, and to draw conclusions to explain a man's questionable death—which may or may not have been an accident. At the same time we will look into another matter, for it now appears likely that the death of one Sesto Alva may be related to an attempt on the life of Signor Gian Carlo Lahte—the latter occurrence surely no accident, but a deliberate felony. For this, I have issued two warrants, though the individuals named are presumed to have fled."

Several in the audience were heard to whisper and a few crept away, no doubt to alert others to what promised to be an unusual and entertaining story.

"Some may ask why I am presiding here today," Trowbridge continued soberly, "for though I am a former barrister, I have been elevated in recent years to serve the colony in a somewhat greater capacity. But it is as a Justice of the Peace for Middlesex County that I have heard evidence brought before me in recent days . . . evidence concerning strangers to these shores, whose ways are not our own. In their own land, two at least claim wealth and privilege—and, one supposes, a code of honor, which may also be somewhat different from ours. At any rate, Mr. Alden, a coroner of the county, has agreed that we might work together to illuminate the sequence of events involving these gentlemen, and others. It will then be the duty of the jury," he continued, turning to the twelve men who listened attentively, "to decide whether a Grand Jury of the Superior Court will hear the case, and consider an indictment. While a Coroner's Inquest may seem a less formal setting than a trial, I remind you that oaths which may be given here are not only sacred, but are also legally binding. Are there no acting attorneys present?" the judge asked, looking again to see for himself. "Fine. Though it is allowed, it is not required. There will be time for that later, if anyone here should recognize a need to retain counsel . . . for whatever reason."

Trowbridge and the coroner put their heads together briefly, after which the judge carried the case forward.

"As I see that all who have been summoned as witnesses are present, we will begin by following the events in the order in which they occurred. First, we will learn of the last days of the deceased, Signor Sesto Alva, who came to Boston from the city of Milan in Italy. Captain Edmund Montagu will enlighten us on this, and other matters. Captain?"

Edmund Montagu left his wife's side to enter the witness box. After raising his hand and giving his oath, he began.

"Your honor, it is known that Sesto Alva traveled to Boston as the protector of his cousin's daughter, a young woman now called Elena Lahte."

"I see," said the judge, "that Signora Lahte is here, and will instruct the jury that she was formerly known as Elena Alva. She is the daughter of Don Arturo Alva, of Milan. This lady came to be reunited with her husband, Signor Gian Carlo Lahte, supposing him to be here. It should also be noted that we have cause to believe Signora Lahte's father followed his daughter, surely in the hope of taking her back to his own home . . . for reasons I do not think it necessary to go into."

Captain Montagu went on to speak of the successful search that had revealed Sesto Alva's identity, and the less successful one to locate Elena's father. Judge Trowbridge then dismissed the captain from the witness box, and sought to move matters along.

"Sesto Alva was found dead on August the sixteenth—a week ago Friday—lying by the side of the road near Bracebridge. His discoverer was a farmer of that village who is with us today. We will now hear from Mr. Knox."

After disengaging the arm of his anxious wife, and

looking over to Reverend Rowe, Caleb Knox rose and made his way forward. He raised a brown hand and swore to be truthful, then sat squirming in his chair while he clasped thick fingers together in his lap.

"Mr. Knox. You are a farmer, owning land in the village of Bracebridge?"

"Aye, that's right, sir . . . Your Honor."

"And on Friday last, you discovered . . . ?"

"I found a man dead, as you say, sir, lying in the grass . . . and his horse grazing nearby. It seemed to me the horse might have thrown him off, after some sort of fright—"

Trowbridge quickly interrupted, asking if the farmer had seen any specific evidence of such a thing himself. Knox replied that he had not.

"There is also, I believe, a rather interesting coincidence involving a pin."

The farmer told of picking up the unusual cloak clasp. It was shown to the jury, who took its time admiring the action of the clever ornament, and its strange, serpentine design.

"Signor Lahte," Trowbridge told them, "suspects that this object, which he admits is his own, was taken from him by Sesto Alva while both lived in Milan. You will hear from Signor Lahte later. Have you anything more to tell us, Mr. Knox?"

"No, sir. Only that I wished none hurt, and hope never to harm any man!"

"An admirable aim. You may step down."

Trowbridge conferred briefly with the coroner again, and then called for Richard Longfellow to enter the witness box. He came carrying a small box in his hand.

"You, sir," said the judge, "invited Signor Lahte here from Milan?"

"In a manner of speaking. I once promised him my

hospitality, should he ever have reason to travel to Massachusetts. His recent arrival was a surprise—though a pleasant one."

"Signor Lahte came to your home in Bracebridge on Friday, August the sixteenth?"

"That is so."

"On the same afternoon Sesto Alva was discovered dead on the Boston-Worcester road, not two miles away. Apparently he found out where you were from an unknown person in Boston. But you did not invite Signor Alva?"

"I did not, for I knew nothing of his existence."

"Yet some time later, you went to see the place where his body was discovered."

Longfellow caught Mrs. Willett's eye before he made his answer. "As our constable was absent, and it seemed to be my duty as a selectman, I went to see the area early on Sunday morning."

"And what did you find?" Trowbridge asked, leaning forward.

"First, this object . . ."

Lifting the lid from the box he held, Longfellow produced the granite sphere, and stood to hand it over to the judge. "In studying it closely, I perceived several bits of wool, which I removed. Further examination with the aid of a microscope showed that these strands came from the felt hat worn by the deceased. Thus, I feel certain the wound on Alva's head was made when his hat came into contact with the object you hold."

"But you cannot say exactly how this happened?"

"Not exactly, no, but—"

"What else did you notice there?"

Longfellow described, as he'd done for Trowbridge the day before, the rock's position when he first saw it, as well as the mystery of its apparent position somewhat earlier.

"There was a bottle, too, lying nearby . . ." He finished by telling of the victim's stained coat, intending to tie this to what he believed to have been the state of Sesto Alva's constitution at the time of death—until the judge again raised a hand.

Watching her neighbor's growing confidence, Charlotte suspected that he, too, now believed what she'd first imagined—that the granite orb could have been used as a weapon, and might well have been wielded with the thought of assuring a man's swift and certain end. But had it been held by Thomas Pomeroy? She glanced to see Elena's reaction to the testimony, recalling the girl's fear at her narrow escape three days earlier . . . and its return with the discovery of her husband's recovered pin.

It seemed that Lahte, too, sought Elena's eyes; Charlotte saw the young wife respond by slipping a hand into his own. At least, for the moment, she seemed to feel safe.

"Only days after Sesto Alva's death, an attempt on another life took place in Bracebridge," the judge now informed the courtroom, once he'd allowed Richard Longfellow to step down. "According to witnesses, the perpetrator was a youth named Thomas Pomeroy, lately employed at the Bracebridge Inn. We will hear more of him from the inn's landlord, Mr. Pratt."

"I did find Pomeroy a useful fellow to have around," Jonathan maintained some moments later, "for the short time he was with us. In fact, I believe I shall miss him, even though . . ."

"How did you come to offer him employment, sir?"

Jonathan related Pomeroy's story of his departure from London and his family, the dangerous ocean voyage, and his eventual arrival in Boston. He ended by telling of the yellow diamond he'd been given in exchange for gold.

"On what day did you receive this gem?" the magistrate asked.

"One week ago. August the seventeenth," Jonathan added, concern evident on his round face. "The day after Sesto Alva was found. Though I was able to give Pomeroy the coins he asked for only three days ago—on the day he disappeared. I have the stone here." He reached into his waistcoat pocket, and began to unwrap the brilliant from its soft covering.

"I will ask you to leave it with the court," said Trowbridge, once he had taken the evidence. With some regret, Jonathan Pratt nodded.

"There is a further somewhat curious thing on which no one has yet touched today," the judge continued, addressing the twelve men on his right. "This is the fact that Signora Lahte went about, both in Boston and in Bracebridge, wearing the clothing of a boy, while pretending to be a servant—first, with the knowledge of Sesto Alva, then with that of her husband."

To a man, the jurors raised their chins, the better to see the beautiful young woman who sat demurely by her protector, her dark eyes cast down.

"It seems Signora Lahte felt safer, while on a foreign shore, in hiding her feminine nature from those who might do her harm—including the father she feared. Yet even under a man's coat and breeches, Signora Lahte captured the attention of Thomas Pomeroy. Mr. Pratt, had young Pomeroy opportunity to meet this lady's protector, Sesto Alva, on the road? Would he not have been missed at the inn?"

"He may have stepped out for some time. After all, the entire village has had Signor Lahte's visit on its mind lately, and seems to have lost half its usual sense. I doubt even my own wife would have noticed Pomeroy's absence."

Upon hearing this, Lydia Pratt glared in such a fashion that her husband had new reason for regret.

"I believe you have told us enough," Judge Trowbridge replied. He indicated that the landlord might step down, and watched as Jonathan went to sit next to a rigid wife. "Now, Signor Lahte, will you speak?"

The musico walked forward, with a noble bearing that captured all eyes in the room. Although told it was not entirely necessary he, too, raised his hand, and vowed to speak truthfully.

"Will you tell us, sir," asked Judge Trowbridge, "how you came near to losing your life on Wednesday morning?"

While Lahte described the course of events, the eyes of the judge watched those before him. When the witness had finished, the magistrate inquired further.

"You did not know this Pomeroy? Never met him, before going to Bracebridge?"

"To me, he was a stranger."

"Signor Lahte . . . when you married your wife, did you not suppose her father had other plans for her?"

"Yes, certainly. But Elena had no wish to give herself to the man chosen for her by her father. I, of course, could not go to Don Arturo—for I knew I would not be accepted."

"If her father ever does come forward, do you believe he will relent, and forgive either one of you?"

"That, I cannot tell. I do know if I had raised such a child myself, I could not bear to see her sold against her will!"

"Possibly not, and perhaps you're right. But to obey the law, we must often curb our sentiments. I warn you— the ill will of your wife's father might still bring about your end. Be cautious as you walk, sir!" Trowbridge looked keenly at the Italian, who returned his stare. Finally the older man sighed, and went on.

"However, as this is a Coroner's Inquest, let us summon

the examining physician at long last, and hear his story. I suppose we will all find it interesting. Dr. Warren, if you please."

Joseph Warren came to the box with a smile for the jury, some of whom grinned back, glad to see a familiar face. Trowbridge remained grave as he studied the confident man before him.

"You have waited a long while to make a small report," he pointed out, holding a single sheet up in his hand, and setting it down again.

"I have brought a broader statement with me this morning, your honor," said Dr. Warren. He held up several sheets of his own, taken from his coat. "Which I will summarize, if you would like, sir."

"I think that would be a good idea," said the judge. The coroner, his lips tightened at the physician's easy demeanor, nodded his own agreement.

"I was recently summoned by Mr. Richard Longfellow, a selectman of Bracebridge," the doctor began, "to examine the body of Sesto Alva."

"The date?" the coroner asked.

"I received his letter late on the sixteenth, and arrived on the next evening. What most thought an accident was supposed, by one or two in that village, to be a more complicated matter. I was taken to a cellar to examine the remains; there I found what I expected to see— a depression in the man's skull, above and behind the right ear. There was, however, no apparent swelling. Nor was there lividity under the hair. I immediately laid back a section of the scalp, and found little evidence of extravasated blood. By this observation, I concluded that the man died very soon after his head was struck by a hard and rounded object—possibly a rock. Perhaps even before," the physician added, his attention seemingly caught by a new idea.

"Struck once, or more?" asked the judge.

"Perhaps only once—I can't be sure. The injury occurred a day before I saw him."

"Had you no further thoughts?" the coroner demanded.

"My next concern was the yellow fever—"

A murmur of alarm rose from the room; each summer, fears of fresh epidemics ebbed and flowed over all the colonies.

"—due to the obvious presence of dark vomit on the man's coat and shirt. Yet when I opened the mouth and examined it carefully, I found it oddly irritated, as if by some corrosive agent. There was a marked hemorrhaging in the tissues of the mouth and esophagus, which I'd seen before in cases of poisoning. To be perfectly sure—and with a view to the public's safety, on the chance I was wrong—I arranged to take the corpse away, so that no other person might become contaminated. Eventually, I saw it safely buried in Dorchester."

"Eventually," Trowbridge replied dryly, keeping to himself thoughts of overcurious physicians with ready scalpels.

"Was the damage to the mouth and throat, sir," asked the coroner with greater interest, "due to one severe episode, or was this a case of long suffering?"

"I suspect his malady was chronic, sir . . . and yet, the final damage seemed to imply that if an irritant was present, it was last taken in a very strong dose—certainly one I would imagine large enough to cause great discomfort, and the loss of his stomach."

"You give us detail, but your considered opinion gives us little help here," Judge Trowbridge returned testily. "Which was it? Pitched onto a rock, pummeled, or poisoned? Have you even reached a decision as to whether this was an accident, or something more?"

"No," Warren admitted, his smile almost contrite.

"Though I cannot, as I've said, believe the death *entirely* the result of a fall from a horse. . . ."

Mrs. Willett, who had been listening carefully, sat up with even keener attention. Might Dr. Warren now say something more about the neck? For it had seemed undamaged to her, when she felt it. And didn't most who died so soon after suffering such a fall have some part of their spines broken?

"I would ask you further, sir—" Trowbridge began again. But before more could be said, a fresh sound of bustling came from the back of the room, in answer to a commotion outside. The doors were then flung open to reveal several men jostling, as two of them half-shoved and half-carried a third in between them. Edmund Montagu leaped to his feet and hurried down the center aisle to confer with the pair of captors, who held a young man between them.

Several on the frontmost seats recognized Thomas Pomeroy, though his head was bowed as he fought . . . not, perhaps, with a hope of attaining his freedom, but to make a show of his anger. Upon seeing Captain Montagu the boy seemed to change, and stood more quietly. Yet in response to a new blow, he soon lashed out again.

"What is all this?" asked the judge. When no answer was forthcoming, he stood and slapped down a book lifted from the bench before him. "*What is going on?*"

"Your honor," Montagu called, turning toward the magistrate, "if you will allow me a moment with these men, I will relate something that should have great bearing on many of the questions before the court." As he finished, another flurry broke out—this time, at the front of the room. With no warning, Signora Lahte had fainted.

A call for sherry sent a quick-witted boy running off to

a nearby tavern. Meanwhile, Charlotte and Gian Carlo Lahte knelt to hold the motionless body of Elena between them. Richard Longfellow looked to his sister, fearing that this new tumult might have caused her some distress as well. In fact, it had—for Diana, who had often been the object of such attentions, felt little pleasure when another suffered the effects of unbearable emotion. However, she soon found a more charitable sentiment as she remembered that the girl's nerves must have been long and truly strained by her peculiar situation.

"These two men," said Montagu, striding back toward the judge and the coroner, "are in my employ. Having learned from me that Thomas Pomeroy was sought by the Crown, they were directed to search the wharves for information on recent arrivals . . . information of a particular kind. After broadcasting word of what they soon learned, they found the boy, hidden by a cart-wright whom he has obviously misled. For Thomas Pomeroy is actually one Matthew Beaulieu, lately brought here from London on the ship *Swallow* as a transported felon, who escaped a guard responsible for several others like him. From that man, we know Beaulieu is a thief of long habit, recently given the choice of working in this colony for seven years, or staying in London to be hanged!"

Thomas Pomeroy had now been dragged to stand in front of the judge; yet his attention was drawn to the activity that still revolved around Signora Lahte.

"What have you to say for yourself, young man?" Trowbridge asked. "Are you this Matthew Beaulieu, as well as Thomas Pomeroy?"

The boy wrenched free an arm, so that he might point in the direction of Gian Carlo Lahte.

"*I saw him*, there on the road—I saw him with the

dead man that afternoon! *He held a rock*—and I told her he was the one who must have killed Sesto Alva—her husband, the musico!"

"And the diamond, boy? What of the diamond? How did you, arriving here with no more than your shirt, manage to come by that?"

"*It was mine!*"

"We have a good amount of gold coin here, as well," said one of the thief-takers in a deep, pleased voice, "which we found on him." He took from the pocket of his long coat a soiled linen purse, half full, and set it on the bench.

"I see," said Trowbridge, frowning anew as he looked inside. "One thing is clear. This man's oath, be he Pomeroy or Beaulieu, is worthless. As a felon, his words may not be considered by a jury. I suspect that his claims may even persuade us of his guilt, as he appears to hope he can cause another to pay for his own wrongdoing. Take him to the jail. Later, I will speak with him, and ask him to explain his recent attack on Signor Lahte."

"*No!*" Pomeroy screamed as they dragged him back down the aisle. "It was only to frighten him! It was all the fault of her father—you must believe me— *please—please!*"

Thomas Pomeroy was then hauled, still screaming, out of the courtroom, and the doors were slammed shut to the relief of all inside. Edmund Montagu moved to speak with his wife, but encountered her brother first.

"What was it that made you suspect?" Longfellow asked eagerly.

"The pistol, of course. You said he found it hidden in the room of a man he did not know. That suggested to me more than a passing interest in crime."

"But how is it that his earlier escape was unknown to you?"

"There are several ways for a man to be lost, while crossing the ocean. Beaulieu was reported drowned. I think he may have been clever enough to spin out promises of future reward, which convinced his jailer to look the other way as he walked off. Or, quite possibly, Don Arturo Alva sought out just such a lad to do his business, and paid his keeper for him at the wharf when they landed. We'll know soon enough—they rarely keep silent for long about such things, once they're carefully questioned. But now, I must go and see to my wife."

Longfellow stepped aside, then made his way to the judges' bench where Trowbridge sat shaking his head.

"Hutchinson shall have all of it, with Lynde and Oliver, as soon as they sit. Quite a spectacle, Mr. Longfellow! I cannot say I am entirely sorry. But I pray you will not lay such a thing at my feet again any time soon."

"I hope not, sir," Longfellow answered sincerely.

"But here—take this to your friend Mr. Pratt," the magistrate instructed, picking up the bag of gold, "and have him count it. By rights it is his, in payment for the diamond. *That* I would be glad to see you slip quietly into your pocket, to keep until it is again called for—only give a receipt to the clerk before you go. It is not that I do not trust our fellows here, but it is sometimes difficult to keep things so small from falling through cracks."

"What do you think of my guest's position?" Longfellow asked, his voice lowered.

"I think that a man of Lahte's standing need not worry. His life has been unusual, to say the least—and it is one I hardly envy. I believe we have heard enough to keep him out of custody. Yet I can't help thinking Massachusetts would be a calmer place if he were to move on. Is that likely, Richard?"

"Il Colombo may well fly, as soon as he sings for us

a final time. If you would care to hear him, I'll send you an invitation."

"Lately I find I am much occupied, with one thing and another."

"In that case I will see you another time, sir—though I, too, hope it is not in court."

His only answer was a surprising wink, and a nod. Judge Trowbridge rose with a glance around the room, which showed him most of it was already on its feet. Then, he went unnoticed into his chambers.

Chapter 20

BEFORE BREAKFAST WAS OVER, the Longfellow household came alive with the efforts of list-makers and furniture-movers; soon, it opened its doors repeatedly to delivery men, who came between a stream of servants bearing notes of glad acceptance for the evening's musical gathering.

Longfellow had the pleasure of telling Gian Carlo Lahte he would be accompanied by at least a dozen serious musicians, all of whom looked forward to presenting a part of Gluck's newest Italian opera, which described the dramatic descent of Orpheus into the Underworld. One had sent several pages of music, while another promised to bring a glass harmonica recently arrived from London, as well as his cello. Signor Lahte took up the sheets full of musical notation with interest. Clutching these and a biscuit, he then went off to practice.

Meanwhile, Diana received a dressmaker, hurrying her up to a room on the second floor; there, they began to alter a tight, trained gown of embroidered white silk for Elena, who stood stoically as she was pinned. Gossip flew between Diana and the dressmaker concerning many of the several score invited for the evening's concert and dancing—guests who could also look forward to a table of whatever delicacies might be teased from the city's warehouses, and from the ripening countryside.

Lem, too, would be there, Charlotte thought with satisfaction as she wiped a cloth over a set of crystal glasses. As one by one they glowed with perfection, she listened to the arrival of the other responses. Lieutenant Governor Hutchinson had declined, due to a slight fever within his family, but they could look forward to seeing Dr. Warren and his wife. Most of the others who answered were little known to her, and some were complete strangers. Missing her own hearth, she wondered if her own Orpheus fared well under Henry's care . . . or if, perhaps, the situation might be just the reverse.

As Charlotte continued to work, she was occasionally asked for her advice by Rachel, and even Hephzibah. Both women were glad to approach her for a sensible ear, and were greatly relieved by the current cloistering of Mrs. Montagu. Before long, chairs were polished, flowers ordered, another large box of candles sent for, and the livery stable told to look for business from those who would come some distance, for Longfellow's invitations included guests from towns all around the Bay, and some well beyond.

At midday, Captain Montagu came to collect Diana so that she might rest at home—an offer his wife declined, at least for another hour or two. Still, he reported before taking himself back to Town House, nothing had been heard or seen of Don Arturo Alva. At least Elena's father had been unable to stop her remarriage on the previous evening, when a simple ceremony had been performed by Reverend Eliot at New North Church, which stood not far away. Edmund went on to presume Alva was on his way to Canada, where he would no doubt arrange quiet passage to England, or to Madeira, or the Azores. There now seemed, he told Richard Longfellow, little chance that the scoundrel would ever be made to pay for his crimes. Somewhat to the captain's surprise, Longfellow showed little concern. He appeared to have more interest in the arrival of an ancient tuner who hammered at the strings of a harpsichord, when he was not attacking its tight pegs with a small wrench.

All in all, thought Charlotte, with a twinge of sadness, the capture of Thomas Pomeroy would be enough to satisfy most who heard the story, if a bigger fish had gotten away. At least, Don Arturo Alva could hardly threaten any of them tonight, in a houseful of people.

"Mrs. Willett?" Longfellow asked, interrupting her reverie over a small plate of ham and cold potatoes. "Have you need of anything more? An addition to your costume, perhaps? For it seems I must go out again."

"If the kitchen is happy, then so am I."

"You're certain? Cicero has gone to talk with a man about the oysters, and I am taking Lahte with me. You ladies will have an hour of quiet without us."

"I doubt that! But I think we'll manage."

With the departure of the men, Diana and Elena came down to see the seamstress off with the newly marked dress, then found something in the pantry for themselves. They joined Mrs. Willett to eat from their laps in a small, beautifully papered room that faced a secluded garden.

"It seems the worst is over," said Charlotte, as she

noted that a peace had fallen over the house, and that
Mrs. Longfellow's roses did well.

"For the moment," Diana agreed with a sigh. "Though
now, I will have to think of my own manner of dress. With
Elena quite striking in white, I shall choose something
dark. And I think you will all be surprised—"

Diana broke off to look toward the open door that led
into the hall. "Whatever it is," she said crossly, "leave it
there, and send the bill to my brother—unless he has already paid you."

"Signora," came her answer, which made Diana frown.

Though her back was to the door, Charlotte watched
Elena's head revolve swiftly; then, the girl cried out.
Turning herself, she was shocked to see the face of a dead
man—for if it were not for a scar along his cheekbone, the
man before them might have been Sesto Alva, risen from
the grave!

"Elena," came the harsh voice again, this time with
greater authority. The girl responded in Italian, her fear
swiftly changing to anger. Neither Charlotte nor Diana
could comprehend the phrases that flew over them, yet
it seemed clear that father and daughter harbored little
respect for one another. Don Arturo Alva approached
Elena, raising his jeweled hands to take her by the shoulders; then he shook her until she lost a small lace cap
she wore, and appeared to swoon. Her father dragged
her to a chair and stepped back, his eyes defying her to
move again.

"Sir," Charlotte heard herself say in a strained voice,
"you must not treat a daughter so—"

Alva looked at her with curiosity, and she supposed he
had not understood her. She tried again.

"You are at this moment being sought by the law . . .
vous êtes . . . appelé, no, *recherché—par la loi!*" Again, he

only stared. But a calculating smile appeared on his face while she continued.

"*L'homme Thomas Pomeroy—il est saisait; il a donné son histoire . . .*"

"Madame," he replied, "I believe even my poor English is better than your halting attempt at French. You say I am sought, and someone is seized by the law—and his story is—?"

"But we thought—"

"That I have come here with the mind of a child, knowing nothing of your tongue, or your ways? It is you in America who know nothing of the great world, madamina."

When used by Gian Carlo Lahte, this odd name had seemed endearing; now, Charlotte imagined it was used mockingly by the man before her.

"Then I can tell you simply," she replied, "that the authorities seek your arrest, for which a warrant has been signed. Thomas Pomeroy has been taken, and charged with attempting to kill your daughter's husband. It is supposed you may have had a hand in this, and in the death of Sesto Alva, as well."

"Sesto?" The man seemed incredulous.

"Of course!" Diana interrupted. "For we know he has been poisoned!"

Alva looked to Diana; then, his eyes moved to his daughter. Elena had revived, and seemed triumphant at her father's unmasking.

"No!" he shouted, startling them all anew. "Who is Pomeroy?"

"He is also known as Matthew Beaulieu," said Charlotte.

"*È pazza,*" Alva growled as he stepped forward and took his daughter by a slender wrist.

Elena now echoed her father's earlier refusal, pulling back while Charlotte and Diana moved to her side, threatening to thwart at all costs the man before them. Alva blew out his cheeks in frustration. "I warn you," he threw back at them, "the wolf will remain nearby! Do not rest—*never* close your eyes, signore!"

As he finished his threat, they all heard the front door open and close. In another moment, Cicero passed by. Don Arturo sidled into the hall, and the women heard the door open again. By the time they ran to it themselves, Alva's dark-clad figure had disappeared.

When Diana let out a whoop, Charlotte's eyes searched Elena's pale features. "Have no fear," Mrs. Montagu then crowed to the girl, "for Edmund will find him again before long, and you will be safe here with us. For now, we have proven ourselves the superior force! What an insufferable man to have for a father," she added under her breath to Charlotte, before rustling off to give Cicero new instructions.

And how tragic, Charlotte concluded, to be a daughter unable to love her only remaining parent. She had seen Elena's bearing, like that of her father, show more outrage than sadness, or even censure. She wondered again at the strength shown by young Signora Lahte—strength surely due, in some part, to the stubbornness of youth. Had Elena been wise to run away, to oppose her father's will? If she had not done so, Sesto Alva would still be alive. With this knowledge, how could she ever be entirely happy again? And what of the continuing threat to herself, as well as her husband?

It would be wise, Charlotte thought further, to watch how this brave but vulnerable girl bore the further strain of an evening of great excitement—an evening which would soon begin.

· · ·

AT SEVEN, UNDER a milky sky, a rumble announced the arrival of several carriages at once. Soon they disgorged two dozen individuals—all ready to worship the saintly Cecilia, or perhaps her elder sister, Calliope.

As Longfellow greeted each group at the door, Charlotte stood waiting to be introduced, and to have her own hand taken in turn. Though she did not know many, it appeared many had heard something of her; more than one gentleman, she noticed, looked back to Longfellow with a grin.

The growing crowd appeared to be made up of good, well-nourished people, each of them splendidly dressed. Near the stalks of candelabra that stood about the floor, as well as in more shadowy corners, bright coats in many hues glowed above lace both white and gold, which ruffled playfully at throats and sleeves. As for the ladies, the occasion allowed them to wear their most ornate silk gowns, though some of the younger ones had chosen gay cherryderry and kingcob, summer cotton and patterned satin from India. Most of the fine jewels in the room were from handed-down collections, removed from trunks and drawers to rest briefly on pretty dimpled fingers and perfumed throats. But these gems hardly sparkled more than the smiles exchanged between old friends. Occasional attempts to discuss serious matters were soon met with raised hands, and a quick return to happier subjects.

At least, thought Charlotte during a lull at the door, she had brought one good gown of dark green lustring; over this, she wore a nearly transparent apron of tiffany, with a crossed lawn kerchief at her bosom in place of frills. Still, she could have passed for a milkmaid in such elegant surroundings—something which, she thought with a blush, she was, after all.

However, it was clear that her neighbor felt quite at home tonight. For the first time she saw Longfellow as the sole master of this house, with his stepmother temporarily out of it. One day, it would be his to do with as he pleased, when the last Mrs. Longfellow's dowager claim expired—along with that lady herself. Yet it seemed he would have to wait a while. And he would probably continue to avoid that woman of restless habits, with the repetitive, nasal voice of a nuthatch, and a plump white breast to match. It was one reason Richard Longfellow had gone to Bracebridge in the first place—to make a second home for himself and for Eleanor, as long as his Boston house was occupied. But had he reason enough to stay in the village forever? Or did he already look forward, Charlotte asked herself, to his eventual return to town? The thought unsettled her as she watched him entertain old friends with better grace than he showed most on his country estate.

Another rustling at the door preceded an ordinary-looking man in brown, who accompanied a tall young woman fashionably attired in a riding habit. Her collared coat and deep skirts were cut from black velvet; a neck cloth was wound about her throat. Mrs. Willett imagined this particular lady could hardly have arrived on horseback, given her apparent condition, but the impression Diana's friend Lucy Cooper made (though she suffered from the heat) was a striking one.

When Diana entered a moment later, she, too, was on the arm of a husband; but this one wore a handsome, deep blue military coat with much gold, set off by a thin ceremonial sword on an elaborate frog, while his cockaded hat nestled under an arm. Like Lucy, Mrs. Montagu had made good use of her own natural reason to abandon stays and let down her hair. In fact, her thick auburn curls hung in daring simplicity down her back, softly framing a newly rounded face which this evening seemed nearly seraphic—though its radiance probably owed less to heaven, thought Charlotte, than to country sun. Her low-cut dress was of the sack style, its flowing material a pale blue edged in flashing silver; long, close-fitting sleeves and a train behind added to a nearly medieval picture as Diana proceeded slowly into the room. Many were the heads that turned to watch, and to congratulate her fortunate husband.

A growing stridency of voices and an increase of heat in the great room beyond the entry hall proclaimed that nearly all who had been invited had arrived. A few now began to find places among chairs that had been arranged in rows. The musicians, too, sat and began to tune their strings, creating a familiar cacophony that called the room to order. Something else, hidden beneath a drapery of green baize, stood between them on a table with spindled legs, promising another treat for the evening.

Longfellow led Charlotte to a chair near the center of the first row. Spying a trio of guests standing in the arched entrance to the room, he quickly promised to join her later. While the three newcomers bobbed to survey those before them, Longfellow hurried to make them welcome.

"Mr. Wainwright! And what rabble have you brought in with you? Warren! And Josiah? I'd heard you would be away from town this week—your appearance is a fine surprise! But why have you come without Mrs. Warren, Doctor?"

"The answer to that might surprise you, too, Richard," Josiah Quincy broke in with a strange laugh. "I fear you no longer have your finger on the pulse of Boston society. But then, that is our physician's job, is it not?"

"What do you mean?" Longfellow asked, worried by the young man's excited manner.

"I have advised Mrs. Warren to stay at home this

evening," the doctor replied, "for I'm afraid she is not entirely well."

"Nothing serious?"

"Only enough for me to hesitate to have her travel through the streets," Warren answered cautiously. "But here, you have abundant beauty and wit of your own. Mrs. Willett!" he called over the room's buzz.

"Go to her, Lem. She might enjoy seeing an old friend tonight," Longfellow instructed the young man. "But first, tell me what it is that I should know, but don't."

The boy looked uncomfortably at Dr. Warren, then at his shoe buckles. Though Longfellow's eyes snapped with suspicion, a deep cough from Josiah Quincy captured his attention. Josiah had taken out his handkerchief, and now glanced swiftly at its contents with a practiced eye, before putting it away again. At twenty-one he looked forward to a brilliant future, if the consumption in his chest gave him sufficient time. Fair-haired and slight like his friend Warren, though somewhat taller, he cut an arresting figure. His wandering eyes crossed on focusing, giving him a further air of gravity—though hardly tonight!

Longfellow considered that Josiah was one of the youngest to meet in the long room above the office of the *Gazette*, with company that included Warren, John Hancock, Dr. Church, Jeremy Otis, the artisan Revere . . . occasionally John Adams and Richard Longfellow (though he had seen them little, lately) . . . and always, Sam Adams. Most were Harvard men, reasonably well-to-do. All hoped to keep their world safe from harm by walking a path close to the black leads of treason. None of the rest was here tonight, though some had been invited. Was something else on, then? Perhaps there would be another round of protests in the streets, yet another bonfire, some new effigy thrust up into the Liberty Tree. Who would they choose this time, to mark with public scorn? Whoever it was, when an odd whistle was heard in the streets and alleys, many hundreds of men would join together. That, Longfellow *did* know. And despite his curiosity, he also knew he preferred to spend this evening inside, surrounded by light and music.

"Lem," he said at last, "go on—take my seat by Mrs. Willett." Glad to obey, the boy walked away. "I will see both of you when we have our supper," Longfellow said to Quincy and Warren. "And gentlemen, I would be obliged if you would not alarm my guests, as you have already alarmed me! It isn't much to ask. If the place should clear itself to follow other events, my sister, I can assure you, will not be pleased!" It was enough to put a new face on things, for they all knew of Mrs. Montagu's ways, as well as her growing influence upon the many females of the town.

Something new stirred the room; each head turned to admire the guest of honor. Signor Lahte had come in quietly to stand under the tall arch, as if he were waiting on a stage. Applause soon rose in anticipation of enjoyment to come, and the musico's lashes dropped humbly. He bowed low, before raising his shoulders and last of all his face, in a practiced, flowing movement that he repeated as the clapping continued. He retreated through the arch, to return with his young wife. Another burst of approval swept through the room as all admired the white gown with its long train, and a tall silver wig with dancing white feathers, set off by a necklace of borrowed emeralds on a slim neck as smooth as polished marble.

Diana looked on, proud of her creation, convinced that Elena could have gone without shame even to the Bourbon court. But Boston would do for now.

Her brother, too, admired the youngest of his guests with pride. The City on the Hill, built by exiles, had reached a degree of civilized behavior that could match

London's, he imagined with a smile—even though the beauty of the hour was a daughter of Milan. But she and her husband, in his rich court attire of silver and gold, would make a beautiful pair wherever they landed. That, no one could deny. Except for one man, Longfellow realized with a swift frown. As the applause finally abated, he took a new look at the windows whose heavy curtains remained open, and recalled what he'd been told of the brief appearance of Elena's father, only hours before.

At last, the moment had come for the music to begin. When he had helped Elena to her seat, Lahte joined the musicians, to whom he had earlier spoken of the particulars of the performance. To open, an aria from one of Handel's operas, *Giulio Cesare*, had been agreed upon. The musico would become the Roman general in Egypt, about to step into a snare baited by beauty, and pride.

A French horn's first rousing fanfare was joined by an oboe's curiously eastern note, and the jingle of the harpsichord; now, two violins soared majestically, while a pair of cellos set a succession of determined footsteps beneath the whole. In the New World, the voice heard next had always belonged to a woman or a boy, for what man among them could hope to raise his voice to the necessary pitch, in full force? Here, finally, they would be able to enjoy the role as the composer had intended.

Lahte sang with fewer frills than many had expected, but with a strength of feeling that was deeply moving, and remarkably satisfying. This, his audience concluded, was a true Caesar at last, standing heroically before them!

> *"Va tacito e nascosto*
> *quand' avido è di preda*
> *l'astuto cacciator . . ."*

Richard Longfellow had slipped forward to reclaim his chair at Charlotte's side. He began a low translation, while Lem bent down and scuttled toward the wall.

"Silent, secret, hungry for his prey . . . the cunning hunter goes," he whispered, leaning toward her ear. "And the man who would do evil . . . wants no one to see . . . the deceit that is in his soul."

Something rose to niggle at Charlotte's mind, reaching it through senses greatly distracted by the mingling of many delightful sounds. In another moment, she was again carried away.

Over and over, Lahte repeated the same words, in varied form, to new combinations of notes. Seated behind his host, Edmund Montagu felt as if he were being gently lifted; he, too, found it difficult to concentrate on his own thoughts. He had seen Warren and Quincy enter, and as they spoke with Longfellow it had seemed Richard was genuinely at sea. That was not surprising—after all, he was now little more than an amusement to these dangerous men. Yet what, exactly, were the rebellious fools up to? Outside, the pearly sheen of the sky had turned to a darker gray. Soon, lanterns or torches would be needed, and faces in the streets would be obscured. He had insisted on more sentries at the Neck's gates, when he last spoke with the governor. He had also sent some of his own men to the ferries, where they would keep their eyes sharp. Montagu was certain the atmosphere of the night would be unsettled; even the air was curiously thick and electric. For a moment he took the beringed hand of his wife, and asked with his eyes whether she had any reason to complain. Her ecstatic gaze assured him that she did not. Then, he went back to his own worries, while the room continued to swell with song.

When the piece was over, wild applause demanded

bow after bow. The musicians, too, got up and began to congratulate each other, until all felt the need to sit down again.

As the hour progressed, other songs washed over the great room and out into the halls of the house, as well as through its tall, open windows. In the street, several who were headed for the Common, or the Green Dragon, or across the mill stream drawbridge that led to the North End, stopped to listen. Then, more than one forced himself to hurry on, having something of even greater interest in mind for the evening hours.

Chapter 21

EVENTUALLY, WHEN THE need for stretching and other refreshment grew stronger than the thirst for novelty and beauty, the music ended for a time. Longfellow's guests wandered about his house, gravitating to a pair of long tables that offered food and drink. Here ladies and gentlemen picked up plates, and filled them with tastes of the season: black, red, and blue berries, soaked in liqueur and topped with whipped cream; lady's fingers painted with apricot glaze; slices of lightly smoked trout on fresh-baked cracker, and red roe spooned from bowls seated atop blocks of melting ice. A treasure trove of ice, too, floated in a silver bowl of citrus punch liberally laced with rum, while wine, decanted into cut crystal bottles, awaited those with more refined appetites.

Tongues loosened, and toasts were thrown like garlands onto Signor Lahte and his lovely bride. Nothing could be more enjoyable, at least in the social world, thought Charlotte as she sat down with her glass replenished. By the reflected flicker from a mirrored sconce behind her, she saw Lem return with a plate in one hand, punch in the other.

"You say he's lived next to us for a full week?" the youth asked, continuing their previous conversation as if he still shared her home.

"Nearly that."

"He is handsome, I suppose."

"Yes."

"And everyone else thinks so, too?"

"Most do. Even Lydia Pratt." At the mention of the landlady's name, Lem goggled, his mouth full of cake, while Charlotte suppressed a laugh. "But not quite everyone, I think," she added gently.

"How is . . . how are they?" Lem managed.

"Jonathan is quite well. So is Nathan. And you must mean Hannah, and Henry. They are well, too . . ." Teasing her young friend with an intentional omission, she let her voice trail away.

"And the rest of Hannah's house? Martha?" Lem finally asked, almost strangling on the name.

"Mattie? I believe Henry did say she has been worried lately."

"Worried? Why is that?"

"She heard from her brother that you will join the town militia, and may be swept away by its glory." Charlotte had expected a chuckle at this, but Lem seemed unamused.

"Join the Boston boys and their old uncles on the green? Not likely! I would sooner eat cod every day. You can tell Martha, if you happen to see her, that I will be coming home to do my marching." The young man rose abruptly. "But I see, Mrs. Willett, that you've finished your wine. If I may, I will fetch you another."

As he moved off into the crowd, Charlotte was once again surprised to see that the boy she'd long known was now nearly a man. There was still an occasional movement that betrayed his uncertainty, yet he clearly felt a new ease in his approach to nearly everyone. And he did employ his eyes well, paying proper attention to the needs of those around him. Perhaps, she decided, he might thrive in the city and its elevated society, after all. Wasn't that what she, and others, had hoped for?

"What I meant to say," said Lem when he returned, ". . . what I've decided, is that I won't stay at college this year. *Nor go there any other.*" He handed her the glass, and waited for her thoughts on the matter.

"Have you told Mr. Longfellow?"

"No. Not yet."

"I'm certain he'll tell you that if you stay, you might one day use its scientific laboratory, with equipment you'll find nowhere else."

"That would be interesting . . ."

"But not enough?"

"I would rather be among friends again."

"Richard may say you'll miss finding new friends, and living among scholars who will direct the future of the colony. Bonds are often formed, I think, between those who suffer life's trials together."

"So I've heard," Lem returned, recalling warnings of the pranks he might expect, and descriptions of the great discomfort of cold weather in Harvard's drafty halls.

"There is another side, of course," she went on. "In Bracebridge, you have a room of your own. I will also give you permission to speak to females . . . something I believe the professors at the College consider a dubious pastime."

So Mrs. Willett, thought Lem, had no great faith in

the men who attempted to guide them. In this, lately, he found he agreed with her.

"There is, too," Charlotte continued, "the question of what Boston may do to make its own future. As I know very little of these things, I doubt that I should advise you. Still," she finished with a smile, "I have hoped you would not be 'swept away' by those who arrange the town's politics. And from what I have heard from Captain Montagu . . ."

"Mr. Longfellow hoped I would stay, I know."

"But he may begin to see that you can assist him in his experiments in Bracebridge, and continue to help us both. You could mention to him that his great hero Dr. Franklin did not attend Harvard College, or any other."

"Then do you think he'll agree to my return?"

"In another day or two, ask him yourself."

"I *am* going home, then! And my cousins are welcome to make of Boston whatever they care to—for there's far too much racket here for me."

Charlotte said a silent word of thanks. He had come to her a cast-off, driven from a house more full of noise than joy. Together, they had been content with a quiet life—and now it seemed they were to enjoy each other's company again, for a year or two. Beyond that, who could ever say?

Her wine finished, she felt like dancing—as others had begun to do—or at least catching her breath in the fresh air. She and Lem soon walked through the house to the double doors that opened onto the rear yard, where they expected to find a breeze. Find it they did, along with something else entirely.

In the shadows of the stone porch, two figures stood with their backs to the new arrivals, gazing into the eastern sky above the rooftops. Charlotte felt Lem hesitate as he, too, recognized the two men. Dr. Warren was the first to sense their presence.

"Mrs. Willett! What a pleasure to see you again. Do

you know Josiah Quincy? I believe he has heard of you, and some of your good work in Bracebridge, from young Mr. Wainwright. Has Lem told you about our life in town, as well?"

"We've just been speaking of the ways of the greater world, in general, and the future of Boston in particular."

"Have you?" Warren asked, his eyes moving back and forth between them.

"Though I must also suppose," she assured them, "that some of the subjects you discuss together are not for my ears."

"Your ears, I imagine, do not close themselves to much. Did you enjoy the Coroner's Inquest, by the way?"

"Enjoyment is not quite what I would call it . . . though several interesting questions were raised—but, oh! look—what is that fire? Off in the distance—"

"Nothing to worry us, madam! Not a house, surely, for it seems to be on Fort Hill. Possibly a carriage lamp fell into a dry field. Perhaps we should go and see, nonetheless. Josiah, shall we walk together for a while, to clear our heads? And Lem, will you follow us?"

"I have a first duty to this house, Doctor," the young man answered, more sure of himself than the physician had expected.

"Oh? I see," said Dr. Warren, again sizing up the boy, and then the woman at his side.

"I hope, Mrs. Willett," said Josiah Quincy, "that we will meet again."

"Thank you, sir, and a safe night," Charlotte replied. At that, the four parted company, two stepping back into the light while the pair of gentlemen disappeared into the streets, to join a growing throng that had already begun to revel in the dark.

. . . .

IN THE NEXT hour, the London *harmonica* was uncovered and tried, to the delight of the assembly. One of Europe's newest instruments, it had been made to Dr. Franklin's specifications, like the one in Philadelphia which had been displayed during the previous winter. Longfellow soon explained to Lem, now stationed at his side, that rather than having rows of beer glasses of varying sizes like the old German *Glasspiel*, Franklin's instrument was composed of three dozen open globes, ground to produce tones and half-tones, nested in one another and joined through central holes to a metal rod—the whole rotated with pressure supplied through a foot treadle. Wet hands on the polished glass rims produced a series of penetrating sounds that spanned three octaves. The notes were different, yet each had the clear, sharp quality of chimes.

The other musicians took turns accompanying the owner of the *harmonica* as he played airs from several nations, some reproduced from purchased sheets, others learned by one or another of the group in cities as diverse as Dresden, Florence, Vienna, and Dublin. Still other songs, thought by some to be equally charming, were of Philadelphia and Boston manufacture. And, of course, the works of London's (and the Queen's) current favorite, Johann Christian Bach, were not neglected.

Finally, after playing a piece composed for the musical glasses by Gluck many years before, one of the maestro's newest operas was introduced as the evening's pièce de résistance.

Settled next to Diana, Charlotte had to strain to hear Longfellow explain the story to Lem, who had accepted her chair, while the musicians took time to tune again.

"Orpheus, himself a mortal, was the son of Apollo and Calliope. He had the misfortune to lose his wife when she was bitten by an adder—something I hope you ladies will take pains to avoid in your own outings. Then, just as Eurydice began to enjoy herself with the other shades in the Elysian Fields, Orpheus decided to go down and carry her home. With his lyre and his honeyed voice, he soon soothed the Furies who guard the gates of Hades. They allowed him to lead Eurydice back to the light—but he was not to turn to her, nor to answer. You can imagine what this might do to a lady! She finally convinced her spouse to ignore his orders, and so she was lost again, through her own folly."

"Thank you, Richard," replied his sister. "I am sure Lem appreciates your insight into a woman's soul, and her inevitable silliness. All of which is worth about a fig."

"That you may keep, my dear—for a man should also be wary of a woman bearing fruit," her brother returned jovially, perhaps beginning another lesson.

"Richard! I believe we are all waiting . . . ?"

Longfellow sat back with a smile, and with a wave of his hand bade the music begin anew.

The notes that now came from the musico brought tears to the eyes of many, as Orpheus mourned the loss of his beloved. A few others felt their hackles rise, reminded of the plaintive howl of faithful dogs who sang their misery after a death in the family—or, on occasion, before one.

With an eerie presentiment of her own, Charlotte looked to Elena, who sat several chairs away. Although the young woman had earlier seemed to warm to the looks of admiration around her, she now appeared to have tired. Like many others, she had taken out a lace fan, and wielded it for its cooling effect.

Abruptly, the room was starkly lit by a sheet of silent lightning. The guests braced themselves for the shock of thunder. When it came, Charlotte saw that Elena retained a child's fear of the noise, for she got up, took her flowing train in hand, and moved toward the hall. Further flickers, however, fit surprisingly well into Il Colombo's musical description of his anguish in Pluto's realm, and the rest of the audience remained spellbound.

Moments later, there came a note higher than anything heard that night—a shriek of fear, rising from the darkened hallway Elena Lahte had just entered! Charlotte was among the first to rush forward, for she imagined Don Arturo Alva there, attempting to pull his daughter out into the impending storm. But the scene that met the eyes of all who crowded under the arch was something none, including Mrs. Willett, had expected. Before them, they saw a dark old man—Cicero, to be exact—holding a pistol to the head of a young man in dirty clothing, while Elena cringed against a wall, a hand to her face, her pretty fan trampled on the floor.

"Pomeroy!" Longfellow bellowed, pushing forward. "Is there *no place* in this town that can hold you? And what do you want here? Has Alva sent you on more murderous business? What is this?" He reached down to the carpet to pick up a long-bladed knife. "I see you have come for more than supper—and this time, I can assure you that you'll pay for your presumption, by finding yourself soon in shackles! But Cicero—how is it that you came to be standing in the hall, with a weapon?"

"He was under my orders," Diana called out as she made her way through the crowd, her hands prying apart the shoulders of her brother's guests. "When the madman Alva came in earlier, I told Cicero to arm himself and watch for intruders, whenever the rest of us might be occupied. It appears that he saw more than we, hiding behind his screen in the corner there. Though I never supposed he would catch *this* goose, once again!"

Charlotte had now helped Elena part of the way up the stairs, so that she might lie down in one of the bedchambers. Pausing, they both looked back to see Thomas

Pomeroy staring up at them one last time, his face bearing the stamp of defeat, and perhaps something more. After a moment, the girl continued to rise proudly, white as the dead Eurydice, her train trailing behind her. Pomeroy watched them disappear. Then, he gave a whimper and sat down on the floor of the hall, his grimy fists pressing into his eyes.

The music started again, soon reaching a level that rivaled the flashing storm. Yet Charlotte could not remove from her mind the pathetic image of a young man without a hope, without a friend, who had been swiftly taken away. Though he was a thief—even, perhaps, a murderer—she wished he could have been helped, somehow, to a better life. But Thomas Pomeroy had long ago been caught up in devilish clutches, and these had urged him along his own road to Hell—a road from which not even the golden voice of Orpheus would save him.

Chapter 22

Further grim tidings came in through the kitchen door of Richard Longfellow's town house, early the next morning. Because of her habit of rising to milk the herd, Charlotte was already enjoying a last cup from the housekeeper's teapot, wondering what to do with herself next, when the woman ran in from the street.

"Oh, madam—the news!" cried Hephzibah. Rachel craned her neck from the pantry. "Such a thing was never seen before! And to such a fine gentleman, too! It is Mr. Hutchinson," the housekeeper wailed. "His house—his beautiful house is *gone*!"

"What?" Rachel gasped in disbelief.

"Razed clear to the ground! I had it from a barrow man, just come from there. Only the walls left standing, he says, and the lovely gardens all destroyed. Even the trees chopped down!"

"Who?" Charlotte exclaimed, though in her heart she knew.

"Townsmen," Hephzibah spat out, "an army of *brave* townsmen! Oh, the shame will be on us forever—"

Seeing the old eyes brim with hot, angry tears, Charlotte hurried to the hearth for water. As she found a tin of tea, Hephzibah sat to be comforted by young Rachel at the long wooden table. Once new leaves were wetted, Mrs. Willett joined them.

It was more than a little strange, she thought; while they absorbed the awful news, little sound came from the usually busy street above. They could hear only occasional footsteps, or the distant, hollow ring of iron horseshoes on the cobbles. Perhaps the city lay hushed in its surprise—yet many must have participated in such broad destruction. How many more had stood by, doing nothing to stop it? And what possible good could it bring to anyone? For revenge was more than likely—

A rapping at the front door disturbed the house once more, and Rachel ran to answer. She called out from the hall that it was Captain Montagu, for Mr. Longfellow. Charlotte joined Edmund moments later, in the small morning room where he'd gone to wait.

"Mrs. Willett." He spoke in a voice that was oddly flat, as he rose from his chair.

"Edmund, we've just heard—"

"The place has been utterly destroyed. They have stolen his plate, his jewels, his money—even the servants' clothing. It is beyond belief! It is open rebellion against the King...."

Falling silent, the captain walked stiffly to the hearth mantel, where he began to finger a fragile crystal ornament turned to fire by the sunlight. Charlotte, too, was now at a loss for words. But before another minute ticked by, Richard Longfellow strode in on stockinged feet, his shirt still hanging half out of his breeches.

"Edmund! How did this happen?"

"How indeed, Richard?" asked Montagu, looking up with an exceedingly solemn face. "Can you tell me you know nothing of this matter?"

"I? Last night I suspected *something* might occur, as you did, I'm sure. But to destroy the man's home—the pride of this entire town! Where is the sense in that?"

"Do you finally believe, then, that some of your circle have lost their reason? Or is it *treason* that has been their aim all along?" countered the captain, as a vein at his temple throbbed.

"You seem to have ways of knowing what the town is about. So perhaps you will explain to *me* just how this—"

"Richard!" Charlotte cried out.

"I suppose," said Longfellow, relaxing at length, "that it must be called no less than an act of terror, whoever its instigators might have been."

"Agreed," Montagu returned sharply.

"But how is Hutchinson? They haven't dared to harm him—?"

"Safe, thanks to the warning of a friend. Yet the curious fact is that the lieutenant governor of this colony has not even a coat in Boston to call his own, as he escaped in his shirtsleeves. A neighbor saw the entire family run through the back garden, while the mob went in at the front. And all the while these men looted, they were actually heard to call out for the defense of liberty and property. *Liberty, and property!*"

The captain's harsh laugh broke the tension, while both men paused to consider this new proof of blighted humanity.

"Word came to me in the early hours, Richard, that Hallowell, the customs commissioner, was another of the Liberty Boys' targets last night. Three days ago the Admiralty records he kept were looted, no doubt to save someone's skin; but this time, attacking his house, they stole or destroyed more, including his personal belongings. Judge Storey—Deputy Register of the Court of Vice Admiralty, no less—was deprived of court records and personal papers when his home, too, was ransacked. Both men had their cellars emptied, of course! Those bottles must have provided fuel for the later attack on Hutchinson. . . ."

"I suppose all of them will eventually receive compensation from the town."

"Do you?" asked Montagu, with a look of disbelief. "I doubt it. At the moment, I believe the town's latest victims are surprised to have come away with their lives!"

"Well—let me buckle my shoes, and find my coat."

Longfellow hurried from the room, to be stopped by Signor Lahte and his wife as they came down the stairs. They, too, sought a reason for the general alarm that had, by now, run through the household.

And so five walkers, including Mrs. Willett, went out minutes later, to see for themselves.

"I HAVE WATCHED riots before, certainly," Montagu asserted as they walked down Hannover. He looked coldly at a pair of familiar gentlemen who passed with quiet faces, going in the opposite direction. "But even in London, I've seen nothing like this. Never!"

"I doubt," said Longfellow, "that it began as it ended. The heat is known to encourage a thirst, as even your wife has declared. And once started, unfortunately . . ."

"No—this mob of yours comes and goes like a wild

animal that has been trained. Yet even a dancing bear may call his own tune, one day. And when that happens, what man, what woman or child in its path, will be safe?"

The captain turned to watch a rider coming toward them, thinking it was fresh news—but he was disappointed as the man rode by.

They approached North Square, and saw many others who had come to observe the scene. Even Montagu was moved by their chagrin. What had once been a proud home on a busy street, across from Old North meeting house, was indeed little more than a pile of rubble. There was no sense of victory in the air—only genuine sorrow at the terrible waste.

The house itself was but a skeleton. Slates from the roof, even from the cupola, had been thrown down onto the grass, or out into the street. Carved woodwork lay ruined beside costly panels ripped from interior walls. Over all fluttered a rough sea composed of papers, books, and branches—for even the fruit orchard behind had been hacked with axes. Flowers had been trampled, rare bushes uprooted, a glass house and its plants smashed down. Slashed portraits sat on top of jagged pieces of painted china. All that remained of the home of a man and his five children was an open grave, proclaiming the sudden death of respect, and decency.

"Even his papers," Charlotte said softly, looking down.

"Including the history he had barely finished," Montagu informed her. It pained him to see her face become even more pinched at the news. "However," he continued, "a neighbor picked up much of it, including many of the old documents. Not all are in the best of shape, but most have been preserved. Reverend Eliot was a brave man last night, if another clergyman may feel some blame for what has happened."

"What's that?" asked Longfellow, looking up from the

destruction. He forced himself from his recollection of the magnificence he had seen just days ago, when mansion and owner had welcomed him.

"Reverend Jonathan Mayhew, it seems, gave a sermon on Sunday that many took to be a call to action, in the name of God. That, at least, is what I am told. If it is true . . . then may God help the Reverend Mr. Mayhew!"

Longfellow knew the popular minister had long ago proven himself to be a man of great vision, or of madness. Who else among them had dared to preach England had a constitutional right to remove the head of a king? He also had the notion that British subjects might some day span the continent, settling all the way to the Pacific Sea. With a wrench, Longfellow brought himself from this unlikely idea back to the moment.

"Your letter, I suppose, is gone," he recalled suddenly, looking to Gian Carlo Lahte.

"The proof of my marriage," sighed the musico.

"It was here?" asked the captain.

"Hutchinson was to have had a copy made and filed."

"And duly stamped?" Edmund Montagu replied in a flash of grim humor.

"That, I think, would have been impossible," his new brother retorted, unable to keep a challenge to the Crown out of his voice.

"Do you *still* defy Parliament's right, and the King's?"

"You see before you, Edmund, one house that has been destroyed—but how many more do you suppose will go, if this continues? I tell you, your game is a dangerous one for us all!"

Charlotte closed her eyes; still, she saw the scene of destruction before her. She knew the Hutchinsons were one of the town's first families, long a part of Boston. Surely, they had all read the lieutenant governor's views in the newspapers—even she, who paid scant attention, knew Thomas Hutchinson disliked the stamps. But was it truly the stamps that had again kindled men's passion? Or were they only an opportunity to continue a greater fight, which none of them might live to see finished? The thought appalled her as she stood, far from her quiet farm, in the midst of Boston's woes.

As the party began their walk back to Sudbury Street, Charlotte considered that two among them were even farther from their homes, with little chance they could ever return—at least, together. As if he shared this thought, Signor Lahte dropped back to walk slowly beside her. Meanwhile, Elena went on ahead, her eyes alert, confident as only youth can be when faced with destruction. Though the night before the girl had suffered a serious threat at the hands of Thomas Pomeroy, today her step was light, and she was charming in a borrowed bonnet trimmed with little curling feathers, worn above a vermilion gown. What next, Charlotte wondered, would the world offer young Signora Lahte, as she attempted to settle into the rhythms of wedded life?

"I'm sorry for the loss of your letter," she eventually said to Gian Carlo Lahte, noting that he, like the captain, appeared weary despite the early hour.

"It is very little, compared to what Mr. Hutchinson has lost."

"But the new ceremony should be honored here— perhaps even more than the first."

"Here, yes—here, it may be honored, madamina."

"But . . . ?" she asked, her eyes searching his still handsome face.

"In Europe, I do not think so. And as Elena wishes to return there . . ."

"In England, surely, your union will be allowed?"

"I cannot say. It is something that has not often been

done. But I feel—it is as if her first promise to me has been taken away—destroyed. It is only a feeling, perhaps."

"Won't Elena's love continue to bind her, no matter what a paper or a court might say? Can you forget that in marrying you, she has defied even the will of her own father?"

To this he made no reply, other than to turn his face away.

When they had drawn near the bridge over Mill Creek, Charlotte heard the sound of another horseman hurrying toward them. Once more, she saw Edmund turn to be recognized by a possible bearer of official news. But when she looked up to see for herself, she knew immediately that it was not for the captain that this rider had come.

Something like a dark cloud swallowed the sun, as a black cape was flung out over Elena Lahte. She leaned away, but it was too late—caught in the rider's clutches, she was hauled up to sit across the saddle before him, her waist clasped tightly. At the pull of a rein, the horse wheeled with a neigh that did little to mask the scream that trilled from the girl's throat, when she recognized her father.

His mount lifted its forefeet and lurched wildly ahead, kicked hard by spurred heels. Then it took to the walk beside the street, forcing those on foot to dodge out of its way. In an instant, Longfellow put himself before Charlotte, and Montagu made a futile grab for the horse's bit. At the same time, Lahte attempted to save his wife in the only manner he could—by clutching her skirts and laying hold to a foot. Arturo Alva's arm went up; his whip cracked down against Lahte's shoulder, shocking him into releasing the slight advantage he'd gained.

The animal stumbled again as it continued to snort in a panic of its own. Then, it ran for the harbor. At the end of the short street, the horseman forced the beast to stop, not sure which way to turn. A boy who pushed a barrow full of squash around the corner caused a further delay, as the horse reared up once more.

Gian Carlo Lahte cried out, running after his wife and her captor. It appeared that he might reach them, until Don Arturo turned the horse from the barrow, and spurred it on.

Edmund Montagu now saw another mount coming down the slope of the cobbled street. He soon had its bridle in hand. "Officer of the Crown, in pursuit of a felon," he shouted, forcing the rider to abandon his seat. The man then stood astounded as he watched his own horse turn the corner, and disappear.

Richard Longfellow had less luck, but he did know where to find the nearest livery stable. Leaving Charlotte, he ran to the next block. There, he gasped out a request to the proprietor, motioning frantically for something to ride. Marveling at his distress and excitement, Angus Jones gave over a horse that had just been brought in, its saddle still on, and Longfellow was again off, ducking his head at the door.

Meanwhile, Montagu continued to follow Elena and her father, watching them twist around carts and carriages, and dodge horses that turned away in fright at the strange thing coming toward them with three heads, and several flailing limbs. Down Wood Lane to Fish Street they went, past the wharves and warehouses that stretched out into the water—then up by Old North again, and on to Fleet. After crossing North, they turned into an alley. Here Montagu lost them, forced to halt by a group of women whose skirts startled his horse as they whirled in confusion. Hearing cries ahead, he wheeled and took the fastest route to Salem Street, where he saw his prey fly by while the Christ Church bells began a stately peal. The captain then jogged to Charter, and hurried toward the nearby burial ground. Now, he heard the approach of another steed coming up from behind, and jerked his head around to observe Richard Longfellow gaining ground.

Longfellow raised an arm, pointing to the right. After that he turned left on Mill Street, riding toward the windmill just ahead. Montagu kept to his own way, hoping they might pinch their prey like a lobster. Soon, Don Arturo would run out of peninsula, and would be forced to turn one way or the other. And then, whichever way he went, one of them would be there to cut him off.

It was at windswept Hudson's Point, near the shipyards across from Noddles Island, that they finally caught up with him. Trapped, with the waters of Boston Harbor preventing his escape, Alva held in his prancing horse, while his daughter's struggles increased. She had tried to twist free on numerous occasions, but still sat with her breast facing the horse's neck, caught by her father's arm. Now, seeing a new possibility for freedom, she gave a final pull.

The moment could not have been more ill-chosen. As Alva's strength lessened in his moment of indecision, Elena's thrust broke his grip and she went flying, backward, from the tall horse. Her head hit the hard stones; her body lay still.

"*Figlia!*" Alva screamed, seeing his daughter motionless in the road, while his horse continued to prance, wild-eyed, about her body. Leaping down, Alva allowed the animal to dance away. As Montagu and Longfellow reached them, the distraught father raised his daughter's head to his thigh, cradling her as he tried to brush the hair from her face, while her skirts billowed up in the harbor's brisk breeze.

"Stand aside!" Montagu thundered, but Don Arturo did not seem to hear. Longfellow, too, dismounted, and took hold of the captain's shoulder to pull him away.

"If she's dead, you do her no good," he said logically. "And if she is alive—what then, Edmund?"

"We'll need a wagon, in either case," Montagu decided, controlling his anger and his fears. He walked rapidly to his obedient horse, and picked up the trailing reins. "I will go and find one."

"Good. I'll see to the girl."

When the captain had gone off, Longfellow went to the crouching man and knelt to take up Elena's hand with experienced fingers. There was a pulse—quick and weak, but discernible. And yet, her eyes would not open, even after an effort was made to rub her hands and pat her cheeks. He had known others to fall into such a state and never leave it—at least, not alive.

While an anguished Alva watched closely, Longfellow felt the long bones in Elena's arms and legs, and discovered no breaks to concern them. He nodded with a brief smile, hoping to relieve the man who seemed to shrink before his eyes. The sound of Alva's sudden weeping came as an unpleasant surprise, and he started to pull away. Then, recalling that he had once suffered similar agony himself, he gently placed an arm over the grieving father's shoulders.

When Montagu approached them only minutes later, a wagon could be seen coming behind him. Longfellow walked to the captain's side.

"She is still alive."

"Thank God for that."

"But she'll need to be watched closely."

"As will the father." Montagu indicated the man who again rocked his child. "He will have to be placed under arrest, Richard."

"My house should do. He can continue to see his daughter, which may help her to regain her wits. Warren is not far from me."

"Yet in the same house, with Lahte?"

"For the moment, I think their pain will unite them."

"All right, then. But I'll post guards at your doors—something I should have done before! Here is a wagon, and some sail. If Alva cushions her head, we may get the girl to a bed without further harm."

The wagon stopped and its young driver joined the others in lifting up the still figure. She was, he thought with pity, a small thing, nearly as light as a sparrow, though she surely sported far prettier plumage.

Chapter 23

ELENA LAHTE LAY in a darkened room, her spirit deadened to the life that went on around her. For three hours, since she had been carried up the steps of the house on Sudbury Street, she had shown no sign of awareness.

Joseph Warren had come and gone. After he examined the girl, he could only suggest that time might accomplish her cure. Meanwhile, he admitted, there was little a physician could do. He did promise to return in the evening, or whenever they might perceive some change and call for him. His eyes lingering on Captain Montagu, the doctor had again seemed about to speak. But he added no more, and went away.

Now Elena's husband and father flanked her bed, while Mrs. Willett sat in a chair at its foot, watching them all.

What would happen, Charlotte asked herself, if Elena should awaken suddenly? How would she feel, seeing her father there, when her last memory was of her abduction? And what of Gian Carlo Lahte? How could he forgive Don Arturo, if he, too, believed Thomas Pomeroy had been sent to end his marriage, and his life, with a pistol? Though hard to believe, how else could she explain what she'd seen with her own eyes? Further, how could Lahte excuse the fact that Elena's fall had been caused by her father? And if she had not fallen, Alva would have stolen her away, taking her to a ship, then removing her to his own city, and his sole control.

But was there not also, she reasoned, something understandable in a father's shock and anger at the loss of his only child? For with a husband such as Lahte . . .

Charlotte closed her eyes and recalled questioning looks on the faces of those she loved, when they wondered why she gave no children to her husband. In her case, the situation was unexpected. But what if a man *knew* no son or daughter could ever be born of a union? Would he then have the right to demand so much—even for love? It was a question Lahte himself had asked her. But then, after all, it was Elena who had decided to follow a husband who'd left her behind.

She opened her eyes to find that nothing had changed. At least while they watched over the girl, the two men kept a kind of peace, only occasionally glancing away from her motionless face. Neither spoke, other than to utter an occasional sound of distress. Another such groan came from Lahte at that moment, causing Charlotte some alarm, before she calmed herself once more. She watched him take a cloth from the basin of water beside the bed, and wring it before applying it to the girl's moist brow.

What kind of home might Lahte and Elena eventually find, she wondered, if they were given the chance? Elena was unwilling to stay in Boston. That was not surprising. But would her husband's many admirers in London bring her joy? Or more unhappiness? Would Lahte continue the life of a musico? Or might he seek, for his wife's sake, a less public occupation? Like Longfellow, he could become a landowner in some country spot, where he might experiment with a large estate. But would that satisfy the girl?

There was also her father. Don Arturo had come after them once. Charlotte suspected he would do so again. Still, it was very likely he would now be forced to stay in Massachusetts, to be tried. And if convicted . . .

It was all so sad. Studying the older man's features, she noticed his expression change as he watched the care his daughter received from her husband, saw it alter from a look of worry to something softer. Was compassion growing within him? At least, there was no fire left in Don Arturo's manner. Perhaps he had given up his own desires, hoping that by doing so he might persuade Heaven to return the thing he treasured most. What else could a father pray for, at such a moment?

There was little anyone could do for Elena. However, thought Charlotte, there might perhaps be something she could do to improve the lot of *someone* . . . if she could only understand what remained unclear. She was now in possession of a good many facts, and they did seem to fit together. But curiously, they reminded her of a child's Chinese puzzle, which mocked one's efforts to reveal its interior. Two men meeting, somehow, on a hot afternoon, in an empty road . . . a cloak pin, with no cloak . . . the musico's anticipated visit to Bracebridge . . .

Now, she decided, would be as good a time as any to try shifting a few of the puzzle's many pieces, in the hope that the whole would fall apart, revealing something of interest at its center. Taking a long, quiet breath, she folded her hands, and began.

·   ·   ·

WALKING SOFTLY THROUGH the house, Diana Montagu
continued to think as her brother's hostess, deciding how
to deal with yet another crisis. Elena already occupied one
of the bedrooms; Lahte, of course, would stay with her
there, though he might prefer a cot or a pallet to the bed,
should he feel the need to sleep.

The father would be shut into another bedroom for
the night, and the key removed from his door. Diana did
not like the idea that it was next to her own. But when her
husband had announced he would stay, she did not like to
think of going back to an empty house—nor did Edmund
wish her to leave, with the town in its current mood. But
what if this man Alva became crazed again, and somehow
managed to escape during the dark hours? She would take
care to lock her own door when she went to bed; it might
be hours before Edmund would think to join her. He had
much on his mind, she knew. In a way, it was fortunate
that *something* drew his thoughts from their neighbors. For
he had started the morning by reviling the people of
Boston in a manner quite horrible to hear! Now, she supposed he eyed even his wife with something less than
complete trust . . . but was it *her* fault if some people did
not appreciate good furniture, china, and painting, and
all the rest that it took to make a home? Surely, if the fools
who had gone to Hutchinson's house with their axes and
crows owned things as fine themselves, they would think
twice before destroying the property of others! But what
was one to do with men who had poor taste, few possessions, and little civility?

However, Diana told herself as she climbed the stairs,
things were no better in Edmund's dear London. She had
heard of that city's riots, and the upheavals occurring
around the countryside. At least in her own colony, she

thought, while there were criminals, there were none who could be called peasants!

Having reached her bedroom, Diana lowered herself with care onto the bed, and stared at the tall wardrobe that stood against the opposite wall. In another few months, she would be able to unpack and wear her old gowns. Though when she thought of it, how much better to suggest a journey, perhaps even to London, to buy new ones. This reminded her of the charming vermilion muslin Elena had worn that day—before Charlotte removed it. Diana's chest tightened. Then, a jabbing pain came as she recalled the girl's body, lying so very still. She *must* make herself think of something lighter—something foolish! That way, surely, the child within her would have no excuse to shift again so sharply. She had been warned that these continuing pains were an unhappy omen—that they might foretell the death of a child, and even a mother. Yet she would *not* shrink before Fate like a cowslip in the heat, she told herself stubbornly.

A sweeter memory came of a fragrant yellow bouquet, offered to her when Edmund took his leave the previous summer, just before her inoculation. Edmund, she thought, might hear her grumble, but he must not know of her real trouble—especially now. She would make sure all ran smoothly around him by taking care of her brother's guests—even if Richard *had* sent Cicero off again to enjoy his new laurels among old friends, while her mother's servants were nearly overwhelmed. She must order more china and linen for Alva's room, and she had already instructed that another place be set at the table—if tomorrow was not too hot for any of them to eat! If only she had not driven Patty away, she might have one pair of hands she could be reasonably sure of. But Patty was gone for good, the wicked thing. Or was she? Perhaps, with an increase in what she was paid . . . possibly with a room that included a bit more furniture, or a new hat in a brightly ribboned box? That might do. She would have to see. After all, Bon Bon had been sent off to live with Lucy, fortunate to have been banished, rather than run through! For he never should have nipped the captain—

As if he had heard her call out to him, Edmund Montagu entered just in time to help his wife sit up.

"Is there any change?" she asked.

"No, my dear."

"Elena is no worse?"

"No different . . . but no worse."

"When will Dr. Warren return?"

"Soon."

"And where is Richard?"

"In the garden, clucking over the state of his privy. He is pleased to announce he will sink a new shaft this fall."

She smiled at that, as he had expected. But before long, Montagu returned to his wife's former concern.

"I hardly know how we'll tell the daughter, if she does wake, that we may now have to hang her father—as well as that wretched boy. I wish to Heaven they had all stayed at home!"

"In Milan? Is it an attractive place, Edmund?"

"It is not Paris, nor even Rome—"

"How I will enjoy seeing them all one day, with you! Though I know Rome is very warm, and has smells."

"Unlike Boston?"

"At least here we speak a single language, so that we may all understand when we complain to one another."

"Do we? Sometimes, I doubt it. Diana, you know there are many here who wish to thwart me, and do real harm to government. That is one thing. Yet should any harm come to you, during this unrest—!"

He added no more to his threat, but asked shortly, "Do you look forward to living in London when we return, sweet? Or perhaps somewhere nearby, in the country? Would that please you?"

"Not now, my love," his wife whispered, drawing him near.

But when he left, Diana knew her husband believed that she, too, entertained the idea of leaving Boston.

He was wrong, of course. Though she may once have considered such a suggestion with pleasure, it now gave her a far different sensation. That was curious. Perhaps it was the child, voicing his own desires? It must be one further proof—if more were needed! For there was little doubt left in her mind at all.

The first would be a son.

CHARLOTTE CONTINUED TO sit quietly at the foot of Elena's bed, reviewing possibilities that swirled around her like mist before a rising sun. Something, surely, was behind it all, attempting to break through.

Don Arturo was obviously a man of great pride, who had had something precious stolen from his home. But did he want his daughter returned to him, when he came to Boston? It would certainly seem so, watching him now. She glanced up once more to assure herself.

But then, would not *this* desire have been first in his thoughts, well above a lust for revenge? And if that was so, why should he have ordered Sesto Alva killed?

As Elena's traveling companion, Sesto was the only man in Massachusetts who knew where she was. No, that might not be so. Don Arturo could have followed Sesto to his rooms in Boston . . . but if he had, why did he not take his daughter then? Thomas Pomeroy might have told him later of Elena's appearance in Bracebridge—but how could he have known of it *before* Sesto's death, when she did not arrive until a few days later? And if Don Arturo did engage Thomas Pomeroy to assist him, would he not have told the boy that his first duty was to retrieve his daughter?

There was, too, the underlying nature of Thomas Pomeroy to consider. A criminal, perhaps—but she could not bring herself to think of him as truly evil. What reason could he have had for committing the terrible sin of murder? Money? When he came to Bracebridge, he already had the gem that he gave to Jonathan—which might even, as he claimed, have been his own. It was not impossible, she decided. And if it *had* been sewn into his clothing, then might another like it, also hidden, have bribed his shipboard jailer, giving the boy his freedom when he landed? Either way, once he'd received the purse of gold from Jonathan, *why* did Thomas Pomeroy return to Boston? Was his freedom no longer precious to him? He had remained in town—had even come into Richard Longfellow's house. Was this, too, done at the order of Don Arturo? Elena's father had claimed he did not know Thomas Pomeroy, or Matthew Beaulieu. And how could Thomas believe he could abduct the girl against her will, from a houseful of her friends? Yet could he have come for any other reason?

Suddenly, something occurred to her that she supposed might explain the boy's return, as well as his earlier actions. What if . . . what if Thomas Pomeroy had been moved by something more powerful than the thought of further wealth—something strong enough to lead him to risk his very life? *What if he had come back for love?*

She closed her eyes and saw his face, as she and Elena climbed away. Had the loss of love been the real reason for the boy's pathetic collapse the night before? It was no more than she had guessed at the very first—that somehow, something happened between them in the dining room of the Bracebridge Inn. But as her mind decided that it had touched at the puzzle's final secret, another distraction arrived in the person of Dr. Warren.

Closing the door softly, the physician walked across the carpet and motioned for her father to move away. He knelt by his patient. He spoke her name once, again. He reached out, but the girl's eyes suddenly opened on their own. Seeing him, Elena managed a painful smile. Then she raised a hand to her husband, who took it joyfully.

"She'll soon mend," Warren assured them, after he had felt her pulse, and asked the girl one or two questions. "You may give her some watered wine, and in an hour, some broth and weak tea. If she's no worse tomorrow, I think she might resume her usual diet, and walk about a little."

"Thank you, Doctor!" said Gian Carlo Lahte, his voice weak with emotion.

"I am glad to have been of service. Now, as it appears you two gentlemen could use some rest and sustenance yourselves, perhaps you will leave Signora Lahte alone with Mrs. Willett for a little while?"

Father and husband each kissed the girl before going, and Charlotte heard them descend the stairs together. A quarter of an hour later she, too, left Elena to rest, and went to find Richard Longfellow with an unusual request.

"Richard," she asked when she had found him in the library, "you were given Thomas Pomeroy's diamond for safekeeping, I think, by Judge Trowbridge?"

He put down a volume of Voltaire. "Would you like to see it again, Mrs. Willett?"

"I would like to borrow it."

"Why, I wonder? Wait—I've heard from Diana that there is a vogue, among the ladies, to scratch a memento of a visit into window glass, using a finger ring. But you, Carlotta . . . ? No, I imagine you've been sent as a messenger. Well, if Diana wishes to try such a thing with someone else's stone, she may borrow it—for it can do Thomas Pomeroy little good."

Longfellow went to a painted vase that stood at the end of a shelf of books, tilted it, and let a bit of velvet slide out into his hand. "Go, and have my sister leave for posterity what she will. Surely a little more history won't hurt anyone."

Charlotte thanked him and went away. It was an intriguing idea, but not quite what she had in mind. Yet it was best to keep what she suspected to herself, until she knew for sure.

She walked to the dining room, where the Italian gentlemen sat silently over a cold supper, which Rachel served.

"Madamina!" Gian Carlo Lahte called, leaping to his feet at her entrance. "Have you come to join us?" He helped her into a chair.

"I would like a little something," she admitted, and the girl went out to find more ham and salad. Lahte himself poured her a glass of wine, from the sideboard behind them.

Some minutes were consumed by small talk between the two, while Don Arturo watched them carefully, his eyes seeming to gauge the meaning of references he did not entirely understand. Bracebridge was recalled, and the wonders of Boston alluded to as being well worth further exploration. But as yet, the musico was unable to discuss his plans for the more distant future. And there was something else between them that remained unsaid, underlying Lahte's new happiness. Something that seemed, somehow, impossible to remove.

Finally, Charlotte brought the conversation around to town fashion, and found a reason to bring the scrap of velvet from her pocket.

"I am thinking of having this set into a ring. It is unusual. . . ."

Lahte picked up the diamond, holding it to the light with a discriminating eye.

"Not a new stone, I am sure, for the cut is old. Though yellow is not the favorite of many it is still beautiful, I think—like the autumn sun. It reminds me of something else, though I cannot quite recall . . ."

"I've only recently obtained it. From Mr. Longfellow," she added. Then, watching closely, she turned and offered the gem to Don Arturo. Elena's father looked at it carefully, and she saw that his eyes grew as hard as the thing he held.

"This," she said softly, "was given to an innkeeper in Bracebridge—by Thomas Pomeroy."

Alva handed the gem back, and looked away. She saw the ugly scar on his cheek grow livid, as the rest of his face whitened. Perhaps aware of this, he reached to touch his own memento, then rose slowly from the table. "I should like," he said, "to rest."

Don Arturo took up his glass; he went to the sideboard and picked up the decanter of Madeira, nearly full, with his other hand. Taking both with him he left, and they heard him slowly climb the stairs.

"I do pity him," Lahte said with apparent sincerity. "Even though he has been my enemy. But if he can forget this, I will try, as well. Do you not think, madamina, that we must all try to forget . . . and to forgive?"

"I think," said Charlotte. "that I will rest a little, too." She extended her hand in friendship before leaving the musico to sit alone, as the long afternoon wore on.

Chapter 24

THE SUN HAD fallen, but the last light of day remained as Mrs. Willett steeled herself and walked out of her bedchamber. She knocked on a nearby door. Receiving a faint reply, she entered.

Elena Lahte was brushing her dark hair, leaning back on a pile of pillows.

"How is your head now?"

"Better," the girl replied with a smile. "But . . . I would not like to dance!" She laughed with pride at her increasing grasp of English, which Charlotte suspected had long been greater than Elena felt it wise to admit. For the moment, both shared a memory of the dancing that had taken place on the previous evening, which now seemed, somehow, long ago. Charlotte felt a new pang, but went on.

"Elena, when you came here, I wonder if you suffered from the sea's movement? The *mal de mer*?"

"The sea sickness? No, my stomach is strong."

"And Sesto? Did he suffer?"

"Sesto?" The girl seemed confused. "I think . . . he was ill, yes; but before, too. He was not well."

"Then you were often alone, I imagine, while at sea?"

"On a ship with so many, it is not easy! But I did not want to be with Sesto."

"Was he cruel to you, Elena?"

"Yes!" she said, suddenly expansive. "Cruel, with no proper feeling!"

"But the captain of your ship was a kind man, I hope?"

"Yes. Many times we spoke, when I walked, as he suggested, for my health."

"I suppose he encouraged all of his passengers to take the air on deck, to avoid sickness?"

"That is true. It was very hot, below."

"When you finally arrived here in Boston, it must have been a great relief! How many days passed, after you came ashore, before Sesto left you?"

"Not many. Three? Four?"

"Then your ship arrived on the twelfth, perhaps. What was it called?"

"Called?"

"What was its name?"

"The *Nantes*—or the *Neige*, I think. Some things are difficult to remember." The girl raised a hand to her head.

"You did board a French ship, I believe, at Marseilles— but it's very unlikely that it brought you to Boston. Heavy tariffs are placed on such direct trade to these colonies. So, I will guess that in Funchal, in the Madeira Islands, you waited for a British ship, which would bring you here. Or perhaps one was already refitting, after a great storm that blew her far off course, to the south? Could it have been the *Swallow* you next boarded?"

"The *Swallow*? Ah, *sì*!" Elena agreed.

"When did you first notice Thomas Pomeroy? For we've all heard that he, too, came here on the *Swallow*. He would have been kept on the lowest levels of the ship, of course."

"Of course. There, I could not see him."

"But you did say the captain allowed *all* of his passengers on deck, at least part of the time, because of the August heat. In the hull, it must have been dangerously hot. And if a keeper was instructed to sell Pomeroy on his arrival, so that he might work—"

"Yes; I remember these men did come up, sometimes."

"I'm sure he noticed *you*, Elena. I suspect he saw you often enough, and long enough, to speak with you—even to fall in love. Did he find a way to come onto the deck in the night, while you, too, walked there? While Sesto lay in agony below?"

At this suspicion, Elena smiled.

"I imagine that's why he stared at you so, when you met again in Bracebridge—during our dinner at the inn. You stared back, making your husband unhappy."

"But Captain Montagu says not so—he says my father saw Thomas Pomeroy on the dock—paid him to come to find me. That is why this boy was in Bracebridge—why I was afraid, too, when I saw him."

"Yet if your father saw Pomeroy on the docks, and purchased his freedom, why did he not see you, or Sesto?"

"We were gone, then," the girl tried.

"When your father found you here yesterday, he told us he did not know Thomas Pomeroy, or Matthew Beaulieu. He also told us to be careful."

"My father lies!"

"Last night, Pomeroy returned for you—hoping, I

think, that you would love him enough to go with him, leaving your husband—a man you must have told him you did not love. Did you also tell him you hoped to hurt your husband, in some way?"

"How could I," Elena objected, "when I love Gian Carlo?"

"Wasn't it you who gave Thomas Pomeroy a yellow diamond, Elena? A gem left to you, perhaps, by your mother?"

Unable to stop herself, Elena glanced to a high chest of drawers across the room.

"Did you give him one or two others? From a pair of earrings, or a necklace? Did Thomas, or Matthew, buy his way clear of the *Swallow* with one stone, and with another, perhaps, purchase his freedom from a Boston prison two days ago?"

"Tell me all you think, then!" Elena challenged angrily. "Tell me, and be done!"

"I think, while on the *Swallow*, you and Thomas Pomeroy planned to run away together. When you landed, he went ahead to Bracebridge, leaving you and Sesto to wait for word that your husband had arrived. Perhaps Sesto, too, hoped to gain, if he could manage to blackmail the famous Il Colombo. But you had other plans, I think, for Sesto."

"He was *ricattatore*—a man who demands money, for secrets! He took from me all that I had—my mother's necklace of yellow stones, the pin with green eyes, given to me by Gian Carlo—all, to take me away from Milano. Now, again, these things are mine."

Charlotte considered carefully before asking her next question, which was the crux of the story. "Is it not sometimes said, Elena, that poison is a woman's weapon? *L'avantage d'une femme?* Did you begin to practice on Sesto when you started your travels . . . or before? Did you sometimes put something into his wine, to see what would happen?"

At this Elena shrugged her shoulders, though she still listened intently.

"That, I think, would explain why some of his ulcers had healed, while others were fresh, as Dr. Warren told us."

"It is not easy to be sure of such a thing," Elena replied.

"Nor, I suppose, to prove that Thomas Pomeroy borrowed someone's horse to visit you in Boston one evening, after hearing that your husband was to come and dine with Richard Longfellow the next afternoon. That night, I think, the three of you talked together—and Sesto must have agreed to set out in the morning. But you also gave Thomas a bottle of wine, telling him to meet Sesto on the road, and offer him refreshment. You may have told Thomas to drink none, himself. Or, perhaps, you did not. . . ."

"And then?"

"Then, when Sesto was dead, or lay in agony, Pomeroy picked up a rock. Perhaps he used it to end Sesto's suffering; surely, he hoped the blow would draw suspicion from the poison, masking its use—protecting *you*. I think he did truly love you, Elena."

This seemed to produce a smile of satisfaction.

"And here is the last of what I suspect," Charlotte said, after a deep sigh. "I think you gave Thomas the clasp to drop near the body, so that you might later accuse your husband of Sesto's murder. For if he were tried and found guilty, then you, as his widow, could claim his fortune—most of it already removed to London. Or perhaps you only wanted something to hold over his head. Did you never love him, Elena? Do you not love him now?"

"Carlotta," came her cold answer. "You, too, have

feelings for Gian Carlo. I saw this at first. I hated you, of
course. But think of my life! I must be pitied, for though I
am young, and beautiful, my father would give me to a
man both old and ugly—a man to take me away from the
world, even before I see it! To give him children—no
more. Him, I truly hate! Then, I see Gian Carlo in the
cathedral. He is so handsome, so kind. He teaches me—I
tell him I love him. But he goes away too soon. He will
not touch me. Then, it is *him* I hate! But the old man,
more. So, I come here. Again, I see Gian Carlo. Again, he
is kind, gentle. And handsome. Soon we are husband and
wife—*vero e proprio*. I do not tell him what I wished to do,
before. I think he must know. He is afraid. But for me!"

Elena Lahte's face softened briefly; then her eyes hardened as she went on. "He is only castrato. He cannot give
children. He cannot marry, in Italia. Soon, I know we will
part. But now, I will not marry the old man in Milano!
Gian Carlo will give me more jewels; then, I will become
free. This is not a tragedy, madama. It is only like the
opera—sad, perhaps, but not true."

"Perhaps," Charlotte responded, thinking that Elena
was right. Her love had never been a real one, but a play
put on for profit . . . and at what a cost! She wondered how
long ago the girl had lost her innocence—or was it possible that she had been born with none? Elena clearly
knew how difficult it would be to prove what her plans
had accomplished—unless Gian Carlo Lahte spoke
against her, which he seemed unwilling to do. And how
easy for Signora Lahte to deny all but a natural desire to
be with her husband!

Yet ships did submit lists of passengers, as well as
cargo, to the authorities. These lists Edmund Montagu
could check. And Thomas Pomeroy might yet tell of his
part in the deadly plan. But would the word of a transported felon be taken seriously? Don Arturo had recog-

nized Elena's yellow diamond, Charlotte was sure. Would he admit to what he suspected, even to save himself? Or would he, too, forgive his child?

There was a knock at the door. When it opened, Elena's father stood with a glass of wine in his hand. Humbly, he bowed to both women.

"For my daughter," he said. Charlotte nodded.

He entered and gave the crystal glass to Elena, who took it as a queen might, from a servant over whom she held ultimate power. Again, there was a look of triumph in her face, and Charlotte began to feel ill.

In another moment, her head swimming with what she might say, what she might do, Charlotte rose and said nothing at all, but left father and daughter together. After going down the stairs for a candle, she had a glass of wine from the decanter which had been replaced, to restore herself. After that, she made her way up to bed, looking forward to a night so lonely that not even sleep, she imagined, would come to disturb her.

YET SLEEP SHE did, with the rest of the household, until some time after the sun had risen the next morning.

Feeling warmth on her face, Charlotte opened her eyes to realize that something was far from right. For one thing, her head felt thick, and she knew of no reason why it should ache so.

Swiftly, she dressed in her clothing of the day before, and swung open her door. No other in the hall stood open. Presumably, she was the first to wake. Walking to Elena's door, she recalled the glass of wine she had taken from the decanter below . . . and the one brought to Elena by Don Arturo.

She knocked, but received no answer. She opened the door, and saw the long body of Gian Carlo Lahte lying on a straw pallet. The bed beside it was empty. His wife was gone.

Praying that he still breathed, Charlotte crossed the room and watched until she saw, to her great relief, his chest rise and fall. After that, she suspected she should summon someone to look for Elena. But to what end? What earthly good could come of finding either of them, now?

She knew Don Arturo had sufficient means to leave the city undetected. It would not be difficult for him to reach another port, and there quietly arrange further passage. If Elena remained drugged for a few days more, she could be taken out to sea in a small boat, on her way to a larger. After that, her fate would be sealed.

Would that not be the best thing, after all? Charlotte asked herself this question as she continued to stand over the unconscious form of Il Colombo, listening to a faint memory of angelic song. Would this husband have been able to protect his young wife forever? Or might he, too, have died at her hands, one day?

She hardly knew what to think. And so, she sat down and wept for Elena, Don Arturo, Sesto, and Thomas Pomeroy, and most, perhaps, for the kind and gentle soul asleep beside her. Seeing only Elena's suffering, he had offered his heart, and his hand, too soon—an action he would long regret.

Was there not a lesson in that, Charlotte wondered, for herself?

Chapter 25

Several days later, Charlotte was home again, in her orchard, standing on one side of the knoll that divided her brother's land from the estate of Richard Longfellow. Orpheus sat nearby as she looked up at a few shrunken apples clinging to the crooked boughs of an old tree. She heard a whistle, and turned to see her neighbor ascending, a large scythe cradled on his shoulder.

"I believe, madam, you have some grass to be cut?" Longfellow called.

"Quite a step down, for a gentleman of the town."

"'Let not ambition mock their useful toil, their homely joys, and destiny obscure. . . .' No, Mrs. Willett," he continued, while he still smiled at Gray's familiar lines, "I seem to have lost the temperament for life in Boston. Rather like young Mr. Wainwright. Although I believe our last fête will keep up my reputation, and my welcome, for years to come. A mixed blessing, I suppose."

Charlotte, too, smiled at the wry face that accompanied this sentiment. "But what of Bracebridge, considering the trouble you've brought back?"

"Do you refer to yourself, or to Gian Carlo? He, at least, will be on his best behavior while he stays. The poor man has been greatly subdued by his misfortune—and by Elena's. Still, it's far better to know, and to remain healthy! And there is a new sister he assures me he is glad to have found. But I think we will find him an even better life somewhere else, before long."

"Assuming the three of you are not first blown up to the rings of Saturn."

"We only plan a simple test—of Watt's improvements for the fire-driven steam pump, which we spoke of at length last week. Now, perhaps, the attempt will draw Gian Carlo out of himself. It should also teach Lem a thing or two he would not have learned at Harvard."

She shivered at the thought of compressed steam under her neighbor's hand, yet Mrs. Willett was glad to see him courting his old mistress once more—though she was frequently a danger to them all. "What will you do with this engine?" she asked. "Surely there are no mines near here to drain?"

"Who can say?" Longfellow replied, unshouldering his scythe. He squinted into rays that had begun to slant noticeably, marking the quiet coming of autumn.

"There is another thing I would like to know, Richard," she began again.

"More questions, Carlotta? For instance?"

"What will happen to Thomas Pomeroy?"

"Since Warren has again stated that the rock we found was not the true cause of death, I doubt Thomas will be hung, after all. Still, there will be a trial. Then we'll see."

"What do you think Elena put into the wine? I suppose the Italians know of many mysterious Eastern poisons?"

"I'm sure they do! But we suspect she employed the same old retainer I often put to work in my own glass house. Arsenic is the usual choice, after all—and they have garden pests in Italy, Mrs. Willett, much as we do here. But now, I have another agricultural task to begin—a healthier occupation than discussing poisons, especially with a woman!"

Longfellow tightened his grip on the scythe, and swung his arms so that he laid down a line of grass along its deadly edge; then, pleased with his neat work, he took a step to the side as he brought his hands up again, ready to lay down another swath.

Within the week, Edmund Montagu sent a note to Longfellow, who shared it with Charlotte. The trail of Don Arturo and his daughter had at last been discovered. According to witnesses, a boy, quite ill, was taken on board a ship at Newport; his father claimed the child was in the final stage of consumption, and not to be disturbed. He was attempting to take the boy home, he said, for the blessing of a grieving mother. Their passage was procured by a pair of diamonds, yellowish in cast, and the child had been heard to sob as he lay in his cabin, no doubt as he contemplated his certain future. Montagu also told them that the two thief-takers who had been assigned to watch Longfellow's doors had gone off, as well, leaving no trace behind.

In two weeks more, Thomas Pomeroy was indicted. He was then tried, and sentenced to another seven years of indentured servitude, beyond the original seven given to him at the time of his transportation. His life would not be easy; but in the frontier town where he was being sent to work, he would be exposed to fewer temptations than in Boston. And, Longfellow added one evening in the inn's taproom, where he shared a bowl of chowder with Charlotte, if the lad corrected his behavior, there was no reason he might not learn a useful trade, becoming one day a free man of some worth to his community. At least, that was the hope of the Superior Court, which had sent him off in chains.

Three months later, a final word came on a ship from the Mediterranean, in a letter from Don Arturo Alva that was addressed to Mrs. Willett. She opened it with trembling fingers on a snowy afternoon in early December, while she and Richard Longfellow sat by the warmth of her study's hearth.

"He tells me," she said after a few moments, "that Elena has done her duty. She was married on the week of their return, to the nobleman her father had earlier selected for her."

"Hmmm," was Longfellow's initial comment.

"But there is more—oh!" After another pause, during which she read the rest, Charlotte set the letter down and stared into the fire.

"He congratulates me."

"Does he? For what?"

"For seeing in Elena what he, at first, did not wish to believe. Could not—until, he says, last summer, when he heard his daughter arguing with her governess—moments before the woman fell to her death from a window in the girl's apartment. When he then gave her the choice between a convent and a carefully arranged marriage, Elena attacked her father, as well. With a knife."

"His scar!"

"Yes."

Pondering this horrible knowledge, they sat in silence until Charlotte spoke again.

"Of the two, she would have hated the convent more, I think. And I doubt even the sisters could have changed her. At least in her husband's palace—for it seems he has one, something like a fortress—at least there, Elena may wear fine dresses, and her new jewels. But Don Arturo swears she will be kept closely confined."

"Then she will no longer be a danger to the world. A tragedy, still," Longfellow finally decided. "But would the girl have developed such cruelty, were it not for the faults of her decadent society? Could you imagine such a thing happening here, Carlotta?"

Receiving no reply, he reconsidered before he spoke again.

"Yet perhaps Elena was peculiarly unbalanced, after all. What kind of woman enjoys masquerading in a man's clothing? I ask you, Mrs. Willett?"

Charlotte could not tell if this had been said with a small smile, or not.

"Do you think, Richard," she returned, "that we should pass this news on to Gian Carlo?"

"I'm not sure it will do Il Colombo much good. But I suppose I'll write something of it—whenever I can manage to send a letter off to Vienna."

"Perhaps by then you'll be able to tell him Mrs. Montagu has borne her child safely . . . which I'm sure he *would* like to hear."

"As would we all," said Longfellow moodily, before he, too, turned to observe the crackling logs being consumed before their eyes.

THE END

About the Author

MARGARET MILES lives in Washington, D.C. The author of three Bracebridge mysteries, she is currently working on a fourth.

WITCHCRAFT . . . OR MURDER?

Margaret Miles'
Bracebridge Mysteries

A WICKED WAY TO BURN

___57862-6 $5.50/$7.50

TOO SOON FOR FLOWERS

___57863-4 $5.99/$8.99